FALLING CREATURES

By Katherine Stansfield

Falling Creatures

a&b

FALLING CREATURES

KATHERINE STANSFIELD

Allison & Busby Limited
12 Fitzroy Mews
London W1T 6DW
allisonandbusby.com

First published in Great Britain by Allison & Busby in 2017.

A CIP catalogue record for this book is available from
the British Library.

First Edition

ISBN 978-0-7490-2141-2

Typeset in 12/16.25 pt Adobe Garamond Pro by
Allison & Busby Ltd.

The paper used for this Allison & Busby publication
has been produced from trees that have been legally sourced
from well-managed and credibly certified forests.

Printed and bound by
CPI Group (UK) Ltd, Croydon, CR0 4YY

For my sister, Lil, with whom I've climbed Roughtor many times and who loves a good prison yarn

PROLOGUE

The pony had given in by the time we found her. This was near the ford, halfway between Roughtor and Penhale. The marsh there was broad and very wet.

The creature had struggled, though, we could see that, for the grass was churned brown where she'd fought to stand. Her eyes were rolling white. Sweat was creamy on her shoulders. Her backside was sinking in the pit of mud and black water seeping. She was tired from the pain, from trying to get up. Her breath loud and rasping.

We stood safe at the marsh edge, where the grass was longer. I knew where a marsh started but that was because I was born on the moor. Charlotte was born by the sea. It made a difference, something like that.

Charlotte went to cross the marsh. I grabbed her. Harder than I meant to. She cried out.

'We can't help her,' I said.

The only sounds were the sucking of the water and the pony's hard breath.

'Look.' Charlotte pointed across the moor, towards Lanhendra. Ponies stood watching – four of them.

'They're waiting,' I said.

'For what?'

'Until she's dead. They won't leave her.'

The moor and its marshes were the only things that made Charlotte

Dymond afraid. She put her hand in mine and squeezed it. Her palms were hot, and rough as gorse. We were close as moor stone and the ground that held it.

Until someone uprooted us.

ONE

Charlotte Dymond gifted me blood-heat on the day we met. She took it from another living creature without any cutting. She carried no knife that I saw. She didn't need such a tool. Her workings were in her hands, then later the water. This I would have told the magistrates but they wouldn't hear truth. They would hear only lies.

Charlotte made me the gift at the hirings, at All Drunkard, a place so sinful it was called such even though its true name, as written on the tithe map, was All Worthy. My father had told me All Drunkard was the better name because the magistrates met there and they were drunkards all. He wanted rid of me. I knew he would leave me at the hirings like I knew he'd taken to spirits since my mother coughed her last. It was him deserved to be left at All Drunkard, not me.

To reach the hirings on that Lady Day in 1844 my father and I left our home in Blisland and went across the moor before it was light. My father caught me when I stumbled against moor stone or fell into hollows made by sheep and ponies. I didn't mind him not speaking. I had nothing to say and the wind was cold on my face though it was March and the days were lengthening.

When we came to All Drunkard there were crowds outside the inn. It was easy to make out the masters and mistresses from those looking to be hired because the farm servants had boots like mine, with thin soles and the leather ripped. Our clothes were thin too, clutched against the wind. My father went inside and left me with the horses standing in cart shafts. He didn't come back.

The wind came sharp off the moor and I had no shawl or gloves. I crept to a black carthorse, the creature tied furthest from the inn, and pressed myself into its coat. I was seventeen years of age and my mother had been dead a week. My sister hadn't come home for the burial. I hadn't seen her since I didn't know how long. She might have been in the ground herself.

'You'll not get much warmth from that bag of bones.'

I looked up from the carthorse's greasy hide. A woman stood before me.

'Better than nothing,' I said.

I thought I'd seen her before. But I knew I hadn't. She was the same height as me and had the same dark hair. She wore a fine dress, green, was it silk? And good shoes, with pattens to keep them from dirtying.

She pushed a strand of hair from her face and I felt my own hand move likewise though there was no hair across my face. I bit my lip and she did the same or was it the other way around? We smiled. We were close as moor stone.

'There's always something to be got from nothing,' she said, and she cupped her hands and held them out to me. Her nails were bitten to the quick so bad they were bloodied. There was a smell about her. Like bread caught in the hearth.

'See now,' she said, 'nothing here.'

Then she put her hands on the carthorse's rump, the fleshy part of its back leg. A quiver ran all through the creature, but the woman paid no mind to the horse's discomfort. She dug the heels of her hands into the horse, moving them in a circle, over and over, steady and the same. The horse tossed its head and tried to swing its backside away from her but it was like she held the horse where it stood. The creature made no sound. It had lost its tongue. I was wondering at this strangeness, for the horses I had known were quick to shriek their pain and then, oh then—

Her hands on my cheeks, as hot as if she'd cut the horse's neck and laid me down in its still beating blood. I felt the blood pour over me, soak me to my bones. The creature's heat was mine, its life was mine, even as it stood breathing at my side. She made me warmer than I'd ever been in my life, warmer even than when the gorse was burnt on the moor for clearing ground and the whole world was blazing round me.

'Better now, aren't you?' she said.

'How did you—?'

She put her hands behind her back. The carthorse dipped a mite then remembered how to use its knees and stood straight. It tossed its head once more, coughed, and then there was just her looking at me.

'Quiet now,' this blood woman said. 'Don't you go telling.'

'But—'

'Girl!' a voice behind me called.

I turned to look. A stout old woman was waving at us.

'You not taken?' She reached us through the people and horses and carts and took hold of my arm to feel its strength. 'Scrap of a thing, dear me, yes.'

She wore black and her black hair was piled any old way. She said her name was Mrs Peter and she farmed at Penhale, a short way across the moor.

'You suited to farm work?' she asked me. 'Milking?'

'Yes,' the blood woman said.

The blood woman didn't look a farm servant to me. She was dressed too fine. Mrs Peter didn't see her as one either.

'You're looking for work?' Mrs Peter asked her.

'I can milk cows,' the blood woman said. 'Card wool. Cook and clean.'

She had a long face and large eyes. She looked hard at a person when she spoke to them, didn't look away. I wanted her to speak to me again.

'Well, I suppose I could take you pair,' Mrs Peter said, 'if you know the Good Lord's love.' She turned to me. 'What about you – you can milk cows?'

I wanted to be away from the inn, away from my father and the memory of my mother coughing, her pale face and her eyes no longer seeing me, and I wanted to be with the blood woman who had warmed me, so I said yes. I said yes to everything Mrs Peter asked until she said, 'Have you eaten?' and I shook my head.

'John! John!' she called.

A man lumbered over. He had the same small eyes as the woman, the same black hair escaping from his hat. He looked younger than my father, about thirty years of age. He could have been thought handsome were it not for the largeness of his mouth and nose. He looked about him like he was afraid of the crowds and the noise. This made me think he was slow. But Mrs Peter wasn't.

'John,' Mrs Peter said, 'get them something to eat while I find who they belong to.'

But he wasn't listening. He was looking at the blood woman. His mouth fell open.

'Did you hear me, John?' Mrs Peter took hold of his chin and made him look at her. 'Go and get them some bread.'

'Yes, Mother,' he said.

He started for the inn's door. His steps were plodding as a cow's and he kept looking back at us. At the blood woman.

'Now then, give me your names,' Mrs Peter said.

'Charlotte Dymond,' said the blood woman.

I told Mrs Peter my name.

'Well that's no use to me,' she said. 'We'll have to find some way of telling you apart. Wait here. I won't be long.'

She followed the man John into the inn, leaving just the two of us again, which was better. Then something moved in Charlotte Dymond's hand. Something vanished up her sleeve. She caught me looking and folded her arms across her chest.

'I can't stand cows,' she said.

I didn't see my father again but I dreamt him drawing up the bond with Mrs Peter. I dreamt him making his mark and stinking of drink. There was no one to sign Charlotte away.

TWO

Mrs Peter held the reins. I sat in the back of the cart with Charlotte and her box of belongings. I had no such box and I wondered at her riches. The poor road made us jolt about and knock each other. I didn't mind such knocking. I wanted to keep near her and the warmth she could give. John Peter wanted to sit next to her too but his mother wouldn't let him. He sat up front with her and moaned of the cold all the way.

We crossed the moor and Roughtor came in sight – the sharp hill crowned with towers of moor stone. Blisland, which I had left that morning, was on the tor's other side. Heaven knew where my father was by then. He wouldn't go back to that room where my mother died. I knew that much.

Mrs Peter slowed the cart and we turned down a rutted path that led to a yard in front of a house. Penhale. When I first saw it I was made dumb. The farmhouse was so smart-looking. There were fields all round it and round the fields was the moor. It was a lonely place but I liked the lay of it, the way the house stood firm in the green.

Mrs Peter pulled the cart to a halt. John Peter got down and went straight into the house, saying, 'Cold cold cold' to himself, with no thought for helping his mother. That was what we were for, I thought. Charlotte and me. But Mrs Peter was calling someone else's name. A man came from the barn.

He drew close and I saw he had a face of scars from the pox. His mouth was twisted on one side where he had no teeth. I must have shown my fear but he was used to such looks because all he said was, 'Two of them?'

He helped me down from the cart and then took Charlotte's hand to do the same. He didn't let go once she was standing. He was as mazed by her as John Peter had been. She did something to people. I could see it in the slackness of the men's faces, the way they leant towards her, as if pulled. She was pulling me. I wanted to get hold of her. How did she do it?

'I must see to John,' Mrs Peter said, and she was away into the house, calling for her soft boy to get a jacket on if he felt the cold so.

Still the poxed man held Charlotte's hand. I wondered if she'd take another creature's warmth and gift it to him, or if she only did that for me. Then the poxed man came back to himself and saw he was still clutching at her.

'Forgive me,' he mumbled, and set to fiddling with the harness. He led the horse to the stable built onto the barn and I saw then he limped.

'Tell Mrs Peter,' he called over his shoulder, making sure to look at me rather than Charlotte, 'that Matthew is putting away the cart.'

Then he was gone into the stable and I heard him singing in a strong, clear voice that didn't match his weak face. *Sweet maidens all, pray hear this tale, for I am blind and my heart doth ail.*

Charlotte was by the front door. She ran her hands over the frame like I'd seen men run their hands over horses' legs, like Mrs Peter had felt my arm for strength.

'This will do very well,' Charlotte said, and shoved open the door with her hip. I followed her inside.

It was the grandest house I'd ever seen, though it needed keeping clean. The front door gave onto a porch filled with boots and coats and a musty smell I knew from home. An umbrella was stuck in a tall boot covered in cobwebs. The porch gave on to the kitchen. Three steps in and my heel slid on a twist of mouldy bread. I fell into potato peelings on the flags. Charlotte helped me to stand and I kept hold her hand. I'd met her first. She was mine by rights.

The table was a mess of dirty plates and cups and a black cat gnawed the bones of what I took to be a chicken. One of her ears had torn and not healed closed. It was an ugly thing. I moved to knock her away, on to the floor, but Charlotte stopped me.

'Don't make her cross your path, not so soon after entering a new house. Don't curse yourself so needlessly.'

'There's no curse in cats,' I said. 'That's superstitious talk.'

'There's curses everywhere.'

Raised voices drifted down the stairs, mostly Mrs Peter's. I went to the window seat that looked into the yard. We were to wait, I thought. Wait and then do as we were told.

Matthew the poxed man came in. He was carrying Charlotte's box of belongings and set it by the stairs. He was careful with it, and looked to see if she'd noted his care. She hadn't, but I had. He sat by me in the window seat to take off his boots.

'Horse is fed,' he shouted up the stairs.

Charlotte was at the back of the room, looking out of the second window.

'What stood there?' she asked Matthew, pointing.

'In the Mowhay field?' he said. 'Nothing.'

I got up to look. In the field's right corner I saw the top of a thorn tree. It was bent double like the few that stood on the open moor, made to bow by the wind. Beneath it were tumbled-down moor stone walls, half-hidden by tall grass.

'There's always something to be got from nothing,' Charlotte said. 'The stones. What was there?'

'Grain house, perhaps,' Matthew said. 'If Mrs Peter would cut the field for hay we'd see it better.'

Charlotte spun round. 'She mustn't cut it. Terrible things will happen.'

'Well, I don't know about that. She's left it years without cutting. Doubt she'll do it any day soon. Now, I must ask you.'

15

He fussed with a button on his jacket and I saw how smart he was dressed. Too smart for a farm servant. Just like Charlotte.

'Would you walk out with me on Sunday, on the moor?' he said.

But she was looking at the tree and the moor stone walls and didn't answer.

There was a clomping from above and Mrs Peter called down, 'Dallying is the work of the Devil,' which I took to mean she was waiting for us. The poxed man sang Charlotte and me up the stairs. *For I am blind and my heart doth ail.*

The stairs were dark and the landing darker still. Before me was a closed door and behind it I could hear John Peter muttering. Next to it was another door, next to which Mrs Peter and Charlotte waited. Mrs Peter put her hand on the doorknob.

'This is where you pair will sleep,' she said. 'You'll have to keep it yourself. I won't do it for you. Supper will be in an hour or so, if Matthew will skin the rabbits. You'll do the cooking from now on but I'll make an exception tonight, seeing as you're newly come.'

And then she opened the door to the room.

A low-slung bed with a wool cover. The cleanness of everything. The safe, warm heart of it. Mrs Peter was off down the stairs calling to Matthew that the supper needed getting and would he knock that cat out of the butter dish and Oh, John Peter, Oh, that boy.

Our room shared a wall with John Peter's room and in the wall was a door. Charlotte tried it but it didn't open. I was pleased. I didn't want that slow man coming in when we were sleeping.

There was a small corner cupboard by the window. Charlotte fiddled about in front of it, her back to me.

'What are you doing?' I said.

She looked to be shaking out her sleeve and I thought I heard something scrabbling against wood but when she turned round there was nothing to be seen.

'We must keep the door shut when we're out of the room,' she said.

'Why?'

'Promise me you'll keep it shut?' There was a fierceness to her I hadn't seen before. It was as if a storm cloud had blown up inside her and was about to burst.

I nodded.

She sat on the bed. Our bed. We'd be sharing.

She pitched backwards so she was lying down. I lay next to her. For the first time since my mother had died I felt peace enter me. Even my old need for what I knew to be sinful left me. It was Charlotte Dymond did that.

THREE

The smell of rabbit stew led us from the comfort of our room.

John Peter was waiting at the bottom of the stairs. He took Charlotte's arm and walked her to the table like she was a fine lady and he a gentleman.

'You must sit here with me,' he said. There were warts on both his thumbs. Ugly things, like the black cat's torn ear.

'Don't fuss,' his mother said. She was stirring a pot over the hearth. 'It doesn't matter where anyone sits. Matthew, lift this to the table. My shoulder's paining me.'

'Did you hurt yourself seeing to the pigs?' he said, doing as she asked.

'Perhaps . . . I don't remember twisting.' She tried to roll her shoulder free of the ache but that seemed to make it worse. 'I hope it won't put me in bed. If it does I'll see if Daniel will come and help you.'

'We'll be all right without Mr Carwitham,' Matthew said. 'I can manage—'

'Charlotte must sit by me!' John Peter said. He thumped the table and a cup fell to the floor and cracked. He tried to pick up the pieces but soon cut himself.

'For heaven's sake, John!' Mrs Peter said.

Matthew got down on the floor to clear the mess, telling John Peter not to mind.

Charlotte took the seat John Peter wanted for her. He was master of the farm, after all. He squeezed her elbow with pleasure and she gave a little cry for he'd got blood on her smart green dress. She looked like she would curse him but Mrs Peter banged her spoon loudly on the table and said it was a sin to let good food go cold. It got colder still while Mrs Peter said Grace. At last we fell to eating and Mrs Peter told us of our work, for work was the path to His Love.

'I see to the hens,' John Peter said, before she could finish.

'That's women's work,' I said.

'It is not!' he said. 'It's the most important work on the farm, isn't it, Mother?'

She patted his warty lump of a hand. 'Where would we be without our eggs, eh?' She eyed me sourly over her steaming bowl and began to talk to Matthew of farm matters – the calves' field, broken fences. This Mr Carwitham coming to help.

Charlotte was whispering to John Peter. I watched her slip a scrag of rabbit meat from her bowl to her lap, and then she took hold of one of his hands.

He pulled away. 'I mustn't cut the warts,' he said, looking sideways to see if his mother was listening.

'Not cutting,' Charlotte said. 'I can make them go – disappear, as if they were never there. I don't need a knife.'

His eyes widened, his fingers fussing his warts. 'I don't like them. I catch them on things. But Mother says I mustn't cut them.'

She grabbed his hand again. 'Said I won't cut them, didn't I? The charm doesn't need cutting.'

She rubbed the rabbit meat on one of his thumbs before he had a chance to pull away but he made such a noise his mother ceased talking to Matthew.

'What the devil is that?' Mrs Peter said, getting to her feet.

'Witching, Mother!' John Peter said. 'The girl will make my warts go with no cutting.'

'Sit by the fire, John.' Mrs Peter snatched the rabbit meat from Charlotte and shouted at her, 'None of this wickedness in my house, do you hear me?'

She opened the front door and threw the rabbit meat in to the yard. The black cat bounded out like it was a dog and the rabbit meat a stick. We ate the rest of our meal in silence. I saw John Peter fussing his thumbs, looking slyly at Charlotte every little while. Matthew, too, had to look at her. Only Mrs Peter wasn't charmed by Charlotte Dymond.

We finished eating and Mrs Peter talked very loud of the importance of going to worship regular.

'I expect it of all who live under this roof,' she said, looking at Charlotte. 'Come Sunday you'll be there with the rest of us at chapel and perhaps that will keep you from doing as you shouldn't. May the Good Lord preserve us and keep us from wickedness.'

Charlotte and I were tasked with cleaning the plates and setting the breakfast things, and then Mrs Peter said we must all go to bed. It was barely dark but she took the candles upstairs with her, leaving no chance to do otherwise. I went up myself but Charlotte stayed downstairs. With Matthew. I waited on the landing, trying to hear if they were talking but no voices drifted up to me. I heard the front door open and feared she'd gone out with him but then she was back in our room, more quickly than it should have taken a body to climb the stairs, to my thinking. But what did I know of her then?

She threw something on the bed. It was the rabbit meat.

'For burying,' she said. 'When his warts go, she'll see her foolishness.'

We got in to bed and she seemed to fall asleep right away. I felt her softening. I lay awake, too knowing of her body next to mine to dare move. I heard John Peter murmuring in the room next door, and then I heard Matthew's high voice too. I wasn't certain why he was in that room when it was the master's. I fell asleep to them talking but they weren't in my dreams. I dreamt of the moor. I was climbing Roughtor and as I walked something walked alongside me but hidden beneath the ground. Something with claws that scratched moor stone.

FOUR

I was woken by banging on the door and Mrs Peter shouting that the sun was already risen and the blessed cows wouldn't milk themselves. Did I not know the Good Lord looked well on those who toiled for His lands?

Charlotte was gone.

I ran down the stairs with my hair loose and my untied apron flapping. The black cat winked at me from her curled comfort on the settle. There was bread and tea on the table and I stopped to have it, no matter my lateness. Movement by the hearth made me catch my breath. John Peter was there. He was peering at a knife sharpener.

'We don't hold with idleness here,' he said.

I pulled on my boots and left the breakfast though I was hungry for it.

'No shilly-shallying,' he said. He grinned at the words he'd put together. 'Shilly,' he said, pointing at me with the knife sharpener. 'You're Shilly-shally.'

I left him to his mutterings and ran to the yard. I could hear the cows bellowing though I couldn't see them. Matthew came from the barn. His hands were full of pails and a low, three-legged stool. He gave me the pails and stool and directed me down a path that took me to the fields behind the house. Telling Mrs Peter I knew how to milk cows had been a lie and I made a poor show of it that morning. The first creature stood in my pail just missing my hand. All I got when I grasped its udder was a cow-shout of pain. My back ached within a moment of sitting down and I feared I should have to run away.

But then Charlotte was there, in worn working clothes like mine.

She gave little murmurings to the creature I was working then leant her head against its flank, her dark ringlets pressed into the cow's hide. I watched her ease her hands up and down the teat and the milk came warm, frothing into the pail, like the carthorse's blood-heat had flowed into my flesh.

'You said you didn't like cows,' I said.

'I don't.'

'But you know how to milk them.'

'Had to earn a living somehow,' she said.

She'd been at other farms, then, shared other beds. I wanted to ask where she'd come from, how she'd taken the heat from the carthorse at All Drunkard without cutting the creature. But I knew she didn't want me to. That was enough to hold my tongue.

When we went in for our dinner at midday, John Peter called me Shilly-shally again. Matthew and Mrs Peter laughed and I thought it would be forgotten. But it wasn't. From that day on John Peter only ever called me Shilly. When anyone wanted John Peter to understand that they were speaking of me they had to use that name as well. After a few weeks my real name seemed forgotten by all of them, even Charlotte. I became the name they called me, for I was always running to catch up with myself at Penhale.

In the afternoon Matthew showed Charlotte and me the land. Up the path from the farm to the road, him naming each field we passed – the calves' field next to the house, then higher well park field, great marsh field, square field, higher down field. Aside from the pigs and John Peter's chickens that were kept near the house, the fields were empty. Yet the soft bleats of sheep reached us on the wind. Matthew said we weren't far from Tremail, a hamlet just across the fields. That was where the sheep called from.

He limped all the time we walked but he didn't use a stick and he set a fair pace.

'You've had it a long time, your limp,' Charlotte said. There was no tenderness in her voice. She spoke plainly.

Matthew's face coloured. I thought he wouldn't have minded so much if it had been me that had said such a thing. But I wouldn't have dared.

'Since birth,' she said.

He nodded and walked a little ahead, trying to show he didn't have a limp at all, though it was plain he couldn't hide it and that trying to only gave him pain. His limp meant he put his weight on his left leg and was ungainly. I walked on his right side and Charlotte took his left. With each step he tilted away from me, towards her.

At the end of the path was a strip of moor and then the road.

'Camelford and Davidstow are that way,' Matthew said, pointing right. 'And Altarnun is that way.'

It was the teeth missing that made his mouth strange. There seemed nothing mean-spirited about him.

'If you should get lost,' Matthew said, 'look for Lanlary Rock, there.'

He pointed across the moor at a large lump of moor stone. I thought it to be the size of Penhale's barn.

'You'll find that easy enough,' Matthew said, 'long as the mist isn't low. If you can find that then you can find Penhale. Lanlary Rock is a friend on the moor.'

There were shouts close by. They came from a house with the sign of an inn above the door, a little way beyond the road. There was a sound like furniture breaking.

'That's Vosper's place,' Matthew said. 'You'll meet him soon, no doubt.' He kicked the ground with his good foot.

At the sight of the inn the shake was on me, though I fought it. 'Such places lead to sin,' I said.

'Vosper's certainly does,' Matthew said.

'Humphrey Vosper?' Charlotte asked.

'You know him?'

'What happened to Mr Peter?' she said.

'He's long dead,' Matthew said. 'Before I came to Penhale and that was years ago now. How do you know Vosper?'

'How did Mr Peter die?'

'An accident. In the Mowhay. Fell and hit his head on a lump of moor stone, they say.'

'Were they cutting the hay?' Charlotte said.

He frowned at her. 'How did you know that?'

'The field hasn't been cut for a long time,' she said. 'I thought Mr Peter dying there might be why.'

He looked at her for a moment then brushed his hands down the front of his white shirt and it struck me again how smart he was dressed for a farm servant.

'Where do you get the money for such good clothes?' I asked him. 'Mrs Peter pays you as a farm servant, doesn't she? She's not paying us enough to get such things.'

Charlotte looked him up and down as if seeing him for the first time. She took his arm as we walked back to the house. I was left to walk behind them.

We went to bed, and, just as before, I heard Matthew and John Peter talking in the room next to ours. When the voices stopped there was no sound of the door opening and Matthew stepping out onto the landing. I guessed then that they shared the room, and I said as much to Charlotte as we lay together in the thickening dark.

'John Peter's not master, then,' she said.

'Mrs Peter is. Or she's mistress, rather. It's her we have to please.'

Charlotte must have fallen asleep then for she made no answer.

FIVE

A noise woke me. I thought it was the scrabbling I'd heard in my dreams but the room was quiet. Too quiet. No one breathed beside me.

Charlotte was gone.

I drew back the curtain and saw that it was still night, but a light was burning in the Mowhay field behind the house.

I wrapped my blanket round me and crept from the room, glad of the candle I had kept from Mrs Peter, even though the flame made the landing's walls seem closer. They leant over me and I thought I felt them brush my face as if they had little hands or wings like moths. The wind was throwing itself against the house, making a fuss to be noticed. A draught clutched my legs.

On the last stair my foot touched something soft and yielding, and a cry escaped my lips. The black cat leapt from the shadows with a hiss. She crossed my path. There was nothing I could do.

My candle would be no good in the wind so I set it in the porch window to guide me back. I went round the side of the house. In the field the light was still burning. It was bright and steady though the wind should by rights have blown it out.

I made my way through the Mowhay's long grass, the light keeping my path true. I could smell water, heard it gurgling close by but couldn't see it. As I drew close, I saw the light was set on the tumbled walls I'd first seen from the kitchen window, the stones watched over by the thorn tree that had forced its way to being so wide and thickety, had forced the wall apart, perhaps. Bright ribbons and scraps of white cloth were tied to the branches, and beneath them, in a tangle of ferns, Charlotte was seated. Her eyes were closed. Her face was bathed in the light of the flame. She held something in her hands.

'What are you doing?' I said.

She gasped and opened her eyes. The flame died.

'You shouldn't creep like that!' she said.

'Charlotte – your hands!'

Blood seeped between her palms still clasped together. She opened them and a piece of mirrored glass fell to the ground, smeared red.

She licked each palm to rid them of the blood and she was like the black cat washing herself.

'What is this place?' I said.

'A well. An old one. It would have had a roof once, somewhere to sit. Mrs Peter should have tended it better – it's on her land. *This* is wickedness. At least the water still flows. That's something. Look.'

Charlotte parted the ferns beside her and I saw the water. The pool was large as a good-sized cooking pot, the water shaking with the spring's life.

'It's why the grass has grown so well,' she said, plucking the water with her fingers. 'It's good Mrs Peter hasn't cut it for hay.'

'Why? What would happen if she did?'

'Bad things. I've seen them. Last place I was, there was an old well in the Mowhay, just like this. The farmer who owned the land, he said the hay would be cut. I told him not to, that it would bring harm, but he didn't listen. He called me names of spite.' She took her hair into her hands and coiled it so tight I thought she'd pull it out. 'When his son's leg was cut by the scythe he knew my words to be true but by then it was too late.'

'The boy died.'

'Not right away. His leg was taken off below the thigh. I heard his cries from my bed. He died a week later when the rot set in.'

I thought she was smiling but it was hard to be sure in the dark.

'But how did the boy get hurt? Was he lying in the grass?'

'He was hurt because the well was hurt. It wasn't an ordinary well, Shilly, and neither is this one. Such places are old – old as the earth. They must be cared for, tended. Every well has a power, just like every person. Some cure sore eyes, some mend broken bones. I've known some that keep a body from being hanged. This one . . . I don't know yet what it can do.'

'Perhaps it could help Mrs Peter's bad shoulder,' I said.

'She'd have to be kindly to me first,' Charlotte said.

And then I screamed. Something had dropped in to her lap. Something with claws and a tail. 'Hush!' she said. 'They'll hear us in the house.'

The mouse sat on her knee and looked at me. His tail twitched. I slunk back until I was against the ruined wall.

'This is St Michael,' Charlotte said. 'He's my companion.' She put her thumb close to his face and didn't mind when he set to gnawing her nail.

'You mean he's a pet.'

'No. He's . . . a friend. He understands things.'

'He's a mouse, Charlotte. How can he understand things?'

'He's clever. He helps me.'

'With what?'

'Charms,' she said.

'The rags on the tree?'

'They're clouties.' She brushed the cloth and ribbons with the back of her hand. 'Charms are other things. Things you can hold and things you can say. St Michael makes them strong.'

I peered at the mouse – at St Michael. His tail kept twitching. He looked to be an ordinary creature. I reached to touch him. He darted up Charlotte's arm and hid in her hair.

'You mustn't stroke him,' she said.

'He doesn't like me.'

27

'Because you forget to shut the door. He fears the black cat will get him.'

'You keep him in our room?'

'I don't keep him anywhere. He comes and goes as he pleases. He has a straw bed behind the corner cupboard.'

'Charlotte!'

'Don't tell Mrs Peter. She'd kill him with the poker, I know she would. And you must be careful with the door. Keep it shut or the cat will get him.'

'Living with a mouse.'

'Please, Shilly!'

For her, anything.

'Don't you let him near me,' I said. Then the wind gusted and I remembered it was night and cold and our warm bed waited for us. 'Are you . . . finished here?'

'For now,' she said, getting to her feet.

I followed her, hoping she'd have the makings of another fire to light our way but she didn't and I had to stumble in the long grass and hidden stones.

The candle I'd left in the porch had gone out.

SIX

I made sure to shut the door to our room the next morning when we went out to work. I didn't care for St Michael but I cared for Charlotte and she cared for him. That was enough for me to take more care.

I thought about the clouties tied to the thorn tree. I thought about the child losing his leg. I watched John Peter's hands all through the week that followed but the warts stayed stout on both his thumbs. I asked Charlotte why they hadn't gone.

'His mother stopped my work too soon. She's afraid of such things.'

'But why, if there's only good in them?'

'There's no such thing as only good, Shilly. There's only balance – the good with the bad. You have to have one to know the other.'

We were at evening milking, the light seeping from the sky and disappearing into the thirsty ground that drank it down.

'There's badness in what you do?' I said.

'Sometimes. If people are bad to me. Pass me that pail. I swear these creatures get more wilful by the day. Get on!'

She slapped a cow hard across its backside. The sound rang out like a shot.

After supper she said she was going for a walk. Matthew and John Peter both made to put their jackets on but she said no, she'd rather go alone. She was going to the old well in the Mowhay field, I thought, and though she didn't ask me to go with her I was pleased I knew her ways and the men didn't.

The porch door banged shut and Charlotte was gone. Mrs Peter gave a sigh like she'd been holding her breath.

'There now. Wake up the fire, Shilly. My bones are cold tonight.'

She eased herself in to the settle, the high back good for her bad shoulder, which didn't seem to be getting better. Matthew and John Peter took chairs on either side and we softened to our evening. It was easier without Charlotte there. I hadn't known it until she'd gone but there it was. The air in the room was quieter. Mrs Peter's face lost its sharpness. She didn't speak of the Devil or the Good Lord as much. Matthew looked to the porch from time to time, until Mrs Peter asked him for a song and he gave us his favourite, the tune I'd heard him sing on the day I came to the farm.

Sweet maidens all, pray hear this tale,
for I am blind and my heart doth ail,
my golden lad is gone, is gone,
and on the moor I am undone.

I felt my eyes close. The room was warm from the turfy fire that brought the moor into the house for burning. The dark earth and darker water beneath were thick in my mouth, my throat.

Matthew beat time with the little knife he kept in his belt, tapping it on his chair. It was easy to forget his afflictions when his voice was so beautiful and in the flickering light of the fireside his poxed skin was smoothed. His mouth was eased from the near-sneer that didn't belong on such a kind person. He was made handsome, almost. I wondered if Charlotte saw him so.

The next day was Sunday, chapel day. Mrs Peter said so and we were Mrs Peter's so we were going with her to worship at Tremail, where a chapel was newly opened. We were to meet Mrs Peter's daughter Mary there and we would be on time, Oh heavens, yes, for the Good Lord couldn't be kept waiting.

But milking took too long. The creatures were wilful and stamping in the pails and pushing their nasty, wet noses in our faces. We smacked them and shouted and made Mrs Peter late. And then I shamed her for I had no Sunday clothes.

'What will people think?' she said, seeing us still in our working dresses, covered in mud and cow dirt and sour milk.

'You can have something of mine,' Charlotte said to me.

'So you do have something in that great box of yours,' Mrs Peter said. 'Get up the stairs, then, and be quick about it. We'll have to go on foot across the fields for you've left us no time to take the road.'

'But my good trousers!' Matthew said. He was in the porch, waiting to leave. 'The fields will dirty them.'

'You've Charlotte and Shilly to thank for that,' Mrs Peter said.

Charlotte's box of belongings was under our bed, where it had lain since we first came to the farm. She and I knelt on the floor and together we pulled it out.

'Close your eyes, Shilly.'

'Why? What have you got in there – more mice?'

She reached for my face and before I knew what she was doing she'd run her hot palm over my eyelids to close them, as I'd seen my mother close the eyes of the dead.

I heard the creak of the box opening and thought I would look a little. What could be the harm? But my eyes wouldn't open. I clawed at them. The lids had gone. There was just a spread of skin. She had sealed them closed.

'What have you done to me?' I screamed.

'Easy, easy,' she said, as if I was a horse. 'I said not to look.'

I felt her take my hands and then there was something on me, on my legs and across my front.

'See what I've given you,' she said.

My eyes opened to patterned cloth, red with white shapes. So much cloth I could bunch it and bunch it and there was still more to hold.

And it was on my body. I was clothed in it. My working dress lay on the floor, a heap of rags. But I hadn't put this new dress on. Hadn't felt Charlotte put it on me, either. She was changed too, wearing the fine green dress she'd worn at the hirings. She'd managed to clean John Peter's blood from the elbow, though I hadn't seen her scrubbing anything. St Michael's tail hung out of her sleeve.

'How . . . ?'

'Have you pair expired?' Mrs Peter shouted up the stairs.

Charlotte kicked the box back under the bed then grabbed my hand and we were away down the stairs and out the porch door into the sunlight of the yard. My heart sang and I felt like the whole world was mine, because she was mine. I knew it.

I knew what she was too.

SEVEN

We were too late to find a seat near the front of the chapel, where Mrs Peter said her daughter would be, and could only press in at the back instead. The draught came cold and keen through the poorly shutting doors and the service was too long. The singing helped me bear it, and Charlotte's fine voice joining in, for she could read the words in the hymnal.

'Who taught you to read?' I asked her, amazed that she could. Jealous, too.

'My mother,' she said. She stopped singing for a time after that.

At last the service was over and the doors were opened, but no one was in a hurry to be home. The bare ground between the chapel and the road was full of the lingering, and in their press and gabble Charlotte and I were parted.

'It's Shilly, isn't it?' a voice beside me said.

She was older than me. Fair-looking, with a wide mouth that was the spit of John Peter's but it gave her a pretty smile. Her hands were broad.

I nodded. 'You're Mrs Peter's daughter,' I said.

'Mary Westlake,' she said, and bobbed her head like saying *how do you do*. 'Not much to look at, is it?' she said, waving at the chapel. 'But I like the hymns better than in church.'

'It's good to hear singing that isn't "Sweet Maidens All".'

Mary laughed. 'Matthew still going on about that poor woman, is he? Some things don't change.'

33

'You know his songs?'

'Too well. Matthew came to Penhale before I married.'

I wondered where her husband was. Mrs Peter hadn't spoken of him. Perhaps he was as dead as Mr Peter, killed by the cutting of hay.

'Tell me, how do you find my mother?' Mary said.

'She's crosser than a baited cat sometimes, and she takes all the candles to bed with her.'

'I meant her health,' Mary said.

'Oh! I shouldn't have said—'

But Mary laughed and said she'd wanted for candles of an evening too when she lived at the farm, so it was all right and I liked her.

'My mother looks worse each Sunday,' Mary said.

Mrs Peter was leaning against the chapel's wall as she talked to the women. Her Sunday hat had slipped.

'Her shoulder's giving her pain,' I said. 'But Charlotte could mend it, she knows things.'

'The other girl?'

'She rubbed John Peter's warts with rabbit meat.'

'I shouldn't think that pleased my mother,' Mary said, and then she said something else but the noise of other people's talk had grown louder around us and I didn't catch her words.

Nearby a crowd of men were jostling – Matthew, John Peter and some others. One was a heavy-set man who stank of spirits. I could smell him from where I stood. I was taken bad then, needing to do as I didn't ought to. My skin went clammy. I swallowed the need, fought it, not wanting Mary to see.

'Who's that there, with John Peter and Matthew?' I asked her.

'You've not met Humphrey yet? He's at the inn. Has eggs and milk from the farm.'

There was a lanky boy too. Thin as a willow. He shoved John Peter in the ribs. Mary sucked in her breath.

'That Tom Prout. There's a relation I would happily be without.'

John Peter rammed the boy Tom with his huge shoulders but it was poor Matthew who was knocked to the ground. His right leg, his lame one, twisted under him and he cried out. I couldn't see what was making the men so devilish, and when I turned to ask Mary she'd slipped away. Then the heart of the crush came clear. Charlotte was in the midst of the men.

Mrs Peter appeared at that moment, looking grey about the face. Her mouth was pulled into a line.

'Your shoulder?' I said.

'Giving me some pain today.'

She leant on my arm and we went slowly to the gap in the wall that marked the path home.

Someone called Mrs Peter's name. A gentleman was hurrying towards us. A tall man with blue eyes and brown hair the colour of good chairs.

'I was hoping to catch you,' he said to Mrs Peter. 'I must speak to you about—'

Mrs Peter held up a gloved hand. 'Not today, Daniel. I won't talk of business on the Sabbath. And besides, we must get home to start the dinner.'

'Phillipa, I really—'

'Come tomorrow,' Mrs Peter told him. She turned for home. 'Where are Matthew and John?'

The men were following us slowly, looking back at Tom Prout whispering in Charlotte's ear.

We were granted a half day Sundays so the afternoon was our own. Matthew went out before dinner was done, before I'd even cleared the plates away. He didn't say where he was going but wherever it was, he went there in his good Sunday clothes.

Charlotte looked to be going out too, putting on her pattens and her bonnet. When she opened the porch door John Peter got up from the table to follow her, like a fish drawn on a baited hook. But his mother pulled him back.

35

'You'll stay with me this afternoon, John.'

'No, Mother, I—'

'It'll soon be dirty out. Rain's coming.' Her hand tightened on his arm.

The porch door opened and Charlotte was gone. I felt a dark weight settle on my shoulders, across my back. But then she called me from the yard and I was lifted into the light.

We took the path up to the moor, crossed the road and walked on to the big lump of moor stone that was Lanlary Rock. She whistled and St Michael scrambled out of her sleeve. She let him gnaw on her already bitten thumbnail.

'Where are we going?' I said.

'To see what the land will give us. And isn't it good to be out of the house, away from that woman?'

'Mrs Peter isn't so bad,' I said, thinking of my father and what I'd left behind. His breath burning with spirits and his fists too often finding my flesh. 'She's not mean with feeding us, and we've half days.'

'And that's enough for you, is it, Shilly?'

It was, but I didn't say so, because I didn't want her to think me foolish. That was what her voice was saying to me.

For a time Roughtor sank below the horizon because of how the land rose and fell. It was strange that such a thing as a tor could disappear but that was how the moor was. Something could be there one minute and gone the next, though of course it wasn't truly gone. It was hiding in plain sight.

The ground sloped and then there were marshes. Charlotte's walking slowed. She took a step then stopped. Took another, sideways, then stopped again. St Michael shot up her arm and clung, shaking, to her shoulder. Charlotte plucked at the strings of her bonnet, plucked at her lips. Looked about her like a lost child.

'You've not been long on the moor,' I said.

'It's so open. Not like . . . I can't see . . . There's nowhere to hide.'

'Why do you need to hide?' I said. 'I'm here with you.'

I took her hand and for once it was cold. I showed her where to put her feet so as to cross the marsh without sinking because there was a means, if you knew it. We made our slow way on and Roughtor rose again on the horizon. I wanted to climb the tor, get a purchase on the land by getting up high. But Charlotte pulled me from that path.

'The water,' she said, and I saw that below us was a stream, fed by the marshes and forded beyond. She led me along the bank and was herself again, without fear.

There were trees by the ford and many plants, with flowers and without, with long trailing parts and with thorns. This pleased her and she set about collecting things, St Michael running at her feet. Comfrey for sprains, she said. Rosemary for love. Thyme to keep dark dreams at bay. Hazel for wisdom. My head was too full – her words running over and into one another as she told me how to make use of the world. The power of a bird's heart if taken while the creature lived. The secrets apples could spill.

We'd brought no bag or basket so Charlotte stuffed my clothes with our takings. I was her scarecrow, with twigs and roots poking out the sleeves of my dress. They scratched me as we walked back to the farm but I didn't say so. I would have borne anything for her.

EIGHT

The man who'd spoken to Mrs Peter at chapel came to the farm the next day. I learnt from Matthew that this was Mr Carwitham, a gentleman farmer from Lanhendra. I'd heard his name before, of course. He was much talked of with farm matters, and likewise his stockman who was called Roe.

Because Mr Carwitham was a gentleman he waited in the parlour instead of the kitchen, which was a room Mrs Peter never used but which she said had to be kept neat. To have rooms that went unused – such wealth Mrs Peter had.

She'd woken with the pain in her shoulder worsened and couldn't rise from her bed, so she asked Matthew to talk to Mr Carwitham. I was cleaning the plates after dinner, half listening to the men's voices coming from the parlour.

'I need to see the tithe map, Weeks,' Mr Carwitham said, and it took me a moment to understand who Mr Carwitham meant because no one at Penhale used Matthew's last name.

Matthew came into the kitchen with a roll of paper and spread it on the table, meaning Mr Carwitham had to follow him, had to do his business in the dirtiest, most used part of the house. Mr Carwitham wouldn't like that, I thought. Not by the smart look of him.

Mr Carwitham leant his cane against the table and ran his finger across the map, following its lines.

'This field,' he said. 'I need to move more of my stock to Penhale. Some of my fields are unusable at present, given the rain.'

Had it been that wet? I'd spent time with Charlotte in the Mowhay without my skirt becoming damp. But I'd never been to Mr Carwitham's farm at Lanhendra. Perhaps the fields there were low-lying, flooded by Roughtor Ford so close.

He pointed at the map again. 'Have you room for twenty bullocks or so? I don't want them on the moor this summer. Too costly to risk them with the marshes. I know all about you losing—'

'Which field?' Matthew said.

'This,' Mr Carwitham said, still pointing, not understanding.

'You must tell me the name of the field, sir. I cannot read the words.' Matthew's cheeks didn't colour. He didn't lower his eyes.

'Of course,' Mr Carwitham said quickly. 'Higher well park field.'

I left the kitchen to scald the pails for evening milking, and met Charlotte coming in the porch door.

'They're talking in there,' I said. 'About the fields.'

'Who?'

'Matthew and that Mr Carwitham, from Lanhendra.'

Raised voices drifted out. Mr Carwitham was close to shouting, about due care for prize stock, the money he'd spent on his animals.

'You must help me with the cows,' I said to Charlotte. 'I can't be seeing to them on my own at every milking.'

But she was carrying on into the house, giving no sign she'd even heard me.

Clanking the milk pails together made a good noise and rid me of some of my temper at Charlotte not heeding me, but not enough, for in my raging I pinched the soft udder of the cow I was milking. She kicked out, knocking over the pail and the thin stream of milk I'd got. I was cursing the creature when a hand fell on my shoulder. It was John Peter.

'You scared me!' I shouted at him.

'One of my girls, she's stopped laying,' he said.

I wiped my milky hands on my apron. My hands came away more dirty. 'Do you want me to do it?'

John Peter nodded. I went with him to the worn patch of ground where his chickens pecked their days away. I could see which hen it was. She was thinner than the others and some of her feathers were missing.

I stepped over the low wall that made one side of the chicken run. The hens scattered in a flurry. The old hen didn't move when I picked her up. She knew. I sat on the wall and got her back end tucked into the crook of my arm. I was setting to wring her neck when John Peter laid his big hands on the hen.

'She's mine, Shilly. I should do it.'

He held the chicken as he'd seen me hold her but his hands trembled on her neck. Then his hands jerked and the chicken thrashed. But he hadn't broken the neck, only crushed it. The chicken kept thrashing. John Peter tried to wring the neck again but each time his hands slipped or he was too slow. The poor hen was suffering so I took her from him. I snapped the neck. It was done. I left John Peter sobbing. I took the dead hen to the house.

Charlotte and Matthew were talking by the hearth. On seeing me they stopped. Mr Carwitham had gone.

Matthew said he had to see to higher well park field while there was still light, that Mr Carwitham's bullocks would soon be driven to the farm.

'His best stock,' he said, puffing out his chest like one of John Peter's chickens. He put on a fine coat, too fine for working, surely, if he had any sense. It was almost as fine as the one Mr Carwitham had been wearing.

I slung the dead hen on the table. Her snapped neck lolled and her head dangled over the edge.

NINE

A few nights later I woke to find her gone, but I knew where to look. A light burnt on the old well's walls.

Her eyes were closed and she didn't open them when I drew near but I knew she knew I was there. Bunches of herbs and flowering plants hung from the thorn tree. A dead magpie lay at her feet, a white ribbon round its neck.

I sat beside her. She was warm and warmed me.

'Did you kill the bird?' I said. There were no marks on it. It looked as it would have done if it was perched in a tree rather than lying in the mud and weeds of the old well.

'You think I would harm a creature like this?' She kept her eyes closed. Her fingers were turning over a bent pin.

'You sealed up my eyes,' I said. 'There was harm in that.'

'That . . . That was nothing.'

'There's always something to be got from nothing,' I said.

She laughed and opened her eyes.

'So you are learning from me.' She tossed the bent pin into the well water. 'Watch,' she said.

Nothing happened. Then a bubble rose and broke the surface. Then another. Charlotte whistled and St Michael pattered out of the ferns. He ran up her arm and into her hair.

'Two to beware of,' she said. 'Two to cause harm.'

To cause her harm? Or would she and St Michael do the harming? She and I? I didn't have the words to ask because I didn't want to know the answer. I picked a fern then picked it to pieces.

'Can I trust you, Shilly?'

'I won't tell Mrs Peter about . . . about this, what you do.'

'Good. But I need you to keep another secret. As soon as I can I'm going to Boscastle.'

'Where's that?'

'By the sea. Not many miles from here.'

'Your family's there?'

She nodded and I saw that she was scritching, though she made no sound to match her tears. The flame on the wall jumped but didn't go out.

'What's wrong? Don't you want to see them?' I said.

'I was turned out.' Charlotte pushed away her tears so hard she looked to put out her eyes. 'My mother, she's a schoolteacher in the village. She and my father weren't wed.'

We were silent for a time. Bats swooped overhead, making for the barn. Their bodies were flickers of black in the already black night.

'She'd lose her work if people knew,' Charlotte said, her voice colder now. 'It was my aunt took me to All Drunkard for the Lady Day hirings the first time, years ago now. They wanted me far away.'

She was telling me her secrets, which meant she trusted me and that meant she loved me. I put my hand on her knee to let her know I felt the same, that she could tell me anything.

'All my family are in Boscastle,' she said. 'Hat-makers, apart from my mother. Do some fine work, too, I've heard. Not that I'll ever wear such things. This is all I have. My mother gave it to me before my aunt took me to the hirings.'

She reached inside her shift and drew out a string of beads. It hung so low beneath her clothes that I hadn't seen it before. The flame on the wall made the red glass shine but the beads were misshapen and chipped. The string was dirty. It was a poor piece for her who wore such good clothes, her smart silk.

42

'Do you mean to live in Boscastle, find work there?' My heart hammered in my chest. She would leave me.

'That wouldn't be enough, she won't . . .' Charlotte wiped her face but I couldn't see or hear more tears. I moved close to her and put my arm around her. I felt her ribs through the shift, the heaving of her chest.

'Shh, shh,' I said. 'It's all right. You have a home here now, with us.'

'But I . . . I have to . . .' She pulled away from me. 'I need more than this.'

She tugged at her thin and worn shift, meaning everything else as well, somehow – milking, barely owning anything, sharing a bed, being bound to a mistress. Being a farm servant, as we were.

'I need to be better,' she said. 'My mother will have me then. If I can just change things somehow, then I can go back.'

'How will you do that?' I said, for our lot in life was fixed as moor stone. It couldn't be cast anew.

Charlotte tucked the string of beads inside her shift. 'You mustn't tell anyone I'm going to Boscastle. She won't admit who I am, not yet. But she will. I'll catch the carrier's cart from Camelford. It'll take me to Boscastle and back the same day. I've checked. You know the moor better than I do. I need you to show me the path through the marshes. Will you do that, Shilly?'

Anything to keep her from harm.

TEN

Morning came too soon. The cows were clamouring to be milked and the pigs were calling their hunger but I was so weary after staying in the Mowhay that I couldn't rouse myself to care.

Matthew, too, seemed to be behind, but he was rushing when I was resting. From the kitchen I saw him hurrying down to higher well park field as fast as his limp would let him. And then I saw why, for coming into the yard was a herd of bullocks, followed by Mr Carwitham and a man I took to be Roe, his stockman. The pair of them were on horseback.

The field wasn't ready. Part of the wall had tumbled and the gate looked like it would drop from its hinges any moment, such was the rot. Matthew had forgotten. It was Charlotte did that. She sent his thoughts far from mending walls, just as she sent mine from milking cows.

Mr Carwitham didn't hide his annoyance. He had no cause to, him being a gentleman and Matthew a farm servant. Mr Carwitham wouldn't have such poorly kept fields on his own land, given his standing. I said as much to Charlotte. We were in the window seat, watching the men trying to herd the creatures through the yard.

'If he's got so much good land himself, why's he bringing his animals here?' she said.

'He must have too many,' I said.

Strands of her thick, dark hair had slipped from the knot she tied while working, not that she did much of that, truth be told. I tucked the strands behind her ear, and stroked her ear too, but she didn't notice. She was watching the men. Mr Carwitham booted his fine bay horse and shouted. Even with the porch door closed we could hear him cursing 'Weeks this' and 'Weeks that'.

I moved my fingers from her ear to her throat. I could feel her blood beating but I didn't like that so much because with every beat I worried the next wouldn't come, so I stroked her cheek instead.

'Am I a cat?' she said, leaning her head on my chest so that I should stroke her more easily. Still she stared into the yard, at the men.

'St Michael wouldn't have lasted so long if you were,' I said.

She laughed and the sound thrummed through me. There was clomping above us and then it was coming down the stairs, but slower than usual. Mrs Peter was out of her bed where her bad shoulder had been keeping her.

'Whatever will Daniel think of us?' she said, and then she saw Charlotte and I curled together in the window seat. 'What are you pair doing sitting there? Go out and help, for Heaven's sake!'

She shooed us into the yard like we were John Peter's chickens, and shut the porch door to keep herself from harm for it was bedlam in the yard. The bullocks were charging about, all hooves and tails and fear, unable to see their way out of the yard and down to the field in all their rushing. Charging here and there between the frightened creatures were Mr Carwitham and Roe on their horses, whips raised. I caught sight of Charlotte pressed against the wall of the barn, trying to keep herself from being knocked to the ground and likely trampled.

All at once Roe's horse was bearing down on me. I only just got out of the way of his flailing whip. It was then I saw the smoke swirling at my feet. It stretched like fingers and the fingers clutched the legs of the charging herd, pulling them to where they belonged to be. Mr Carwitham and Roe couldn't see the smoke from up on their horses. They thought they were getting somewhere at last, that it was their doing. Mr Carwitham crowed like a cock.

The creatures stopped running and walked down the path to the field, where Matthew was hurriedly shoring up the tumbled walls. The yard was suddenly quiet, like the peace when a storm has blown out.

But the peace didn't last long.

Charlotte and I went back inside the house and set the breakfast things. Or rather I set them. Charlotte was in the window seat. For once Mrs Peter didn't tell her to stir herself and help me, for Mrs Peter was in pain. She cowered on the settle, but there was no escaping her own body.

Mr Carwitham charged into the kitchen like one of his mad creatures, like the house was his to do with as he wished.

'Phillipa, you must see that the man's incompetent.' He stopped raging when he saw Mrs Peter's face, the way she held herself.

'Daniel, you must forgive Matthew. We've been hard-pressed, my shoulder the way it is.'

Matthew was coming into the house just behind Mr Carwitham. His face was a deep red and he was panting. But he heard Mrs Peter's words and they took away some of his fear.

'Of course,' Mr Carwitham said, fiddling with the head of his whip. 'I . . . You must let me help more. I can do your accounts, and Isaac will help Weeks in the fields.'

Roe had slipped in from the porch without a sound. He nodded at Mr Carwitham's words.

'Lord knows you need more able-bodied men,' Mr Carwitham said.

A creak on the stairs put a stop to the talking. John Peter peered down.

'Mother?'

'It's all right, my dear. The bullocks are safely away.' She tried to rise but the movement clearly pained her.

Mr Carwitham gently put a hand on her arm. 'Don't get up, Phillipa. Let me.' He went to the bottom of the stairs and called, 'Is the Master of Penhale at home?'

After a moment the stairs creaked again and John Peter came down slowly. Mr Carwitham steered him to the table.

'I've just been saying to your mother that I'd like to help more at Penhale, with Isaac here. You'll let us do that, won't you? Set the farm right again?'

The porch door banged shut. I saw Matthew's back crossing the yard.

'I don't like cows,' John Peter said, and I could have kissed him.

'Now, John,' his mother said. 'You know there's always been cows at Penhale. Daniel's brought a few more, that's all.'

'And I must thank you for letting me, Phillipa.'

'Nonsense. It makes sense to run your stock here, given the fields I have empty. You must think of Penhale as your own land, Daniel.'

'But Penhale is mine, Mother!'

'Of course it is,' Mr Carwitham said. 'Nothing will change, with Isaac and myself helping. Life might just be a little easier, that's all. And wouldn't that be better for all of us, eh?'

To my great surprise, and Mrs Peter's too, Charlotte said we should all have a dish of tea. She even set the water boiling herself. But I had no thirst for it, not for tea at any rate. I helped get out the better cups and then went to the cold-shed for milk. When I came back Charlotte was seated next to Mr Carwitham, listening to his talk about the best grass for bullocks, and making a good show of looking like she cared.

ELEVEN

After breakfast I got her to myself again as Mrs Peter told us to clean out the pigs' small field. Mr Carwitham's offer of help didn't mean dirty work of that sort. The air was thick with flies. Wet, whiskery snouts sniffed and barged us as we dug. We stank of our own bodies and those of the pigs.

Charlotte rested on the handle of her shovel. I looked where she was looking and saw Tom Prout coming through the fields. She raised a hand in greeting. I fell to working again to show we were too busy for idle talk. When would these men stop coming to bother us?

'They're working you hard, then,' Tom said, reaching the field's low wall.

'Told you at chapel I was needed here,' she said.

'There's need for you at Tremail too.' He swept the flies from his face. 'If you're looking for a change.'

'Penhale is fine enough,' Charlotte said. 'For now.'

I stopped digging the muck. She wanted to leave me?

Tom leant his elbows on the wall and cupped his chin in his hands. 'Mother sent me to see how my aunt is.' But he made no sign of leaving.

'Mrs Peter is your aunt?' Charlotte said. She let her shovel drop. The old sow trod on it and pushed it deep into the mud.

'By marriage,' Tom said. 'She's related to nearly everyone in these parts. Mother says to the whole county.'

'Is she?' Charlotte said.

'Even to well-born folk. She was a Billings before she married. They're an old St Breward family. They built—'

'What do you want?' Matthew said, coming up behind Tom.

48

'To see my aunt,' Tom said.

'You won't find her in a pig pen,' Matthew said. His hand went to his belt where his little work knife hung.

Tom raised his palms and grinned. 'No need for that, is there? I'm not harming anyone. I'll be seeing you, Charlotte. You know you're always welcome at Tremail.' He sauntered off towards the farmhouse.

'Why are you so rude to Tom?' Charlotte asked Matthew.

'Because he's a liar,' Matthew said. He went to the barn and slammed the door behind him.

When we went in to make the dinner at midday Tom Prout had gone but Matthew couldn't rid himself of his anger. He left half his bread and cheese. John Peter fell upon the plate like a starved man, even though he'd already eaten nearly all the loaf.

Mrs Peter was on the settle, leaning against its tall back.

'Is the pain bad?' I said.

She squeezed my hand and there was some of her old strength. 'I'm better for having Tom visit. He's a good lad. And now Daniel will be coming to help, the farm will be looked after too.'

Matthew got up and left the house without a word.

I cleared the table, mostly sweeping up John Peter's crumbs. It looked as if he'd ripped his bread apart rather than eaten it. Then Mrs Peter gave me a job I didn't want. Taking eggs and butter to Vosper at the Britannia Inn, across the road.

The thirst was on me then and I felt the cold sweat come. Such need was always close but I sought ways to quieten its clamour, to keep from being short with others, to hide my hands not working as they should. Mrs Peter saying I had to go to Vosper's inn set the thirst free again and that was frightening for it made me someone else. Someone I didn't like.

I went to gather the things. The butter was in the cold-shed, wrapped in muslin. I put it in my basket with the eggs John Peter had collected. The light from the doorway darkened. Charlotte leant against the frame.

'I'll take them,' she said.

I wanted her to go for me but I feared for her too, so I told her we would go together. It was safest that way.

We walked up the path. The black cat came with us, running a little ahead and then lagging behind. A warm breeze was coming off the moor. The scent it brought was rich and good. The sweetness of gorse. The ripe marsh water. I felt better the closer we came to the end of the path, despite where we were headed. Charlotte seemed to fade with each step. When the moor was clear before us she stopped and reached for my hand.

The Britannia Inn had been built as a house and still looked like one apart from the sign Vosper had placed above the door. There were a few rooms for paying guests, Mrs Peter said, not that many people stopped the night if they could help it. Most would press on to All Drunkard. When Charlotte and I went inside, the black cat stopped at the door. She was no fool.

My eyes came to know the dark and then I saw my father. He was sitting at the bar. I couldn't breathe. I swayed and thought I'd drop the basket but Charlotte held me. I made myself look at the man.

He wasn't my father. Just another drunkard. They all looked the same. Many men were my father.

Vosper appeared at the bar. There was a dirty rag over his shoulder. He leered at Charlotte and me in the doorway.

'To what do I owe this pleasure?'

He knew why we were there. He could see the basket. Wretched man. The room was thick with ale's yeast as well as the reek of spirits that hung about Vosper's person. My shaking grew worse and my hands were not my own.

'We've brought you eggs and butter,' Charlotte said, 'should you ever do any cooking in this forsaken place.'

She went to the bar and I followed like a dog, close enough that I could take what I wanted without being seen. My hand shook as I reached out but when I got hold of a bottle my strength returned to me. It had been too long.

The man I'd thought was my father sniffed and wiped his mouth on his cuff. He looked Charlotte up and down and then fell from his stool to the floor. Charlotte only glanced at him.

Vosper whipped the rag from his shoulder and ran it through his hands. 'I can assure you there's always a hot meal waiting for you here. No charge.'

The man on the floor took hold of Charlotte's leg. Without a flinch or a murmur she lifted her boot and brought it down hard on the man's hand. He cried out. Vosper leant over the bar.

'You won't make that mistake again, will you?'

I darted from the inn. I'd seen she could take care of herself, and I needed a moment on my own, to do as I had need to.

I waited at the top of the path with the back cat nosing my legs. I could see the inn from there but I couldn't smell it, which was something. After a while Charlotte came blinking into the sunshine. I dropped the bottle in a clump of gorse, knowing I could come back for it later.

'Why were you so long?' I asked her as we walked back to the farmhouse.

'I was talking,' she said.

'To Vosper? But he's so . . .'

She shrugged. 'He's harmless. And the others. Now listen, Shilly, I'm going on Sunday, to Boscastle. Remember your promise.'

She grabbed my hand and pulled me up short, studied my face as if looking for lying.

'I won't say anything,' I said.

'See that you don't. I'll go after chapel. You'll come with me, show me the way.'

'We'll go to Roughtor Ford,' I said. 'It's easy to find the path from there, once you've passed the marshes.'

TWELVE

When Sunday came Charlotte told no one else she was going to Boscastle.

Mrs Peter looked at her askance when she came down the stairs in her best dress and with pattens on. John Peter was asleep after a big dinner at midday. His snores made even the black cat wary. It was Matthew that questioned her.

'Tremail you're going to? Who are you going to see?'

She got her bonnet from the table and her handkerchief from the settle. He followed her about the room.

'Not to see Tom?' he said.

Poor Matthew. She smiled at him and wouldn't say. I couldn't meet his eye for feeling sorry for him. He followed us up the path and onto the moor. Charlotte set a smart pace because she had to get to Boscastle and back before the light faded, but Matthew's limp slowed us down.

We reached the ford. Charlotte put a gloved hand on Matthew's chest.

'No further,' she said.

'But if you won't tell me—'

And then she was kissing him, right there in front of me. A long, slow kiss. Her eyes were closed but Matthew's were wide open as if he couldn't believe it. Neither could I. I climbed down the bank. The water had nearly dried up. I was standing in a kind of pit. She was murmuring to him but I couldn't hear the words and I didn't want to. They were for him, as her kisses were. I kicked at the dust.

At last she called my name. Matthew was walking away, back to the farm, doing as she wished. As all men seemed to. As I did. The only person not charmed by Charlotte was Mrs Peter.

I climbed up the bank. The silence between us was heavy, my tongue dry as the old river place when I asked her, 'Are you and Matthew courting?'

She laughed. I started walking again, and she stayed behind me for I was meant to be showing her the safest path through the marshes. She was just out of my sight, keeping from my questions. She did that on the farm too, seemed always to be disappearing, though never for long. I would look in a place – the barn, say – and she wouldn't be there. No trace of her either, no St Michael pattering. And then there she'd be, right where I'd just looked, as if in the time it took me to turn around, walk out of the barn, she'd made herself appear.

She cried out. I turned. She was sinking.

'Help me!'

Black water seeped from the earth at her feet.

She grasped my hand and waded about, trying to free herself.

'Don't fight it!' I said. 'It'll take you quicker.'

I pulled. Her feet rose in the mud. The marsh hadn't got her yet. I pulled her clear without wrenching her ankle. She fell on top of me and we lay in a heap until she caught her breath. Her cheeks were red and wet with tears.

'How did you walk into the marsh?' I said. 'Why didn't you follow me?'

She shook her head.

'Are you hurt?'

'My stockings!' she said. They were streaked with mud and one was torn. 'Look at the state of me. What will she say?'

'Surely your mother won't mind about your stockings?' I helped her to her feet.

'She will mind,' Charlotte muttered. 'Or she'll mind but not say and that's the worst.'

'Do you want to go back to change them?' I said. I would have lent her mine, had I worn any.

'I can't be late,' she said. She started walking again and this time I took more care over where she put her feet.

I went with her as far as Alex Tor, a small tor close to Roughtor. I pointed out the path she should take.

'I'll be back before dark,' she said.

I didn't want her to go. She might get caught in another marsh, lose her way, lose the light.

'I'll come with you, make sure you—'

She put her gloved hand on my chest, just as she had done with Matthew at the ford. And then she kissed me.

She got back safe but tired. She undressed and climbed into bed with me. I asked her how it had been with her family. She didn't answer, only whistled. St Michael came in through the opened window and pattered to his straw bed. I blew out the candle. I held her close.

THIRTEEN

In the morning Matthew sent us down to higher well park field once the milking was done. The weather was hot and Mr Carwitham's bullocks were drinking the water as fast as we could fill the trough. Three trips back and forth from the working well and then came a shout from the field's gate.

Mr Carwitham urged his horse into a trot. I thought of the day he brought the bullocks to the farm, Roe nearly striking me down in the rushing of the frightened creatures. I pressed myself against the trough.

'I trust your mistress is well?' he said on reaching us. He seemed to be asking us both but it was Charlotte who answered.

'No worse,' she said, holding his horse's head as he got down.

His eyes shone an even brighter blue in the sunshine. He smelt of oiled leather and freshly washed clothes.

'Good. When I've seen how the stock are faring I'll call at the house. Ah,' he said, seeing Matthew hurrying towards us as fast as his limp would allow.

Mr Carwitham didn't walk to meet Matthew in the field and so save him effort, just stood and waited. He tapped his whip against his boot with a dull smack. When Matthew reached us he was out of breath. His face was wet with sweat.

'Sir,' he puffed, 'is something wrong?'

'I came to check the bullocks, Weeks, and your mending of the walls. These are prime stock. I don't want them getting onto the moor and into a marsh.'

'Surely your stockman could have called for you, saved you a journey in this heat.'

'Do not presume to counsel me on the best way to manage my animals.'

Matthew nodded, kept his gaze on the ground. Mr Carwitham looked a little sorry for his words.

'Come now, Weeks. I admit I lost my temper when we brought the bullocks.' Here he smiled at Charlotte and I when it was Matthew he should offer such niceness. 'But I'm entrusting you with my best stock.' Mr Carwitham used his whip to point at the wall behind us. 'There are still stones loose near the gate. A determined bullock might find a way.'

'Matthew's doing his best,' Charlotte said. She seemed to have moved without my noticing and now stood closer to Mr Carwitham. Behind him the creatures ambled about, not caring about walls or masters.

'Of course,' Mr Carwitham said. 'You'll see to the walls, Weeks, and that will be fine.'

'You're at Lanhendra?' she said.

'I am.'

'And you have a fine house, I'll wager.'

Matthew's face was white, listening to her. If she was trying to make him jealous then she needn't have bothered. Tom Prout had seen to that already.

Mr Carwitham looked taken aback by her boldness. 'I do, yes. I . . . Weeks, how is the Mowhay faring in this heat? I'll speak to Phillipa about cutting the hay, if she's well enough to see me.'

'She mustn't cut the hay,' Charlotte said. 'Don't you make her.'

'Why ever not?' Mr Carwitham said. 'The Mowhay here is going to waste, and my stock must eat this winter.'

'Don't cut the hay,' Charlotte said. She put her hand on his arm and stared up into his face for he was taller than her. He looked at her hand touching him but he didn't shake her off. He was caught by her as we'd all been caught.

'Water's low again,' I said. 'In the trough.'

Mr Carwitham stumbled backwards, as if my words had freed him somehow, and maybe they had.

'I must see Phillipa,' he said.

Only when he was halfway across the field did he straighten his back and urge his horse into a trot. Only then did he stop looking over his shoulder.

Soon after that Mrs Peter's cows went up to the moor for summer pasture. Matthew said the change of grass was good for them but I feared they'd be the same ill-tempered beasts when they returned, if they could keep out of the marshes. Mr Carwitham's stock was too valuable to wander freely. He never tired of telling us that on his visits to Penhale.

Charlotte still made her way to Boscastle once a fortnight or so. When she was safely back and in our bed she never spoke of how her family greeted her, if her mother had admitted her. I thought there must be some kindness there because she kept making her visits, and she went in all weathers. She knew the way by then and didn't need me to guide her across the moor. Sometimes Matthew went with her as far as the ford. He seemed no wiser as to where she went when they parted.

Most evenings Charlotte and I walked out on the moor. The times it was just us two were the times I liked best. One hot day after our work was done, Charlotte and I were leaving the house when Mrs Peter gave a shout.

'Lord's sake, Matthew, will you sit down?' she said. She shoved him onto the settle. 'You've blood all down your shirt and I don't want it on the floor.'

His nose had bled. His face was white and he swayed even though he was sitting on the settle. Mrs Peter made him tip back his head and cup his nose. Blood oozed between his fingers.

'Don't go, Charlotte,' he said through his hand.

'You should lie down. Rest, Matthew.' And then she was gone. I ran after her.

We reached the top of Roughtor sweating and panting in the heat. There was the whole moor laid out before us. Free from the shadows of clouds it was so beautiful it made me catch my breath.

'By the sea, that's where I belong.' She pointed to the line of light on the horizon. 'That's my home.'

'You'll get back there,' I said. 'Properly, to live. I know you will.' But as I said it I felt low. I would lose her.

On our way back we saw Mr Carwitham and Roe. They were coming up the slope from the ford. We were almost close enough to speak to them. Mr Carwitham raised his hat and looked like he would close the little distance between us. But then Roe said something to him and Mr Carwitham raised his hat to us again, this time in farewell, and he and Roe continued on their way.

'Have you ever heard Roe speak?' I asked Charlotte.

'He's got no tongue in his head.'

'That sounds like something Mrs Peter would say.'

'She'd say the Devil took it,' Charlotte said.

Matthew was waiting for us. His shirt was streaked with blood. I asked him how he was. He didn't answer.

'Take no notice,' Mrs Peter said. 'He's sullen as a cow wanting to be milked. Has been since you left.'

'Come outside,' he said to Charlotte. 'I wish to speak to you alone.' He pulled her roughly by the arm.

The look she gave him put a stop to that. He let go of her. Charlotte went to the yard by her own wish. I caught her words to Matthew as the porch door closed.

'Don't you *ever* touch me like that again.'

All this with Mrs Peter and me to hear it.

'That girl . . .' Mrs Peter said.

I followed her up the stairs and went in to mine and Charlotte's room. The window was open and I heard Charlotte and Matthew below. I moved close to the glass but stayed out of sight. Matthew had his arms around her, holding her close. She was letting him pull her into his bloody shirt. I gagged on the thought of the smell.

She came to our room. The heat of the day was still trapped in the house. She took off her clothes and we slipped into bed. Her necklace of red beads pressed against me. In the morning their shape was set in my skin.

Our walks across the moor stopped not long after. There was more to do on the farm. Mrs Peter said it was time to cut the Mowhay.

FOURTEEN

It was late August by then. Mrs Peter had gone to market in All Drunkard, even though the pain in her shoulder had worsened again.

'Mary says the All Drunkard farms are cutting,' she said on her return, with us all there for dinner. 'Weather's wanting to change this time next week so we must get on. We'll have to have help, of course.'

'Don't cut the field,' Charlotte said.

Mrs Peter held up her hand to silence her. 'Tom will come, and Daniel will send his nice Mr Roe.'

'Mrs Peter—'

'Humphrey has promised me a cider barrel for the field. He might take up a scythe himself, you never know.'

'The old well—'

'For goodness' sake, girl! That field is mine and I will cut that grass if it's the last thing I do.'

'Oh, don't say such a thing!' I said. 'You're asking to be cut down yourself, Mrs Peter.'

'She's not turned your head with this wicked talk, has she, Shilly? Not that I'm surprised, the two of you in the Mowhay all night. Don't think I don't know you're there, doing all manner of devilish things.'

'You mustn't cut the field,' Charlotte said. Her voice was low and cold.

I felt a thrum go through the table, as if it was a bell struck with a hammer. Mrs Peter felt it too for she flinched from the table.

'If you'll threaten me then you'll have a threat in return, my girl. If you don't get hold of yourself about this cutting of the Mowhay then you'll be living with the pigs, do you hear me?'

Charlotte covered her face with her hands, which Mrs Peter took for sobbing but I knew it wasn't.

'It's only a thorn tree and a bit of stone,' she said to Charlotte, almost kindly. 'We'll not touch them. But I must have hay for the winter. Would you have the cows eat the thorn tree?'

'No,' I said, answering for Charlotte.

'Well then. The Mowhay will be cut.' She turned to Matthew. 'We'll have Tom, Mr Roe and Vosper, I hope, for the cutting.'

'Won't Mr Carwitham help with the hay too?' I said.

Charlotte gave a strange laugh and took her hands from her face. 'He's a gentleman, Shilly,' she said. 'He can't be working in the field.'

'He's happy enough to be coming into the field and bothering us when we're trying to work,' I said.

I saw Matthew smile.

'I'll have none of that talk,' Mrs Peter said. She took my plate from me even though I hadn't finished eating. 'Daniel Carwitham has been a great help on this farm. Cutting the hay, I ask you! He'll be joining us for harvest supper once the work's done. It'll be our chance to thank him. Now, Shilly, you and Charlotte will do the raking. Mary will help me with the cooking while you're in the field. I got plenty laid in this morning. We'll have plum pudding for our harvest supper, now won't that be something?'

John Peter was the only one pleased by the promise of plum pudding. The rest of us knew how hard the work would be. And I knew the cutting would bring something terrible, because Charlotte had told me so.

But there was no telling Mrs Peter.

In the afternoon Matthew looked out the hay-cutting tools at the back of the barn. The two rakes were in a good state, as were the pitchforks, but the only scythe Matthew could find was long rusted. Mrs Peter said she'd ask Mr Carwitham to lend her some. Enough for all the men to use.

That night in the Mowhay Charlotte said we would try to weaken the terrible things that were sure to happen once the hay was cut. The thorn tree would help us because it was a tree of protection. She told me to pick its leaves and as I did so I must think about what I asked of it because that would make the charm stronger. We steeped the leaves in water from the well to make a wash, using one of the dairying pails. When it was ready Charlotte bade me walk the field's walls and rain the wash on them, as if my hands were clouds. St Michael ran ahead of me through the long grass to show me my path.

Then she bade me cut ragwort from the Mowhay's hedges. It was a plant of safety, she said. She asked the well to make the ragwort strong and then bade me set a clump in each corner of the field. St Michael sat on her shoulder and lastly the three of us walked seven times widdershins round the well, Charlotte counting out loud so we shouldn't lose our place. On her saying 'seven' there came a scream. I clutched her arm and whimpered but she was pleased.

'A fox,' she said. 'The charms have been heard.'

But I went to bed uneasy.

FIFTEEN

The cutting day dawned hot. We woke earlier than was custom, for Charlotte and I had to see to our morning work before the men came. Mary came down the path from the moor while we were in with the pigs. I waved but she didn't see us.

'Why doesn't her husband help with the hay?' Charlotte said.

'Robert? Matthew says he's no farmer.'

I scattered turnip ends and blackened potatoes. The pigs snorted with joy and fell to champing, but the old sow was stiff and slow to join the others.

'So Mary won't have the farm, then?' Charlotte said.

'When?'

'When Mrs Peter dies?'

I gasped. 'Is she going to die when the hay's cut?'

'We're all going to die some time, Shilly. Mrs Peter might be hastening her own end by cutting the hay but that's not for us to know.' She patted the old sow's back. 'What I mean is, when Mrs Peter does die – however that might happen – who will get Penhale?'

'Well, if Mary didn't want to farm it then I should think she'd leave it to Tom Prout.'

'Not John Peter?' Charlotte said.

The sow pushed one of her piglets out of the way so as to get a better bit of turnip.

'She might,' I said. 'Why are you asking?'

But Charlotte was already on her way to the Mowhay.

* * *

Matthew, Tom Prout and Roe all bore scythes. Vosper was settling a barrel by the ruined walls of the well house.

'Little early for cider, Humphrey,' Charlotte called.

He laughed and dipped his cup. I'd wait until it was proper and then do the same. I was glad for the heat. My thirst would be as anyone else's.

Tom Prout took off his hat and made his way towards Charlotte. Matthew shouted at him to get back to work but Tom kept on walking.

'You're not master here,' he said.

'I'm your master today,' Matthew said.

Tom blew Charlotte a kiss and she made out she caught it, tucking it into the pocket of her dress. Vosper was slinking along the hedge. Going back to his inn, I guessed. He was too wicked for honest work. Inns were wicked places for wicked men.

Charlotte and I took up our rakes. My heart was thundering with worry. Would someone cut themselves like the boy Charlotte had told me of, or fall and hit their head on moor stone like Mr Peter?

Charlotte picked up her rake. 'We've done what we can,' she murmured to herself. 'On her head be it.'

A slicing sound, the cry of metal. I caught my breath. Tom Prout had started cutting.

The men worked in a line across the field with five feet or so between them. Every now and then a squabble came from Matthew and Tom Prout. Roe worked steadily and didn't look up at the noise. The only time he made any sound at all was when he cursed the black cat for getting in his way. He gave her a sharp kick and she cried out. I looked for her in the long grass for I didn't want her to be caught by a scythe if she was curled up in pain, but I couldn't find her. I hoped she'd got away from Roe.

We stopped to rest mid-morning and it was a blessed relief to empty my boots of the cut grass making me itch. The dust had sent me coughing and my hands were raw from the rake handle.

The men drank deeply from Vosper's cider barrel but they wouldn't stand together to drink. Tom Prout took a cup of cider to Charlotte. I took mine then, when it was safe. It was good for my thirst but not as good as what I'd left in the gorse bush.

Mary came to the field with a basket for our crib, which would see us through to dinner at midday.

'Have you no "Sweet Maidens" for me?' she called to Matthew.

She looked young as she crossed the windrows, lifting her feet so as not to scat the cut hay. Matthew met her in the field and took her basket. She took his arm. He began to sing, for Mary.

Sweet maidens all, pray hear this tale,
for I am blind and my heart doth ail,
my golden lad is gone, is gone,
and on the moor I am undone.

'Not that wretched song again,' Charlotte said. She dug her rake's teeth into the ground. Mary joined in for the second verse.

Such pretty words he sang to me
beneath the budding hawthorn tree
but now the birds have flown, have flown,
and on the moor I am alone.

The air was too hot, too still. There was a prickling that didn't come from the cut grass. I hoped it meant the rain was coming early. If the hay was ruined and left where it lay then maybe we'd all be spared. But no drops fell. The day stayed hot and dry, and the cutting began again.

By the time dusk came all but one corner of the field had been cut. The thorn tree and the walls of the well house looked too big in the open space. They were unprotected.

Roe took his leave. Mrs Peter had said he could sleep in the barn with Tom but Roe said he would rather go home, to Mr Carwitham at Lanhendra. He'd be back to finish the work the next day.

My hands were blistered and my back ached like it had never done before. Charlotte looked to be feeling the same. Tom Prout lent her his arm and they began the walk back to the house, leaving me behind, with Matthew. I felt I should say something to him but I was tired and what could I say that would make him feel better? I felt sore enough myself.

He and I turned into the yard to see Tom in the barn's doorway, trying to pull Charlotte inside.

'I've a nice soft bed in here,' he said. He pressed his face close to hers. 'Come and feel how soft it is.'

I went into the house and didn't look back.

She came to bed with me. The hay's beery smell was heavy in the hot room. She rubbed my back and I hers. We lay together and we rested.

Roe returned at first light and we went to work. Soon it was only the very last stalks of grass left to be cut. Tom Prout fetched the others from the house so they could see the cutting of the neck.

Then the terrible work would be done.

My heart began to race. The men's scythes lay on the ground. Roe drank from the cider barrel. I wanted to do likewise but I couldn't move for ill feeling.

There was a shout. John Peter was running up the field. Matthew and Charlotte got to their feet. Roe dropped the cup in the cider barrel.

'What is it?' Charlotte called to John Peter.

He didn't answer, just kept running, panting, sweating. Had his mother fallen? Or Mary? Had they been burnt, cut, broken in some way?

John Peter reached the end of the field where we were waiting. He dropped to the ground.

'What is it?' I screamed.

'The neck, Shilly. Mother says we're cutting the neck.'

He was excited, that was all. Roe laughed and reached for the cider cup again.

Mary and Mrs Peter arrived and sat on the wall close to where the neck of grass stood. It should have been Matthew cutting the neck, for he was master of us that day in the Mowhay, but it was Tom who drew back his scythe and struck at the last of the grass. He lifted the handful of stalks above his head and crowed, 'I have ee! I have ee! I have ee!'

'What have ee? What have ee? What have ee?' the rest of us sang.

Tom shook the neck of hay at Charlotte, a huge grin splitting his thin face. 'A neck! A neck! A neck!'

And then, as was customary, we all of us sang, 'Hurrah for the neck, hurrah for Mrs Peter.'

Tom gave the grass strands to Mary for plaiting.

'Do it neat, now,' Mrs Peter said, 'if it's to hang in the kitchen all year.'

Nothing terrible had happened yet, but Charlotte was still uneasy. I could see it in the way she looked about her, the way she wrung her hands. Her worry kept my heart jittering. I didn't feel any better when we turned the hay we'd cut the day before, to let the underside dry. I didn't feel better after dinner when we set to forking the windrows into pairs then pooks. It took all afternoon to build the little stacks. At the building of the last one, Tom Prout made it so that he was working next to Charlotte.

'A kiss from a pretty girl will make the hay sweet,' he whispered.

Then he cried out as my pitchfork clipped his boot. Charlotte helped him over to the cider barrel. He limped as badly as Matthew.

Mrs Peter and Mary had laid the table upstairs in the barn, scrubbed it clean of chicken dirt and mould. Our places for the harvest supper were set with strands of knotted grass. A stone jar of ox-eye daisies sat in the middle. Mary's touch, I was sure.

We were sitting down, aching and weary and burnt from the sun, when boots sounded on the stairs leading to the barn's upper floor. Mr Carwitham appeared and took the head of the table, though he'd done nothing for the cutting aside from making Roe come and work, and lending the scythes. He hadn't touched a blade of grass, yet his precious creatures would be eating it all winter.

For a little time after he sat down no one spoke, apart from Mrs Peter prattling about thankfulness and the abundance of the Good Lord's lands and our toiling to Heaven and His Love.

'What good weather we had for it. You see, Charlotte,' she called down to the other end of the table, 'nothing terrible has happened. We're all still standing.' She almost sounded sorry this was so.

'It can take time,' Charlotte said.

'What's this?' Mr Carwitham said, filling his cup. 'Not more talk of bad luck.'

'Oh, we've had plenty such talk, Daniel!' Mrs Peter said.

'The girl doesn't understand the way of the world,' Mr Carwitham said. 'Cattle have to eat come the winter. We can't have things our own way all the time.'

'Quite right,' Mrs Peter said. 'More bread? Shilly, pass it to me.'

Charlotte whispered in Matthew's ear and whatever she said made him smile his strange, sneering smile.

'And butter, Daniel?' Mrs Peter said. 'Shilly made it. You'll take some with you, I hope. Now, I must trespass on your generosity once again and ask for Mr Roe's help with my old sow.'

'Of course. He'd be pleased to. Would Monday week suit you?'

Mrs Peter raised her cup. 'My dear Daniel, I can't thank you enough for all—'

'Those old wells should be filled with earth.'

Everyone fell silent. It was the most Roe had said in all the time of cutting the hay.

SIXTEEN

The rain came a few hours after the hay was safely in the barn, and seemed in no hurry to be gone again. It didn't stop Charlotte going to Boscastle on Sunday.

She got back to Penhale earlier than was her custom. I was alone in the kitchen, clearing the supper things. She tossed her wet shawl across a chair and kicked off her boots any old way. There was half a loaf left ready for breakfast. She tore a great chunk and stuffed it in her mouth. She didn't even try to catch the crumbs.

'What's the matter, Shilly? Aren't you pleased to see me home?'

I hung her wet shawl by the hearth and set her boots to dry. 'Would your mother not see you?'

She sprawled across the settle. '*Home.* That's a poor joke. I've tried to do what she wants and what good has it done me? Made me a fool. I'm no better than her.'

She wasn't talking to me any more. She wasn't even in the same room. Her thoughts were far away and they were full of spite. I knew there was no helping her when she had such tempers. I went to bed, and I took the only candle with me.

A terrible noise woke me. An animal in pain.

I tried to shake Charlotte awake but she pulled the blanket over her head and shook me off.

The noise had come from behind the house. No one else seemed to have heard it for there was no movement in the other rooms.

Had I dreamt it? No, for it came again. Pain, the noise said. Deep, deep pain.

I got dressed and went into the yard, following the cries to higher well park field where Mr Carwitham's bullocks were gathered by the gate, screaming.

At first I couldn't see anything wrong with them, not counting the noise. But then the creature nearest me began to cough, its whole body shaking and rattling so that I thought all its bones would break and it would be a heap of skin on the ground. The others set to coughing like it. Their tongues lolled from their stiffening mouths and seemed to get longer as I looked. The red tongue flesh turned black as the coughing grew worse. The bullocks were going to die.

I ran back to the house and woke Matthew. In the bed beside him John Peter howled and clutched at me but I couldn't stop to soothe him. At least his bawling would wake Mrs Peter and save me doing it.

Matthew was sleepy and slow as he reached for his clothes, not understanding my gabble about blackened tongues and broken bones. At last I spluttered Mr Carwitham's name and Matthew was rushing, limping, to the field. I followed though I dreaded seeing what had happened.

We found the bullocks still at the gate but their coughing had stopped. Their tongues were back inside their mouths. A faint cloud of smoke hung over the field but as I looked it drifted away.

Matthew checked each creature. Mrs Peter joined me at the gate.

'Whatever was that about, Shilly? Have you lost your wits? Scaring John and all for nothing. It is nothing, Matthew?'

He was running his hands over the creatures.

'I'm sorry, Matthew,' I said. 'I thought I saw . . .'

But I knew what I'd seen. Knew it was true. That was why Charlotte hadn't come out of the house to see what all the fuss was for. I was glad

70

John Peter hadn't come down to the field either. It was easier without his fretting.

'They seem well,' Matthew said. He eyed me warily. 'Dreaming, Shilly?'

But the creatures weren't well. That afternoon they lay down and wouldn't get up. They laid their heads on the grass, which cows weren't wont to do, not ever, Matthew said. They wouldn't eat or drink. Couldn't. Matthew opened up their mouths and peered inside. Their tongues had gone.

It was her anger at her mother that had taken them. The beasts had caught her wrath.

When Mr Carwitham came he didn't shout or curse or threaten with his whip as I thought he would. He fell to his knees by one of the creatures and stroked its still, cold head. He cried. The others died with him there. The stench was bad at once.

It was when Roe came and the talk was of how to get rid of the bodies that the shouting began. It was Matthew's fault, of course. He hadn't checked the field walls for sharp things, had cut the creatures' tongues out himself. He would ruin Mr Carwitham. Take everything Mr Carwitham had. Mrs Peter helped him into the house.

Roe, Matthew and I collected wood to make a fire, which took some time for trees are scarce on the moor and the wood we found was wet from the rain. We didn't touch the thorn tree in the Mowhay. It didn't need saying. We each of us knew better.

The smell worsened once the flames were lit.

On my way back to the house I found John Peter's chickens wandering the yard, paying no heed to the bad feeling that had settled over the farm. I tried to shoo them back to their run and my clucks were joined by another's. John Peter was at my elbow.

'She's mine now, Shilly.'

'Who is?'

'Charlotte. She said so and I kissed her pretty throat and her pretty hair and she liked it.'

I kicked one of the hens and the cry it made was the sound inside me.

Still John Peter was prattling his nonsense. It could only be that. Couldn't it?

'She has always liked me, she said, since she first saw me at the All Drunkard hirings.'

When I didn't look up from shooing the chickens he took hold of my shoulder and roughly turned me to him.

'Aren't you happy, Shilly? Now she'll stay with us always, not going to Tremail with Tom. And I won't let her go across the moor alone on Sundays.'

Yes, she'd stay, but at a cost. She'd be in John Peter's bed instead of mine.

I heard the shouting before I even got inside the porch.

'I'm not asking you, I'm telling you,' Mrs Peter said.

They were at the back of the kitchen, by the window. Charlotte was looking out at the old well in the shorn Mowhay.

'You'll have no trouble being taken on,' Mrs Peter said. 'Pretty girl like you.' She brushed down her dress as if there was something mucky on it. 'You can stay in the barn tonight and you can't say that isn't fair, considering.'

'Considering what?' I said, though I feared I knew already.

Mrs Peter didn't answer me. She went in to the parlour and closed the door. I heard Mr Carwitham in there with her.

'She can't make me go,' Charlotte said. Her eyes were bright and her cheeks were flushed.

I put my hand on her arm. Her skin was warm and warmed me, as it had done so many times. I couldn't lose her.

'You could get work in All Drunkard,' I said. 'I'll come with you. We'll look for a farm wanting a pair.'

72

I would leave Penhale. I would leave it all for Charlotte.

'I'm not going anywhere,' she said. 'I'm so close.'

Close to me, did she mean? Close to our shared bed? No. She didn't want me as I wanted her.

I was tired then. The day had been short but terrible, and now Mrs Peter wanted Charlotte gone and John Peter was saying such bad things. I wanted to crawl in to bed and never get out and then none of it would be true.

I went upstairs but got no rest because I couldn't keep from thinking about the door between our room and that of Matthew and John Peter's. It was closed, as it always was. But Mrs Peter wanted Charlotte to leave, and that changed everything. I grasped the handle. I turned it. For the first time since I'd come to live at Penhale the door between the two rooms opened.

How long had it been unlocked? And which of them had come through it?

Charlotte came to bed with me that night, paying no heed to Mrs Peter saying she had to sleep in the barn. I didn't let her touch me.

SEVENTEEN

She didn't stir when I washed my face and dressed the next morning but I knew she was awake.

'I'll look after your box,' I said. 'I'll make sure no one touches it before it's sent on. Not that Mrs Peter would do anything to it. I know she's making you go but—'

'It doesn't matter about the box.'

'You'll need your things.'

She threw off the blanket. 'They won't be going far.'

I told Mrs Peter. She put down her cup so hard it cracked.

The house felt narrow and dark as the cold-shed. I could get no peace there. The yard was no better – all dirt and chicken feathers blowing, no purpose to their tumblings. I took a shovel from the barn.

She came to me in the pig pen. I watched her scratch the old sow behind the ear, tried to wet my mouth enough to speak my fears. The pig grunted in pleasure, turning her head to show Charlotte where she should put her fingers.

'Is it him you want or the farm?' I asked her at last.

'Who?' she said, not looking up from her scratching of the pig.

'John Peter.'

'I want everything,' she said, and she left me to clean out the pigs like she was mistress of Penhale already.

* * *

When we went in for dinner we met Matthew leaving the house, bread and cheese in hand. He went to the barn without speaking to us. His feelings for Charlotte had cooled so quickly. He couldn't have really loved her. John Peter made her sit next to him at dinner, and Mrs Peter could do nothing but glower at them from across the table.

That night there was no sound of Matthew talking to John Peter in the room next to ours. In the morning I saw why. Matthew had made a bed for himself in the parlour. Mrs Peter said he could sleep there until Charlotte was gone.

But she didn't go. Days passed.

Sunday came again and for once I was glad for chapel where there could be no rows, but Mrs Peter said I had to stay at the farm.

'I can't make Charlotte go to worship now. You see that, don't you, Shilly? She thinks she's mistress here but the Lord will have it otherwise, I know it. You must stay back this morning, keep the farm safe.'

'Safe from what?' I said.

'From *her.*'

'Charlotte's a good person, Mrs Peter. You don't have to be afraid of her.'

But even as I said the words I was uncertain of their truth, for the bullocks had sickened and died. And Charlotte had told me herself, *there's no such thing as only good.*

'She's done to you what she's done to the men,' Mrs Peter said, tying her bonnet strings. 'I'll ask the Lord to keep you.' Her hand was on the porch door. 'Something must be done.' And then she was gone, taking Matthew and John Peter with her.

Mizzle wet the air but Charlotte paid the poor weather no heed, staying out in the Mowhay. I thought to keep to the house, but she drew me to her like she'd drawn so many.

She was kneeling in the mud, her back to me. St Michael was on her shoulder.

'Spying, Shilly? Here, hold it still or it'll tear itself before I'm done.'

A magpie thrashed in the mud, nails driven through its wings.

'What are you doing?' I heard myself whisper, but I knew.

She'd told me, that day at the ford when we gathered the plants. The power of a bird's heart if taken while the creature lived.

I pressed down on the wings with my palms. They felt so frail, so easy to break. All around us was water, tree, mud, death.

She had no blade. St Michael on her shoulder twitched and bobbed as she ripped open the magpie's breast, like he was saying *do it do it*. The bird thrashed harder, then went slack. Charlotte opened the bird's breast. Small bones cracked. Blood coated her fingers. She rootled in the hole she'd made in the bird and pulled out a purple lump. St Michael squealed.

She had pins with her. She stuck them in the magpie's heart, taking care to set them evenly in the flesh. When it was full of metal she held it up to admire it.

'What will it gain you?' I said.

'His love. But not yet. It's not done yet.'

She would never love me as I loved her. My own heart was cold and full of pins.

'Something else has to die?' I said.

'Not today,' she said, closing her fingers round the pinned heart. 'I'll sleep with this under my pillow and tomorrow things will change. His heart. I'll not be made a fool.'

I heard the cart clatter in to the yard. The others were back.

Charlotte didn't come in for dinner. I'd had enough of the mizzle, of her. My hands were shaking, from the cold or from watching her take the bird's heart I didn't know. I only knew I'd do anything for her and that frightened me.

We'd nearly finished eating when Mrs Peter looked out of the window into the yard. She threw up her hands and cursed. I'd never heard her say such a thing before.

'What is it?' I said.

'Tom,' she said in a low voice so only I should hear. 'He wants to see her. I told him at chapel he shouldn't come.'

She shooed John Peter out of the back door by telling him his beloved chickens needed feeding. And could Matthew go and see—

But it was too late. Matthew had caught sight of Tom and Charlotte in the yard.

'What can they have to talk about?' he said.

'Come away from the window,' I said.

He charged out of the front door.

'The sooner she's gone, the better,' Mrs Peter said.

I heard shouting and looked out of the window again. Matthew and Charlotte tumbled together but not in play, not as a couple who'd once been courting. They were fighting over something – a scrap of white. Matthew snatched it from Charlotte. He ran inside and up the stairs. Charlotte came in close behind him but fell over the boots and umbrella left in the porch. I rushed to help her.

'My letter – he's got my letter,' she sobbed, stumbling to her feet.

She raced up the stairs. There was something dangling from her hand but I couldn't see what it was. The something was red. Then I heard her banging on the door to John Peter's room.

EIGHTEEN

I ran up the stairs. She was in our room and changed, wearing her good green silk though only a moment had passed since she'd run past me. She wasn't out of breath or upset as I thought she must have been. Time was different for her than it was for most people. She'd been in the room for longer than it took me to reach her.

She had her back to me. Her dress was open, showing me her pale skin, her tender shoulders. My fingers grazed the downy hair on her neck and caught her red bead necklace.

'Where are you going?' I said.

'For a walk.' She moved away and put on her gloves.

I felt all was not well. I knew it in my pinned heart.

'Let me come with you,' I said.

She gathered my hands in hers and brought them to her lips. She blew in to them. Warmth blossomed in my palms. I could smell the marshes and somewhere a pony called to her friend. The wind lifted our hair. We were on Roughtor, standing on the tallest tower of stones and all the moor below us.

You have it now, she said, but the words were only in my head, not said aloud.

I felt the heat pass through my hands, down my arms, across my shoulders and then into every part of me. I glowed with what she gave me, but faintly. I knew I wasn't as strong as her. But I would be. She would teach me.

And then she was by the door. It was as if we'd been standing apart for some time. She reached for a bonnet I hadn't seen before. It was made of red silk and very fine-looking. That was what I'd seen her holding when she ran up the stairs.

I followed her down to the kitchen.

'What's this – going out?' Mrs Peter said.

'For a walk,' I said.

'It's dirty out,' Mrs Peter said. 'Mist coming, I should think.'

Matthew was waiting in the porch, still wearing his Sunday best. Were it not for his afflictions, he and Charlotte would have made a handsome couple. But he hadn't offered her enough.

Charlotte tied her pattens over her good shoes. She straightened up and looked at me and I knew she didn't want me to go with her. I tried to ask why but my mouth wouldn't move. My tongue was going to fall out. She made my body heavy as moor stone when all I'd done was love her.

The front door shut with a snap.

'Leave them go,' Mrs Peter said.

Her words returned some life to my limbs but I felt like I'd fallen asleep and woken with my arms above my head, the blood drained and the feeling of pins there instead. I had to rub the feeling out of myself as I shuffled stiffly to the window seat.

'We'll have a quieter afternoon without them,' Mrs Peter said. 'If that girl has any reasonable thoughts in her head then she'll be going to find herself a new place. What Matthew's thinking being with her, I don't know. I used to believe he was sensible, more so than Tom, at any rate. She sends men mad.'

They'd been gone half an hour when the mist rolled into the yard, just as Mrs Peter had said it would. It brought a fine rain that brushed the window pane. Charlotte hadn't taken the umbrella. It was still wedged in the old boot in the porch. Her new red bonnet would be ruined.

* * *

When I woke it was dark. I heard knocking. Dusk looked to have come inside and made itself at home. How long had I been asleep? The knocking came again. Mrs Peter was on the settle, just waking. I opened the porch door.

It was Roe. His hat was pulled low over his forehead to keep away the rain. The mist swirled around him. He looked to be rising out of it.

'Let the poor man in, Shilly,' Mrs Peter called. 'And light the lamps. It's too dark to see a thing in here.'

Roe came inside and took off his hat, keeping close to the door.

'It's late to be calling, and in this weather too,' Mrs Peter said. 'I hope there's nothing wrong. Stir up the fire, Shilly. You'll have a dish of tea, Mr Roe.'

'I'll not be stopping,' Roe said. His voice was as gruff as the look of him, all whiskery reddish-grey. 'I just came to check that it was tomorrow you wanted the pig killed.'

'Oh. I . . . Yes,' Mrs Peter said. 'After dinner, if it would suit.'

Roe nodded. He didn't look to leave. He was an odd soul and no mistake.

'Well, thank you for coming to check,' Mrs Peter said. 'Do give Daniel my best wishes, and thank him for letting you do our butchering.' She moved to the door but still Roe gave no sign of leaving.

'Weeks will be here, will he?' Roe said. 'For the kill.'

'Yes,' Mrs Peter said. 'Why?'

'I saw him on the moor this afternoon. Couldn't mistake that limp. He was with a woman, out by Lanlary Rock.'

'That would be Charlotte. They went out together. He should be back by now. Shilly, have you seen him? Goodness, what's the time?'

'She had an umbrella,' Roe was saying. 'And pattens on her shoes.'

'I see, I see,' Mrs Peter said, not listening. 'Get John, Shilly. He'll have to help us feed the pigs.'

I went upstairs but John Peter wasn't there. Nor was he out with his chickens who didn't look to have been fed. I went back to the house. Roe had gone. I told Mrs Peter I couldn't find John Peter.

'Well,' she said, 'we'll see to the animals and then we'll find him. He must be here somewhere. John wouldn't go out on the moor on a night like this.'

She called his name as we crossed the yard. No answer came. I carried the lantern but the mist was so thick the light hardly reached beyond our feet. The world felt very small and very large – so much spreading away from the lantern's light yet hidden in the dark. The pigs were waiting for us by the gate.

There was a scattering of stones close by. I lifted the lantern.

'Mother!'

'My boy, my boy,' Mrs Peter said, running into the night.

I was left with only their voices and the poor light of the lantern.

'She's gone across the moor on her own, Mother, when I told her not to. She promised me she wouldn't but she's gone. And Tom, he . . .' Then came his sobbing.

'Come now, John. Stop your tears. You're wet through. Have you been out here all this time?'

I heard scrambling as John Peter tried to get his big frame over the field wall. The pigs scattered in fright, then Mrs Peter and John appeared together. One of his eyes looked darker than the other, as if he'd taken a blow, but the light was too poor to see. Mrs Peter helped him back to the house, telling me I had to feed the wretched chickens. I tossed the feed into the creatures' run without looking where it fell, and hurried back inside.

Mrs Peter was seated at the table with a candle. Her brow was deeply creased and her cheeks sagged. She looked older than I'd ever seen her.

'I've put him to bed,' she said.

'Whatever do you think—?'

The front door opened. Matthew had returned.

He was as wet as John Peter, and tired, his limp worse than usual. He sat and looked at the cold hearth as if the fire was lit. I watched the porch but she didn't come in after him.

'Where's Charlotte?' I said.

He didn't seem to hear me. I asked him again but he only shook his head.

'Matthew, please,' I said. He looked at me then, at last. 'Where is she?'

'I don't know,' he said. 'Maybe she went to see Tom Prout.'

'But you and she didn't go towards Tremail. You went up the path to the moor, towards Vosper's.' As I said that name my insides knotted.

He shrugged. I looked to Mrs Peter for help but there was none there.

'If Charlotte's not on her way back now,' she said, 'then I'm sure she's found a bed for the night. She seems to have no trouble with that.'

NINETEEN

I went to bed but everything was emptied out without her – our room, our bed, my arms. I tried to remember the things she'd taught me. The thorn tree gave protection. If I said a charm for her with its leaves then I could keep her safe. I would go to the old well in the Mowhay, find my way in the mist—

Scrabbling. Tiny claws. Smoke rose from behind the corner cupboard.

I dragged the cupboard away from the wall. A cloud of black smoke burst in my face, taking my breath. I wrenched the window open and sucked in fresh air. When my chest had eased I was able to look behind the cupboard again.

St Michael was in the straw bed Charlotte had made him, writhing and clawing at his belly. Smoke surged round him, coming from the straw, I thought, but then I saw it was coming from him, seeping from his fur. There were sparks, as if some unseen hand had struck flint, and then St Michael was ablaze. I saw his outline in the flames and then he was gone, burnt away completely. The flames lowered and then went out. The straw was ordinary straw. None of it blackened. I put my fingers to it. It was cold.

Matthew was up and out to work before me. I saw him in higher well park field. I called to him but he must have been further away than I thought because he gave no sign he'd heard me.

I didn't stray far from the house that morning. Mrs Peter grew cross at the sight of me coming to the porch and asking if Charlotte was home. She said she had enough to do looking after John.

'He's caught a chill,' Mrs Peter said, 'from being out in the rain.'

I heard moans drifting down the stairs. When I knocked on his door they stopped. I tried the handle but it was locked. Mrs Peter called me to start the washing, but it felt wrong to go on with work when Charlotte had still not come back.

'We should go and look for her,' I said.

'Whatever for?' Mrs Peter said. 'I told her to leave and she's left. She'll have found a new position and not told us, though I pity anyone foolish enough to offer her a place.'

Charlotte had had a letter. It could have been about a new position.

'But her box is still here,' I said. 'She'd not leave her things behind.'

'She could write for them, couldn't she? She'd know I'd send them on.'

'But why wouldn't she say she was going?' I said.

Mrs Peter had no answer for me, though she looked to be trying to think of one. Then hooves sounded in the yard. Roe had arrived.

We went without dinner because Roe wanted to start on the pig. He needed to get back to Mr Carwitham, he said.

'You'll use the barn, as before?' Mrs Peter asked. 'Shilly will fetch the blood pails and rope. I'll call Matthew to bring the sow.'

She left me there with Roe. Silent, silent Roe. It wasn't just his lack of speaking that made me feel discomfort. His silence took a shape as it seeped from him, and it swallowed sounds that would otherwise be heard – birds, the sheep across the fields at Tremail. Then sound returned, all at once and terrible, as he set to sharpening his knife. It gave a shrill rasping that made my teeth ache.

Matthew brought the old sow into the barn. He tightened the rope against her neck then patted her. He whispered to her that it would be all right. I knelt on the pig's other side and set the pail to catch the first rush when the neck was opened, to keep for blood pudding. The sow must have known something then as she began to scream and buck. Matthew looked very pale and his hand on the rope was shaking.

'You're the man of this farm, aren't you, Weeks?' Roe said.

It was hard to tell whether he was being kind or making fun. Roe's deep-set brown eyes were small and hid everything.

'You should make the first cut,' Roe said. 'Got a knife, haven't you? Stick the pig and then let me get on with the cutting.'

Roe held the sow, tighter than Matthew had, which choked the sow's screams. Matthew drew his farm knife from his belt. It was small, only good for cutting string and flicking stones from the carthorse's hooves. His hand was still shaking.

'Come on!' Roe said.

Matthew lurched at the sow. He slashed at her neck. She tried to shoot backwards but Roe held firm. The knife opened a thin red line on her throat. I tilted the pail but little blood came. Matthew slashed again and again but only made more lines on the sow's flesh. They had no depth and the sow was screaming and screaming.

Roe knocked Matthew's hand away. The knife hit the wall. Roe grabbed his own knife from the floor and dragged it across the sow's neck, deeply, at last.

It took a bark from Roe before I remembered the blood pail. A fair amount of blood had already been lost to the earth floor. I pressed the pail to the thick slice in the sow's neck and felt her body slump and sag as the blood pumped out, hot and fast. I thought of Charlotte giving me the carthorse's blood-heat at All Drunkard. Was she cold, my girl, wherever she was?

Roe looped the rope round the sow's back feet, ready to hang her from the rafters now the first of the blood was out. Then I saw Matthew lying on the floor.

TWENTY

I ran to the house for Mrs Peter. She was feeding something into the fire and whirled round when I burst in to the kitchen.

'Lord's sake, Shilly!' she said. 'You'll do nothing for my nerves.' She raked the fire with the poker. 'What's the matter now?'

'It's Matthew,' I said, 'he's fainted in the barn.'

Roe had hung the sow and was scraping off her bristles. A fresh blood pail stood beneath. Every so often a thread of blood slid from the pig. Matthew was still lying on the floor. I sat him up and called to him through the haze of the faint. Roe watched but didn't stop his scraping. Mrs Peter didn't move to help either.

Matthew's eyes opened and he looked round wildly. His breath was ragged.

'It's Shilly,' I said. 'You're in the barn.'

Blood ran over his shirt front and my hands holding him. I thought it was from the sow but then I saw it was Matthew's nose bleeding.

He came to enough that I was able to get him to his feet, and then I asked Mrs Peter to help me for I couldn't carry him back to the house by myself. At first she didn't move, just watched me trying to take Matthew's weight myself, and then she sprang forward and took his other side. It struck me that her shoulder must have been better because she would never have been able to do such a thing in the weeks before. Before Charlotte went out and didn't come back.

I had no time to think about such things because Matthew was heavy and his feet dragged on the ground as if he'd gone lame in both

86

legs. His head dangled on his chest. He was mumbling. I caught two words – *forgive me.*

Mrs Peter pressed her face close to Matthew's. 'What's that? What have you done?'

He raised his head. Blood was smeared across his cheek. I could smell it. Matthew said nothing, just looked at Mrs Peter and gave what could have been a smile. His misshapen mouth twisted at any rate.

We put him in a chair by the fire and he slumped forward. Mrs Peter had helped him when his nose had bled before, telling him to tilt his head back and fetching a handkerchief to catch the blood. There was no such care now. When I made to help him she stopped my hand.

'Leave him be, Shilly. You've the dinner to be getting on with and those clothes won't wash themselves.' She stirred up the fire, her bad shoulder moving easily, free of pain.

While her back was to me I whispered to Matthew, 'Go and lie down in the parlour.'

He nodded loosely, as if his head wasn't properly fastened to his neck, and shuffled to the parlour like a tired old man.

Mrs Peter and I had a swift dinner. She didn't give Matthew anything but took a plate to Roe in the barn.

'He won't stop for his dinner,' she said when she returned. 'Now there's a man. No womanish fainting. Mr Carwitham is lucky to have such a man working for him.'

'Shall I take John Peter something?' I said.

'Best leave him be.'

I cleared the plates and chided the black cat from the butter dish, then put the copper kettle on to boil. Mrs Peter was going to the washtubs outside.

'Check the parlour,' she said. 'See if Matthew has left anything to be washed.'

I pushed open the parlour door with care. He hadn't fashioned his bed on the floor but was in a chair with his head tilted back. His eyes were closed.

Sure enough there were things that needed washing though I nearly missed them. Matthew's bedding was on a chair by the hearth. My eye fell on a scrap of blue beneath the off-white of the blanket. I got hold of the scrap and made to pull it clear of the blankets. Matthew grabbed my wrist.

'What you after, Shilly-shally?'

'Just the things for washing.' I tried to escape his grip but he held on. 'Don't you want me to wash them, Matthew? You'll have to do them yourself if not. I don't mind but . . .'

He let go of me, gave a deep sigh and closed his eyes. 'Take them,' he said.

I pulled on the blue scrap and drew out a pair of stockings. They were thick with mud.

When I got to the yard Mrs Peter said, 'I'll just fetch the kettle, Shilly.' Then she saw the muddy stockings.

'Whatever was Matthew doing yesterday to get so mucky?' she said.

'Are you sure he was wearing these when he came in last night?' I said. 'They could be from days ago.'

'I'm certain of it,' Mrs Peter said. She took them from me and peered at them. Then to my surprise she put them to her face. 'That's turfy mud,' she said. 'Here, smell it.'

Before I could stop her she pressed the cloth to my nose. The dark, wet smell that came when turf was cut for burning.

'Did you check his clothes for signs?' she said.

'Signs of what?' Matthew was standing in the porch. He was wearing a clean shirt. I didn't know how long he'd been there.

'We've so much washing to do, Matthew, and Charlotte not back yet.' She looked at him out of the corner of her eye as she picked up a washboard.

'Where did you go yesterday?' I said.

My question hung between us. It was an easy one. Something I could have asked him on any day of the year. But that day it was different. Charlotte hadn't come back.

'I went to see Mary,' he said.

'My Mary?' Mrs Peter said. The washboard slid from her hand and clanged against the tub. 'Whatever for?'

'Just to see her. We had a dish of tea.'

'And what did Robert have to say about that?'

'He wasn't there. Mary said he had to see to some papers.'

'But he was in the house.'

'He'd gone out. To the lawyer's house, where he works.'

'So it was just the two of you?' Mrs Peter's face had turned purple and there was spittle on her lips. 'Well I never. Did anyone see you?'

Matthew scratched his head. 'I don't think so. It was the girl's half day so Mary made the tea. And the mist was bad in All Drunkard. More like fog. I didn't see a soul in the streets.'

'Thank the Good Lord for that,' Mrs Peter said. She put herself close to Matthew and her pointing finger made him step back against the wall of the house. 'You will not call on my daughter like that again, do you hear me?'

'Meat's cut,' a voice behind me said. Roe was wiping his knife on a grubby cloth. 'Cat's getting in the blood.'

Mrs Peter smoothed her hair. 'Thank you, Mr Roe. Shilly will get on with salting as soon as we've got this washing hung. We're all behind ourselves today, as you can see.'

'You're short of hands.'

'That we are!'

Matthew was away, down to the fields.

'If she shows her face here,' Mrs Peter said, 'she'll have me—'

'I've got to get back,' Roe said. 'Master needs me.'

I finished salting the meat and went into the house. Mrs Peter was seated by the hearth. She held a bundle of white cloth and I had the sense she'd been waiting for me.

'Did I miss that for washing?' I said.

Mrs Peter pushed the cloth into my hands. 'Something terrible has happened.'

I unfolded the cloth. It was a shirt. There was blood on the front – fat drops near the collar and a great patch reaching round the back of the shirt in the marks of fingers.

'It's Matthew's shirt,' Mrs Peter said. 'It was in the parlour.'

'The one he was wearing just now, when his nose bled.'

'The one he was wearing when he came back last night.'

TWENTY-ONE

Matthew stayed in the fields until the light went. He came in just as Mrs Peter was clucking John Peter down the stairs. It was the first time I'd seen him since he appeared in the dark the night before.

'That's right, my dear,' Mrs Peter said. 'You come and sit on the settle and have some of this good stew Shilly has made for you.'

John Peter let her put a blanket over his knees. The skin round one of his eyes was greenish. I'd been right thinking there was such a mark on him when he'd clambered over the wall.

'How's your cold?' I asked him.

'Cold?' he said.

Mrs Peter moved between us to fetch the bowls. 'He's feeling much better now, aren't you, John? So you decided to come down for your supper. Is it ready?'

I dished up the stew. There seemed a lot left in the pot. Then I remembered we were four bowls, not five.

'Where did you and Charlotte part?' I asked Matthew. 'Did you see which way she went? Did she seem—?'

'I don't know where she went,' he said. He stirred and stirred his stew but didn't eat.

'We'll have to go and look for her,' I said. 'We'll go out tomorrow. Perhaps she's fallen, turned her ankle. Or got lost in the dark.' There was the marsh, too, but I couldn't speak of that aloud. It was too bad a thought. 'We'll find her, won't we, Matthew?'

John Peter began to moan. It was a terrible noise that rose in pitch to a cry. He rocked backwards and forwards on the settle with his mother at his side.

'You must know something about where she went,' I said.

'Yes, Matthew,' Mrs Peter said, 'you must know. You were seen with her on the moor.'

He dropped his spoon. 'Who saw me?'

'Mr Roe,' Mrs Peter said. 'He called here yesterday, before you came back.'

'But I left her at the Altarnun road. She wouldn't let me go any further with her.'

'Where did she go?' I said.

'I don't know. I promise you I don't know.'

When daylight broke into my room I went out to search.

The path up to the moor was churned with mud and the marks of many boots and shoes. And pattens. The circles the hoops made were scattered about. Mrs Peter hadn't been up the path since Sunday, as far as I knew, and I didn't wear pattens. The marks had to be Charlotte's. I followed them to the end of the path but there I faltered.

The moor opened before me, rising and falling and rising again as far as I could see. Ponies, cattle and sheep picked their way through the moor stone and the fern, through the bracken and the gorse. Two riders in the distance.

When I was clear of the path the patten marks disappeared until I came to Lanlary Rock where I found one or two others. At the edge of a marsh I found one, and I let the thought come. The marsh could have taken her, as it had tried once before.

At the ford the stream was full and flowing quickly. I drank a little. It was so cold my teeth hurt. A shadow fell across me. I wanted to look up to see what was there but my knees locked so I couldn't rise. My neck wouldn't turn. The cold of the water crept from my teeth to my cheeks then across my scalp and down my back. It was as if the chill had grown hands and they were trying to push me into the water. My stiff knees began to yield, but not to my will. I felt my body sink. How easy it would be to give in. I let my skirt drop into the stream. The water pulled me as the cold hands pushed me down.

Words came to me. Words I'd heard Charlotte say when we sprinkled the wash made from the thorn tree, for protection. I said the words over and over again, my teeth clenched. The cold hands lifted. My limbs came back to life. I staggered to the bank and made for Roughtor as fast as I could. I didn't look back at the ford.

My heart jittered all the while I climbed. At the top I turned a circle. I could see for miles. If she was out on the open moor she would be easy to see. But if she *was* there someone would have found her and I would have heard. People crossed that part of the moor all the time. Those making for St Breward and Blisland on foot, farmers on horseback checking their stock. But I'd heard nothing. She'd vanished with Sunday's mist.

There was movement at the ford.

A flicker. Not a shadow. Something firmer than that, but black still. A person not a pony. They were walking backwards and forwards on the same spot close to the stream. They were too far away for me to see if they were a man or a woman even. I felt that whoever it was was somehow neither.

There was a cry above me. A hawk passed overhead with some scrap of creature in its beak. I looked back to the ford. The walking figure had gone. But I was still afraid.

I skirted the ford on my way home, keeping to higher ground. I worried that I should be looking back as I went, to be sure the figure wasn't following me, but I couldn't bear to. Some part of me knew it was bad to see such a thing.

At last I came to the top of the path that led to Penhale. My hands were shaking and my tongue was dry. I reached in to the gorse bush but the bottle was empty. I'd forgotten I'd drunk it all. The night she didn't come back. When St Michael had burnt to nothing and left me too. The bed was cold without her and I needed something to warm me. I was cold again standing there, the miserable, empty bottle in my hand. The cold that had got me at the ford was still in my bones. I had to get warm, and there was no Charlotte to help me. There was only Vosper and his inn.

I slipped in the front door. The bar was empty. I would take a bottle and go, just as I had before. Perhaps two this time, to save me another trip. Or three, for the nights were sure to be bad now.

A smarting pain on my fingers.

Vosper looked ready to lash me with his dirty cloth again. 'You'd be my best customer if you paid for everything you took.'

I felt in my pocket for the coins. Mrs Peter wouldn't miss them. I didn't look at him. Reached out for the bottle. So close to it.

Vosper moved it further from me.

'One minute more won't kill you, Shilly, though you look half dead already. No sickness at Penhale, I hope?' He backed away, taking the bottle with him.

I shook my head.

'What's wrong with you then? You've no colour.'

'I saw something . . . At the ford. It made me cold.'

He frowned. 'Pony, was it? Too many go that way, in the marsh. They never learn from the others.'

'Not a pony. Black. It walked but not on legs.'

He poured me a glass. Too small but it helped. He poured another and set it just out of reach.

'Tell me,' he said.

I told him. The cold came back and I badly needed the drink. I'd never needed it so bad in all my life. Not even when my mother died and my father took my bottles for himself.

'Fetch,' he said, and gave me the bottle.

I drank long and deep. Better without the glass. Glasses guessed a person's fill. Guessed wrong for me.

94

Vosper poured one for himself. 'A fetch.' He drank and cleared his throat. 'Likeness of a person living who's soon to die.'

A shake was on me, but not from needing drink. Had I seen Charlotte at the ford? Felt her in the cold creep that travelled the length of me? The pushing hands. And Vosper now, telling me of fetches. What did he know of her going?

'She's not come home,' I said.

'Charlotte?'

'Do you know where she went?'

The door opened.

I took the bottle and slipped away, but not before I saw who'd come in. Tom Prout, looking to have a thirst as bad as mine.

TWENTY-TWO

I put the bottle in the gorse bush at the top of the path. It was already half empty. I cursed myself for not taking more money from Mrs Peter. I had parsley in my pocket. I chewed it as I walked down the path. Parsley for hiding the sins of the throat. I wondered if Charlotte knew that use for a plant.

Mrs Peter was in the yard.

'Where've you been?' she said.

'To look for Charlotte.'

'Did you find anything?'

'At the ford I felt . . . I felt something.'

'Felt something? In the water?' She clutched my arm.

'Not something to touch. But something touched me. It was cold. I couldn't move. Its hands—'

'Ah, it was only that nonsense, was it?' she said. 'Keep to the path the Good Lord shows you, Shilly, and come and hitch the horse for me. I can't find Matthew and I've no time to be hunting him out.'

'You're going to All Drunkard? You can ask if anyone's seen her.'

'I suppose I could. Though I'll have no time for gossiping.'

I walked the horse to the end of the path, as Matthew usually did, and then Mrs Peter took the All Drunkard road. I didn't go back to the farmhouse straight away, for I was at the place Matthew said he and Charlotte had parted on Sunday. I closed my eyes and waited to see if I felt anything like I'd felt at the ford. Nothing. I opened my eyes.

Vosper was in the doorway of the Britannia Inn.

96

A shout from inside made him turn and go in but not before he'd had a good look at me. I felt his gaze all over like a wet shawl.

The washing we'd done the day before was dry enough to be taken down from its high place above the hearth. I was glad to do it for it gave me something to make my hands work, to stop me thinking the worst. I folded the clothes into piles belonging to each person. Matthew's pile looked too little. His shirt and his blue stockings weren't there.

There was a noise outside. I ran to the window. The cart was racing down the path from the moor.

Mrs Peter was seated at the front but her son-in-law Robert held the reins. The cart was full of people. Tom Prout and other men I knew from chapel. More men were coming down the path behind it – Mr Carwitham and Roe on horseback, Vosper on foot.

Tom Prout helped Mrs Peter climb down from the cart.

'Oh Shilly!' she said, falling into my arms. 'You won't believe what's happened, what I learnt in All Drunkard. Matthew didn't call on Mary on Sunday.'

'Why are these men here?' I said.

Mrs Peter got hold of my chin to keep my eyes fixed on her. 'Don't you see what that means?'

I pulled away. Why did it matter if Matthew hadn't been to see Mrs Peter's daughter? It was Charlotte everyone should have been thinking about. The yard was full of men, more than I had ever seen at the farm before. Roe was telling them to stand in groups and the men were pointing to the moor saying names of places and paths in a terrible babble. And then John Peter came charging from the house into the middle of it all.

Mrs Peter pressed close to me. I could smell her sour breath.

'Now listen to me, Shilly. What I've learnt puts an end to our not knowing. If Matthew wasn't with Mary on Sunday then he *was* the man Mr Roe saw on the moor with Charlotte. Matthew didn't leave her at the end of our path like he told us. He lied. He went out to Lanlary Rock with her.'

'But Mrs Peter, Roe said the woman had an umbrella, and neither Matthew nor Charlotte took one.'

'It was Matthew,' Tom Prout said. His lip was split, the sore only just starting to heal. I wanted to tear both his lips from his face to stop him speaking.

'We don't know what happened,' I said. 'We don't know where Charlotte is.'

Mrs Peter patted my cheek. 'We do know, my dear. Matthew has done away with her on the moor.'

TWENTY-THREE

'Matthew wouldn't hurt Charlotte, I know he wouldn't. Ask him. Ask him what happened and he'll tell the truth.'

'We can't ask him,' Tom Prout said. 'Run away, hasn't he. Been seen going north.'

My knees buckled. A strong pair of arms took hold of me. Roe half carried me to the kitchen, Mrs Peter leading the way through the men and horses. Mr Carwitham stayed on his horse by the window.

'Put her by the hearth, Mr Roe,' Mrs Peter said.

Roe pushed me into the chair, sniffed, then stomped back to the yard.

'Now, Shilly,' Mrs Peter said, 'steady yourself and then we must get some refreshments made. We've a lot to feed today. It's a good job we butchered the pig.' She called to Mr Carwitham through the open window, 'Thank you again, Daniel, for sending Mr Roe to stick the pig. It's so kind of you to think of us here at Penhale.'

'You're wrong about Matthew,' I said. 'He wouldn't have hurt her. If something's happened . . .'

Mrs Peter eyed me sadly. 'We'll know soon enough what Matthew did to her. The men are going out to search.'

'I'm going with them,' I said. I tried to push past her but she caught me by the shoulders.

'No you're not,' she said. 'These men know the moor just as well as you if not better. You'll be more use here getting the food ready. Come now, Shilly. I know you cared for her but she had a wicked side. You saw the way she stirred them up, Matthew and John. Tom, too, for that matter. We'll find her, though, and I'll see to it she has a decent resting place. I won't have it said that Phillipa Peter let one of her servants lie in a pauper's grave.' She guided me to the table and set the flour jar at my side. 'I shouldn't think her family would do her such a kindness. Taught her nothing but cheek and witching. Have you ever known such a thing, Daniel?'

I'd forgotten Mr Carwitham on his horse by the window. A white butterfly settled on his knee. He flicked it away but it hovered close then returned to perch on his whip. He let it stay there.

'No, Phillipa. But then we don't all have an easy time of it at home, do we? Sometimes it's the worst place for us.' He turned the head of his whip this way and that, turning the butterfly with it. 'A dangerous place. Mothers aren't always—'

'Sir,' Roe said, 'the men are ready to start.'

I watched them go. It had all the feeling of a fox hunt setting off, such as I had seen on Blisland Green. Everyone seemed in high spirits. Most went up the path to the moor, Vosper leading the way and Mr Carwitham and Roe at the back on their horses. A few went with Tom Prout in the other direction, towards Tremail.

Mrs Peter and I went back into the kitchen.

'I couldn't stop John going with them,' she said.

'He's better, then,' I said. 'His cold.'

'Not fully. He shouldn't be out. You must have seen he hasn't been himself the last few days.'

'Where was he all that time on Sunday?' I said.

'A more important question for you, Shilly, is where is Matthew now? We'll sleep more soundly in our beds once they catch him,' she said.

'What will they do to him?'

'Why, they'll hang him of course. Now, watch the cat with the meat while I fetch potatoes.'

* * *

100

I'd only made a couple of pasties when there was a shout from the yard. Mrs Peter and I rushed out.

Vosper was short of breath. 'The cart . . .' he puffed.

'Have you found her?' I said.

'They've sent me for the cart, Phillipa.'

I got hold of his coat collar so he'd answer me. 'Have you found her?'

Vosper shook me off then spat on the ground. He tried to catch his breath. 'We followed prints to the ford—'

But I was running up the path to the moor, not heeding Mrs Peter calling me back.

They'd found her, they'd found her. The words pounded with my feet as I tore past Lanlary Rock and down the slope to Roughtor Ford. I passed the searchers in ones and twos and then there was a crowd of men ahead. They were on the bank of the stream. They held me back. They didn't want me to see. I reached through the tangle of arms and legs. Somewhere near me John Peter was scritching.

She was in the stream. She was floating there, not moving even as the water rushed away down the moor, through the villages and on to the sea. Was she tied somehow? Was that why she hadn't come home to me?

The men were no use, standing there idle.

'Why have you left her in the water?' I shouted at them. 'She'll be cold. Oh my poor girl.'

None of them moved to help her. Just stared at me and shook their heads. They were cruel creatures, all of them.

I climbed down the bank, my boots scattering the gravel of the dried-out bed. I ran to the water's edge, was close to getting hold of her where she lay in the water. I'd untie her if they wouldn't. I'd carry her home and get her warm again.

But there were no ties. She wasn't floating in the water. The water parted round her, as if she was a lump of moor stone blocking its path. How could that be so? Put something in a river and it got wet. I knew that to be as true as wood burning, stone sinking. But Charlotte Dymond made the world do as it didn't ought to. It was as if the water didn't want to touch her, or couldn't. Like she was covered in fish oil. But she wasn't. She was dry as bone.

A hand grabbed my shoulder, dragged me backwards.

'Don't you go drowning yourself. There's enough loss here already.' It was Vosper.

'What's the matter with her?' I fought him but he only held me tighter. 'The water like that. I have to help her!'

He pushed me back up the bank and then forced me to the ground.

'For God's sake, Shilly. Have you lost your wits? She's in no danger now. Look at her. Look!'

And then I saw why she didn't move, and why the men didn't rush to help her.

Her throat was cut.

TWENTY-FOUR

I was carried back to the farmhouse. You had to wait. The men had to get another man, Mr Good. He was to come and look at you in the river.

Mrs Peter locked me in the room that you and I had shared because I wouldn't stop fighting the men who were holding me. I banged my head against the wood until I fell down in a rush of hot darkness. When I woke it was dark everywhere. My head ached and there was blood where I'd cut myself on the door. Mrs Peter came. She made me promise I wouldn't bite or spit. She let me out. I asked where you were. She said in the barn. I asked if I could see you and she said only if I didn't touch you. Mr Good would come again the next day to turn you over and to smell you. You had to be kept still and quiet and so did I. We would be close and still as moor stone.

Mrs Peter said she would come with me to the barn. Robert stepped back when I passed him in the kitchen. I remembered then that I'd bitten him. The kitchen was dark but the barn was full of light. I thanked Mrs Peter for giving you so many candles after the dark nights you'd spent on the moor. She didn't speak but held me very close. She waited in the doorway to be sure I wouldn't try to hold you again. Then she left us together.

You were in the cart. You were lying on a sheet in the bed of the cart. You were lying on your back. Your eyes were closed. Your lips were parted like you were about to say something. I waited but you didn't speak.

*   *   *

103

You were wearing your dress strangely. Only one arm was sleeved. The dress hung from you as if trying to escape. You were showing your belly and your breasts were bare. You weren't wearing your red bead necklace. You were cut about the neck. You were cut so deeply about the neck that I could see the sheet beneath you where there should have been your neck. The skin above your breasts was torn and the muscle showing was dull red. You were missing pieces of yourself.

You weren't wearing your gloves. Your nails were clean and unbroken though bitten down still from St Michael's teeth. Your bonnet wasn't with you and neither was your shawl. Your boots and pattens too were gone. Your feet were bare and bluish.

I touched you, even though Mrs Peter had said I shouldn't. I wanted you to know I was there so I touched your hand. The cold of it made my own hand ache. You were gone from your body and without you your body was as anyone else's. Flesh. Blood. Bone.

I know you were glad to have me there. You didn't want to be left alone. You'd been alone at the ford waiting to be found and I hadn't found you though I'd looked. Others had found you when it should have been me and another had put you there. Had cut you about the neck. Taken pieces of you. Taken you away from me. They would hang and I was glad they would hang like the pig in the barn they were a corpse swinging I would open the drop below them myself.

TWENTY-FIVE

I left the barn when Mr Good came. Mrs Peter said I shouldn't like to see the body stripped and examined. The body. Charlotte was gone.

I slept. Mrs Peter woke me and made me eat some bread. Then time had passed and I was at the end of the path up to the moor. I reached into the gorse bush. There were two full bottles when I'd left one and that only half full. I opened a bottle and drank until the moor was blurred and so was the pain.

I was in the Mowhay. I had no rags to tie or charms to say. The magpie's bones were still between the nails. I wondered if the black cat had eaten the flesh.

I slept. I woke. Mrs Peter was speaking to me but I couldn't hear her. It was like my head was underwater.

And then there was another voice calling me from the bank.

'Shilly, you need to eat something.'

'He lied then, Mary,' I said. 'Matthew lied about coming to see you on Sunday.'

Her hair had escaped its usual tidy knot. Her apron was coming untied and hung oddly from her hips.

'Matthew lied about everything,' Mrs Peter said. 'The constable has been sent to bring him back.' She put a spoon in my hand and a bowl of stew on the table.

'Did he come to your house, Mary?' I said.

I wanted her to say it with her own mouth. But she covered her face with her apron and sobbed.

The porch door opened. Robert came in.

'Compose yourself, for God's sake,' he said to Mary. Then to Mrs Peter, 'The men are here.'

Mary wiped her eyes and went to the hearth. Her hands were on the cooking irons but she did nothing with them.

'What men?' I said.

'Nothing for you to concern yourself with,' Mrs Peter said. 'Your task is to eat.'

She and Robert went into the yard. I watched from the window seat. Strangers were going into the barn, and men I knew – Tom Prout and Vosper. Past Charlotte still on the cart, under sacking.

'I won't let them take her!'

Mary got hold of me.

'You don't want to hear them, Shilly,' she said.

I went slack in her arms. She smelt of ash and sweat.

'What are they doing here?' I said.

'The inquest. To find the cause of death.' She led me back to the table and made me sit.

'But they know that already, don't they? You can see . . .'

'They must write it down. What they'll say in there, what Mr Good will say . . . It won't be pleasant. Stay here with me.'

'But they won't take her away, will they?'

'Not yet. But someone will soon. She has to be buried, Shilly.'

'It wasn't Matthew. I know it wasn't. He wouldn't—'

'I know.'

I waited in the window seat. Mary sat by the hearth. She kept the fire hot. When the window steamed I wiped it with my sleeve. I wouldn't miss the men leaving the barn in case Mary had lied and they did take Charlotte from me.

A man came down the path from the moor. He was around Mrs Peter's age and had a loose-skinned face. He came to the door.

'Is your mistress at home?' he said. 'I need Weeks's boots.'

'Matthew's boots?' I said. 'He's not here. He's run away.'

The man smiled. 'I know that, my dear. That's why we need them.'

'It wasn't him,' I said. 'You mustn't take his boots.'

But Mrs Peter came back then and got Matthew's working boots for the man she called Constable Rickard.

'Were you the one sent to find him?' I asked the constable.

'No, my dear. It was Bennett went to get him. I'm to look at things here, on the moor.' He thanked Mrs Peter, said no thank you to tea and then left.

'Well, I'm in need of some tea, I can tell you,' Mrs Peter said.

I wiped the window again. The men were leaving the barn.

'You shouldn't have given Matthew's boots to that man,' I said. 'He'll need them when he comes back.'

'Shilly, he's not *coming* back,' Mrs Peter said. 'I know you think he's good at heart but you don't see the truth of it. You'll have to now, though.'

'What happened in the barn?' Mary said.

'They found him responsible. It's on the certificate. *Wilfully murdered by Matthew Weeks*, they put.'

Mary dropped the kettle and water ran across the floor.

TWENTY-SIX

Mrs Peter woke me to say I had to give my evidence, and then she had to tell me what this was.

'Who do I have to give it to?' I said.

'The magistrates. They decide if Matthew will be tried, and he will, I'm sure. The Good Lord will see to it. I've brought you some tea, look.'

'It wasn't Matthew, Mrs Peter. He wouldn't have hurt Charlotte like that.'

'Don't let it get cold.'

'Mrs Peter—'

'Things look black against him, Shilly. It's written on the certificate so who are you to say different? It was Matthew. Now, drink your tea.'

She poked about in the clothes on the floor.

'Is this the best you have? This won't do at all. You're close to Charlotte's height, aren't you, and waist too.' She pulled Charlotte's box from under the bed. 'There'll be something to wear in here. We'll get the lock off. Maybe this will do it.' Mrs Peter pulled a kitchen knife from the pocket of her apron and pushed it between the lock and the box.

'Mrs Peter, no!'

I knocked her hand from the box. The knife skittered across the floor. She gave a cry and clutched her hand. I must have looked a wild thing still in my clothes from the day Charlotte was found, my face unwashed and my hair a tangled mess. I could smell the spirits on my breath and I was breathing hard, like the horse run to foam in the cart. She edged towards the door.

'All right, Shilly. I won't touch her things. Don't go getting upset again. I won't have any more of that and neither will the magistrates. Hurry up and dress. And for goodness' sake pull a comb through your hair.'

I didn't hurry and nor did I comb my hair. When Mrs Peter had gone I knelt by Charlotte's box. I thought of the day she'd sealed up my eyes. She'd wanted to keep her things secret. If I cared about her at all then I should dig a hole in the moor and bury the box so it went to the grave with her. But even as I thought this I knew I would do no such thing.

The knife hadn't come close to forcing the lock, though the lock looked old and worn and Mrs Peter had gone hard at it with the knife. Charlotte had had no key that I'd seen. I got hold of the box and looked at it from all sides. The wood grew warm beneath my hands and all at once there was a clicking sound. I scuttled away. The lid opened, as if some unseen hand were drawing it back.

I waited a moment. When I was certain there were no burning mice or birds pinned alive, I crept towards the open box. Inside were the most wonderful clothes I'd ever seen. I sunk my hands into them and my rough skin caught on the finery. I'd never seen her wear such things. They didn't look as if they had been worn. Her wages from Mrs Peter wouldn't have bought them. Gifts, maybe.

I searched the box. There was nothing in it but clothes. Her other lives.

I put on my working dress and went downstairs. Mary was in the kitchen, the black cat on her lap. She ran her finger over the creature's one good ear.

'Are you coming to tell the magistrates about Matthew lying?' I asked.

She looked like she was going to speak but Mrs Peter said, 'Mary's going to look after John. All these people coming and going, it's unsteadied him. You know he doesn't like visitors.'

I knew no such thing. A cry came from above and the sound of something falling. Mary was away up the stairs before I could ask her anything else.

Mrs Peter and I went out to the yard where a pony trap was waiting. Robert was at the reins. He shifted away from me and rubbed his arm. I closed my eyes as we clattered past the barn, and opened them when we drew near the gorse bush at the end of the path. Later, I told myself.

At All Drunkard the road was full of people. I'd never seen it so busy. I asked Mrs Peter if it was market day. I said we'd had a wasted journey if it was, because we'd left the eggs and milk at Penhale. The cows – I'd forgotten to milk them.

Mrs Peter and Robert looked at each other.

'You have to pull yourself together, my girl,' Mrs Peter said. 'You must be sure to say the right thing.' She looked me up and down and sighed. 'I wish you'd put on a better dress.'

Inside the inn the air was close and the smell terrible – sweat, spirits and animals. It was a worse place even than Vosper's inn. There were people everywhere. They seemed to know who we were but I didn't know them. Tom Prout was already in the back room, keeping seats. The cut on his lip was still sore. He'd been picking at the scab.

A wooden pole ran from the floor to the ceiling. There was another pole ten feet or so away, on the other side of the room. All Drunkard Inn was so consumed by iniquity it needed shoring up, and so did the people crowded there. Charlotte's name was on their lips. They were hungry for her.

'Good turnout,' Mrs Peter said. 'And there's the reason.'

She pointed to a row of men not far from where we were sitting. There were five or six of them. Each clutched a little book and wrote in it. Every so often they glanced up and looked about them before writing again.

'Newspapermen,' Mrs Peter whispered in my ear. 'With some from London, they say.'

One of the men was looking at me. He had a neat little moustache. A pair of thick glasses took up most of his small face. His hair fell to his ears and was a rich brown. His hat was on his lap and he was leaning his little book on top of it as a sort of makeshift table. It was a very fine hat. Like one Mr Carwitham might wear to chapel – tall and soft-looking. Matthew would have loved a hat like that. But I wouldn't be able to tell him about it. Matthew and I were beyond that kind of talking.

There was a fuss at the back of the room. He was led through the crowds.

TWENTY-SEVEN

I gasped at the sight of him. His clothes were muddy, his trousers ripped at the knees. He wore no boots. His wrists were bound with metal rings. His hair was matted. Everything about him was tired and sad apart from his eyes, which were afraid. So terribly afraid. That was why he had run away from the farm.

The man leading Matthew tied him to one of the wooden poles, using the metal rings at his wrists, but the man needn't have done so. Matthew had no more running in him. He could barely stand. He couldn't sit, either, for the pole was in the way. All he could do was lean, his face against the wood, his hands twisted.

Three other men came in and were sworn to be the magistrates. They sat behind the table at the front of the room that was said to be a bench. The magistrates were all old and fat. And drunkards, all, if my father was to be believed. The fattest, oldest magistrate was named Mr Lethbridge. He told Matthew he could ask questions of the witnesses giving evidence if he wished. Matthew said nothing, gave no sign he'd even heard Mr Lethbridge speak.

One of the men who'd brought Matthew in spoke first. He looked like a farmer but said his name was Constable Bennett and that he'd been charged to find Matthew after he'd run away from Penhale.

'I found the murderer on Plymouth Hoe,' the constable said. He pointed at Matthew all the time he spoke so that no one should doubt who he meant. 'The murderer had gone there to visit his sister, he told me, and to see the Hoe. But he had money in his pocket and meant to try for the Channel Islands.'

Matthew had gone all the way to Plymouth? He looked as if he'd walked there, and slept on the open moor.

Mrs Peter went next, telling the magistrates that Matthew and Charlotte had left the house together but only Matthew came back.

'The next day my little maid found muddy stockings belonging to Matthew. He'd hidden them in his bedding. The mud was turfy mud. I knew it from the smell. It was from the ford's cut turf. I myself found a shirt of Matthew's that was bloodied. It too was hidden.'

'I see,' said Mr Lethbridge.

'He was very strange from that Sunday evening on,' Mrs Peter said. 'He kept away from the house and wouldn't answer where he'd put Charlotte.'

'Where did Weeks say he'd been on that Sunday?'

'He had the cheek to say he'd been to see Mary – Mrs Westlake, my daughter. A married woman.'

Robert was sitting straight as a nail. His arms were folded across his smart brown suit and he kept his eyes directed to the floor.

Mrs Peter was still speaking. 'It's a lie, of course. He didn't call on her. I should like to make that known.'

'Thank you, Mrs Peter,' Mr Lethbridge said. 'That will be all. Ah, wait a moment. Your son.' He looked at a sheaf of papers. 'He's unable to give his evidence, I gather.'

'John is unwell at the present time, and he is, sir, John is . . .'

'That's quite all right, Mrs Peter. I know your son is not, how shall we say, not as *able* as others. But we have more than enough witnesses to confirm our suspicions. Please sit down.'

When it was my turn Mr Lethbridge asked me about Charlotte's relations with Matthew. Every word I spoke sent the newspapermen scribbling. The only one not writing was the gentleman with the good hat and thick spectacles. He did nothing but stare at me.

I told the magistrates that I had gone to the ford on the morning Charlotte was found, to look for her, but that she hadn't been there then. It was after that the men went out and found her.

'You mean to say that you were at Roughtor Ford not long before the body was discovered,' Mr Lethbridge said, 'and yet you saw no sign of the deceased?'

His question made me tongue-tied. He saw this and pushed me to answer him.

'I felt a presence, sir, when I first went to the ford. It made me very cold and stopped my limbs. I didn't like it, sir, and ran away when I could. I went up Roughtor and looked to the ford again and there was something moving.' I shivered at the memory. 'A shape. Black, it was. Moving on the same spot of ground.'

'A woman?'

'No, sir, but not a man either. It was a spirit, sir. The spirit of someone who was soon to die. It's called a fetch, sir.'

There was a gasp that seemed to come from every corner of the room.

'Vosper told me the name of it, sir.'

'You talk of spirits at a legal hearing?' Mr Lethbridge's voice was more astonished than raging.

'Yes, sir. It was a sign.'

'Of what?'

I hung my head. 'That something terrible had happened. Mrs Peter made us cut the hay, you see, and then Charlotte went up to the moor and then St Michael burnt . . . When I came down from Roughtor the fetch was gone. Then they found her.'

I heard mutterings and chairs scraping the floor. Tom Prout laughed. So did the newspaperman with spectacles, and the men crowded by the door. Mr Lethbridge let me go and I scurried back to my seat where I was forced to listen to Mrs Peter's whisperings about my place in the Eternal Fire.

Tom Prout went to the bench next. He told the magistrates he'd come to Penhale on Sunday after chapel and had seen Matthew and Charlotte fight in the yard. He said Matthew was jealous because he and Charlotte had been courting. He, Tom, was going to move to Penhale to be with Charlotte. He'd said as much to Matthew on Sunday and that had made Matthew angry. He was bound to hurt Charlotte sooner or later.

Such lies that boy told.

I didn't want to hear what Mr Good said when he went to the front of the room but Mrs Peter held me by the shoulders. I didn't know if she was trying to comfort me or stop me from leaving but either way my legs were soft as butter and I couldn't rise from my seat, no matter my wishing.

What could Mr Good say that people didn't know already? Charlotte was cut about the neck. She was dead. There was nothing else that mattered. But he went into the particulars. He spoke of windpipe, larynx, cartilage. Of the size of the cut, its depth and its width. Of the likely instrument. Of how this had killed her. Of how she couldn't have made the cut herself.

To be out of that stinking inn, to be at the top of Roughtor instead – to be with her with the wind in our faces and the scrap of sea shining a way away. To be free. She had slipped about the farm, disappearing and then turning up in the place I'd just that moment looked. She was always just out of sight. I wished I could do the same and get from the magistrates' hearing. I wished it hard, said the words over and over like I'd heard Charlotte say her charms. And I was taken from that wicked place.

TWENTY-EIGHT

I was in the barn. I pulled back the sacking in the cart. There was nothing there but moor stone. She was waiting for me in the doorway. *Don't listen to them*, I told her. *Don't listen to them any more. I know you best in the world.* She was wearing her green dress. It was done up right and the skin about her neck was smooth. Beautiful. Her necklace of red beads winked at me. We walked up the path to the moor and all at once we were at the ford. The water in the stream was gurgling and in it I could hear a voice speaking though I couldn't see him. Charlotte was trying to speak but I couldn't hear her over the voice of the man. A red line drew itself on her throat and then another crossing it. The gurgling of the stream grew louder. The water was rushing and the lines on Charlotte's throat opened and blood was pouring down her chest and I couldn't look.

I opened my eyes. Roe was in the chair. He was saying he saw Matthew walking with a woman near Lanlary Rock. She wore a red bonnet and carried an umbrella.

'And the next day Weeks couldn't stick the pig,' Roe said. 'He fell into a faint. Guilt, it was.'

Then it was Vosper's turn. Mr Lethbridge asked him to give his name and address.

'Humphrey Vosper of the Britannia Inn. Which, if I may say, is a fine drinking establishment and would have made a much more suitable place for this hearing, given its proximity to the scene of the murder.'

'Thank you, Mr Vosper, that's quite enough. Did you know the deceased?'

'I did, sir.'

'And the prisoner?' Mr Lethbridge said.

'I did,' Vosper said in a sullen voice.

'You were one of the men who found the body, I understand.'

'It was in an old river place a little below Roughtor Ford.'

Was that where I had seen her, in the dry part of the river? No – the water had flowed around her. She was in the water but not in it.

'And was the body in the water?' Mr Lethbridge asked, as if he had heard the words that rove around my head.

'No, sir,' Vosper said. 'It was in a kind of pit, which looked as if it had lately had water in it.'

He was saying it badly. He should have said she made the water bend.

'She was laid on her back,' Vosper said. 'I saw what had killed her straight away, her neck all cut like it was. There was no blood, though.'

'None at all?'

'None that I could see. Rickard has the dress, he'll show you.'

A man got to his feet. I knew him to be the man who'd come to the farm and collected Matthew's boots. Now he tried to give the magistrates Charlotte's dress but Mr Lethbridge waved him away, told him to wait.

'Rickard and I found the body together,' Vosper said, 'after we'd followed the prints.'

'Please describe these for the bench.'

'Patten prints,' Vosper said. 'They led up Penhale's path to the moor and then we found some near Lanlary Rock where the ground was wet. I'd seen the two of them together, the woman and Weeks, walking away from me on Sunday, going towards the rock. There was boot prints too. We found those between Lanlary Rock and Roughtor, and where the body was. Rickard has brought the boots to show you as well.'

Once more the constable set off towards the bench.

'You will please wait until you're called!' Mr Lethbridge shouted. Once more the constable had to sit down. 'Can you describe the couple, Mr Vosper?'

'Well, I knew it was Weeks by his limp. The woman wore a red

117

bonnet and carried an umbrella. The weather was very dirty that day. The mist had brought rain by the time I saw them.'

'Thank you, Mr Vosper. That will be all.'

Matthew hadn't said a word, not asking any questions, even though Mr Lethbridge had said he could. He stayed slumped against the pole, neither sitting nor standing, neither wakeful nor sleeping.

At last Constable Rickard was asked to show the magistrates Charlotte's dress and Matthew's working boots. He laid the dress across the bench and set the boots next to it. The sleeves of the dress were puffed and the skirt bagged as if her body filled it.

Mrs Peter was made to come back to say that this was what Charlotte had worn on Sunday afternoon. She said Charlotte had also had on striped gloves and a red bonnet when she left the house. These hadn't yet been found, and neither had her shoes and pattens.

'And carried an umbrella too,' Mr Lethbridge said.

'No, sir,' Mrs Peter said.

'So Weeks held the umbrella, then.'

'No, sir. Neither carried one, though I'd told them the weather was dirty.'

'Well that is curious,' Mr Lethbridge said.

Roe and Vosper were asked to come back to the chair and say that the woman they saw had carried an umbrella. They said she had, though Roe became uncertain about what he'd seen. All the time the talk was of the umbrella I saw the spectacled newspaperman with the fine hat scribbling in his little book. None of the other newspapermen were writing.

Then Constable Rickard came back to the chair. He was asked about Matthew's boots.

'I took the prisoner's working boots from Penhale farm yesterday, sir, and first thing this morning Mr Vosper and I went up on the moor where we'd seen boot prints, that's to say north of Lanlary Rock as well as on the bank close to where the body was found. The boot prints show the wearer was lame. They was all round the place we found the body, sir, and the patten prints too, as if the man and woman had gone back and forth on that spot many times. Mr Vosper made drawings of the boot prints, sir, which I can show you.'

The constable rootled in his pockets, pulled out a pipe and a handkerchief but then one of the other magistrates stopped him. This one was a wizened man. His skin was so wrinkled his eyes barely opened.

'Constable,' the wizened man said, 'one of these boots has fresh mud on it. How can this be so when the prisoner has not been at home to wear them for several days?'

'Well, sir, when Mr Vosper and I went to the moor this morning, Mr Vosper made the drawings of the boot prints, one for each foot, which I think Mr Vosper must have because I can't find them here about me, sir, for which I'm very sorry, but you see—'

'The mud, Constable,' Mr Lethbridge said.

'Yes, sir, of course, well after we had the drawings, I said to Mr Vosper that to be certain the boot prints were belonging to Weeks we should press his working boot into them, to judge the shape. Mr Vosper said he didn't think that was a good idea but I said that of the two of us I was the representative of Her Majesty and that I should be in charge of the evidence.'

There was a groan behind me. The bespectacled newspaperman shook his head.

'And your conclusion, Constable?' Mr Lethbridge said.

'Once we lifted Weeks's boot out of the print we could see it was the same. By which I mean to say that it was Weeks's boot prints we found with the girl's patten prints. We could tell it by the lameness.'

The third magistrate had fallen asleep. It was hot in the back room and the bad air had worsened. Mr Lethbridge said there was one more testimony to record and then the magistrates would have a talk and say if Matthew should go to trial for Charlotte's murder. He asked to hear Mr Carwitham's evidence but it was Roe who took the seat at the front of the room.

TWENTY-NINE

'You are Mr Carwitham's proxy, I understand,' Mr Lethbridge said to Roe, looking at his papers. 'Please confirm for the bench why your master is absent.'

'Mr Carwitham is unwell, sir. He was out on the moor on Sunday afternoon to check his cattle. He caught a chill in the mist.'

'And what does your master report he saw?'

'A man and woman on the moor,' Roe said. 'They walked from Lanlary Rock, bearing towards the ford. The man dipped a mite in walking and the woman carried an umbrella.'

'Your master is certain of that,' Mr Lethbridge said, 'that she carried an umbrella and the man limped?'

'Yes, sir. He told me that after he first saw them he went round Alex Tor looking for his cattle. The next time he saw them they'd reached the ford.'

I'd never heard Roe speak so much. He'd found his tongue at last.

'Where did Mr Carwitham go then?' Mr Lethbridge said.

'He rode down to the ford. It's on the path to Lanhendra, where his house is.'

'That put him very close to the couple,' Mr Lethbridge said. 'What were they doing at that time?'

'He says they were walking backwards and forwards, though neither spoke.'

'He knew the prisoner and the deceased, I gather. Mr Roe, has your master stated if the lame man he saw with the woman was the prisoner?'

'He believes him to have been the man.'

'Would he swear it?'

'Yes,' Roe said. 'I believe he would.'

That was good enough for Mr Lethbridge. He said the hearing was over and the magistrates would go to the snug to talk. At their leaving, madness came over the back room of the inn. There was a surge of noise as everyone rushed to talk to one another. The newspapermen were the first to leap from their chairs and run to the bench where they turned over the dress and Matthew's boots. Constable Bennett stood guard over Matthew as people came right up close to him to gawp.

Robert helped Mrs Peter to the front bar and I followed, glad of a drink to keep me until I could get to the gorse bush.

'We'll soon be home,' Mrs Peter said, 'and then we'll be back to the usual way of things, once we've buried her, of course. Tom has said he'll come and stay, now we're so short of hands. I'll take more care with my new hirings, you can be sure of that. No more young women.'

Robert took a gulp of his porter. 'When will the next assize be held? Has a session just passed?'

'That would make a lengthy wait for the trial,' Mrs Peter said. 'I'm certain there must be a session sooner.'

'What a curse a wait would be,' Robert said.

'I'll ask Daniel Carwitham. He'll know, I'm sure. A shame he couldn't be here. Still, that Mr Roe is a useful man, isn't he? Perhaps Daniel would let me have him a few mornings a week.'

She had no doubt Matthew wasn't coming back with us, and neither did Robert. And yet Matthew didn't do it. I knew that to be true. There wasn't enough in my glass to take my shaking, but it was worry brought the shakes on, not thirst alone.

The bespectacled newspaperman was moving through the crowds at the bar. He seemed to be looking for someone. When he saw Mrs Peter he hurried over.

Up close I could see that his features were very fine in that they were small rather than handsome. His neat nose and mouth served to make his spectacles even larger. I wanted to take his spectacles off his face to get a purchase on him.

'May I speak with you?' he said, though which of us he was asking, I wasn't sure.

His voice wasn't from our parts. One of the London men, I guessed. And a gentleman. I knew because he carried a cane. Mrs Peter had told me once that this was a sign of a gentleman because gentlemen carried canes when they didn't need them to help their walking, like Mr Carwitham. Matthew wasn't a gentleman because he needed a cane for walking and yet he didn't have one, for it would have got in the way of his working.

'We'll have to go in soon to hear Weeks sent away,' Robert said.

'But we don't yet know that Mr Weeks committed the crime,' the newspaperman said.

'Oh we do, sir,' Mrs Peter said. 'It's written on the certificate.'

The newspaperman laughed like he'd laughed at me when I'd spoken of the fetch.

'You wouldn't laugh, sir, if you'd seen what I've seen,' I said.

'And what's that?' he said. 'A spirit? Crimes aren't solved on the basis of spirits. They aren't solved by village constables either, for that matter.'

'I meant you wouldn't laugh if you'd seen a woman's neck cut so badly that most of it was missing.'

'Shilly!' Mrs Peter said.

I thought she might clamp her hand across my mouth as people did to children. But why shouldn't I say such a thing? This newspaperman needed to know the terribleness of what had happened. He needed to know that he shouldn't laugh.

There was a shout near the doorway. People began to push their way into the back room. I didn't speak to the man again, though he tried to talk to me. I made out I couldn't hear him.

We took our seats and Mr Lethbridge stood. For the first time that day Matthew looked at the magistrates.

'We have heard a great deal of compelling evidence against you, Matthew Weeks,' Mr Lethbridge said. 'The bench has no hesitation in recommending that you be imprisoned at Bodmin pending the next session of the assize court.'

'You're wrong!' I shouted. 'All of you – he didn't do it!' I tried to get to my feet but Tom Prout held me down.

'What did I tell you?' Mrs Peter said. 'No more of this talk.'

Their work done, the magistrates got to their feet and the room began to empty. Robert gave Mrs Peter his arm. Tom Prout offered me his with a bold smile that opened the cut on his lip. I told him I'd rather eat my own arm than take his, and he took his leave quite smartly. Matthew was still tied to the pole. I made my way to him.

'Shilly, I didn't—' he said.

'I know, Matthew, I know it. But she's dead. Someone hurt her so badly.'

We were both scritching. I tried to give Matthew my handkerchief.

'Mrs Peter thinks it was me,' he said. 'What she said about my shirt being bloodied . . . Why would she say those things?'

I had no answer. I wanted to tell him not to worry, that it would be all right. But I couldn't. Then Constable Bennett was unlocking the metal rings at Matthew's wrists.

'Come now, my boy,' he said, not unkindly.

Matthew tried to pull away. 'Where are you taking me?'

The magistrates turned to look. Rickard helped Bennett keep Matthew still.

'You'll eat supper in the gaol if the road's good,' Bennett said.

Matthew's eyes rolled in his head. 'No, no, you can't, not there. Don't take me there.' He lunged at me. Blood ran from his nose and down his shirt front. 'I didn't do it, I didn't hurt her. Tell them, Shilly. She made me leave her at the road. I didn't want to but she wouldn't let me go on with her.'

He fell to his knees and the constables had to drag him from the room. He grabbed at chairs as he passed them. At the door to the front bar he got hold of someone standing there. It was the newspaperman with the large spectacles.

'Help me, please!' Matthew begged the man. 'I didn't do it. They say I did but I didn't, I swear it.'

The constables bundled Matthew into a waiting cart and set off down the long road to Bodmin. His cries were carried back to me, and then they were lost.

I heard Mrs Peter ask Tom Prout to call the next day to help repair some field walls. To do Matthew's work. He was barely out of sight and it was as if he'd never been at the farm.

I climbed into Robert's pony trap and saw the newspaperman again. He was standing in the road watching the cart taking Matthew to the gaol. Robert flicked the reins and we set off in the other direction, back to Penhale. And to Charlotte in the barn, waiting to be buried.

THIRTY

Her grave was ready dug at Davidstow. The vicar sent a cart to fetch her for burying, and a box to put her in. I was glad of the box. I didn't want to see her cuts again. Or her face. I couldn't bear it. But I wouldn't let her go alone on that last journey across the moor.

As I was leaving the house for the burial Mrs Peter took me by the arm.

'After today,' she said, 'we'll be done with her. And I want no more talk about Matthew not having been responsible. The magistrates have sent him to trial. That should be enough for you, Shilly.'

I followed the cart on foot. No one else from Penhale came and that was right because she was my girl. I had known her best, had loved her better than all of them.

At the end of the path that led to the moor I stopped, for my thirst was bad. There were two new bottles in the gorse bush. I hadn't put them there, and I had no strength of mind to wonder who had done so, but I was glad of them. I took one bottle with me, and ran to catch Charlotte who was now on the road.

On we went together, all the long, sad way to her grave. At Tremail chapel there were people waiting, and the cart stopped while a hymn was sung. The singers fell in behind when the cart moved off again. Vosper was amongst them. Rain came, which seemed fitting. I hoped it would keep more people from turning out to see, but several times more the cart came on groups singing, and each time it set off again more people followed. I wasn't to have her to myself.

By the time the cart reached Davidstow church there was a crowd behind it. I looked at the faces by the graveside. Strangers, all of them, apart from Vosper. Were any of them relations of Charlotte? Some spiteful part of me wondered if Mrs Peter had invited all these people to have witnesses for her kindness to her farm servant – the poor, unloved child. But she hadn't been unloved. I had loved her, though she was cruel, though she was sly. She was my girl, and after all, anyone who claimed to have no badness in them was shown to be bad by that lie. She and I were just as the rest of the world – creatures falling, creatures failing.

I saw a face that gave me pause. The newspaperman. He was sheltering from the rain under a tree. Or he was hiding. I turned so that I couldn't see him. It was his kind and their words that had made strangers come to the graveside. He would write about the funeral, letting more people share the misery. Giving them a piece of her.

The service was over. People drifted away. I watched the churchyard men cover her with earth then they left too. I thought I should say my goodbyes in my own way, for the vicar's words had meant nothing to me. The last lines of 'Sweet Maidens All' struck me with their rightness. It had been a day of singing, so why not a little more?

And now I make no sound, no sound
for on the moor I won't be found.

I turned to leave her, but something was rising from the freshly turned earth of her grave. It hung in the air, the shape of an adder uncoiled. I thought it mist brought by the rain. But then it quivered, was . . . looking. That was how it seemed to me, for the shape changed, drifted towards me. Reached out—

I thought of St Michael in his straw bed, how he had burnt and vanished.

I ran from the churchyard. I ran from Charlotte still making the world do as it didn't ought to.

* * *

126

In the lane back to Tremail, back to the farm, a voice called out behind me.

I kept on to where I knew the houses began, and the footfalls following me quickened their pace, became running feet – an uneven tread, he was hurt somehow. But he was fast enough because all at once he was in front of me, barring my way. The newspaperman.

'Stop,' he said.

'Why?' I said. 'So you can mock me again for seeing spirits? No thank you, sir.' I tried to push past him but he put himself so that I couldn't.

'It will only take a moment. My name is Williams. And you are Shilly.'

'How did you know that?'

'They called your name at the magistrates' hearing. It's an odd name.'

'It's not my real name,' I said and then I wondered why I'd told him that. I didn't know him. And I didn't trust him. What was he wanting with a young woman in a lonely lane in the rain when honest souls were keeping indoors?

'It's the name I was given when I moved to Penhale,' I said. 'It's a farm—'

'I know all about Penhale Farm. That's why I need to speak to you. You must listen to me.'

He put his hand on my shoulder to keep me from running on. I looked about me. There was no one in sight I could call. The houses were still too far off. Perhaps if I screamed. I could feel a scream inside me, sitting just under the bones of my shoulder where his hand was.

'You must help me,' he said.

'Help you, sir?' I said.

'Don't call me "sir". Call me—'

'I'll call you Mr Williams, sir.'

He took his hand from my shoulder. The scream inside me slipped down a little, to my belly where it twisted to something else. Something like dread.

'I can't help you,' I said.

'I haven't told you what I want your help with yet,' he said.

'You're a newspaperman. I've got no letters.'

'Let's not concern ourselves with newspapers for the time being.'

He invited me to walk on with him, as if I had a say in the matter.

The rain was growing heavier. Mr Williams had a stout hat and a coat and an umbrella. I was clad in only my dress and shawl and was wet through. Water streamed down my hair and under my clothes. My feet were soaked as we walked down the lane towards Tremail proper. Now that we were side by side I saw that he wasn't very tall. His coat made him look boxy. It didn't fit him well, though it was made of fine cloth. He walked stiffly.

'I'm sorry to detain you in such inclement weather,' he said, 'but it wouldn't be prudent to call at the farm, given my fears.'

I didn't speak. I made to seem like I wasn't listening, my face turned away, but I kept him just in sight in case he should try anything.

'I heard you call out,' he said, 'when the magistrates gave their verdict.'

'Because they were wrong. It wasn't Matthew that hurt Charlotte.'

'Why do you believe that?'

'What I believe is my own concern,' I said. 'I don't want people reading my thoughts in the newspaper.'

'You don't understand.' He came to a halt and faced me. 'I'm not asking because I want to write about you in the paper. I'm asking because I want to find out who did it.'

'You don't believe it was Matthew either?'

His glasses were covered with raindrops but he didn't wipe them away. Perhaps he was close to blindness without them. Perhaps if I ripped them from his face and took them with me when I ran he wouldn't be able to catch me.

'I believe Matthew Weeks is innocent,' he said, and his words stopped my thieving hand.

128

'Then who was it?' I said. In my head I said *Vosper Vosper Vosper*. Three times to make it good. A fox's cry to make it heard.

'That I don't know,' Mr Williams said. 'Not yet. But with your help I will. You were at Penhale. You were one of the last people to see Miss Dymond alive.'

And as if I was back in the kitchen I saw her face before she turned to leave. Saw her in the barn, her neck all cut and raw.

'You'll help me?' Mr Williams said. 'I'm staying at the Britannia Inn.'

So it was a trick – he was Vosper's man, and he had nearly had me. I ran until I thought I'd be sick.

THIRTY-ONE

When I got back to the farm it was dark. I was wet down to my skin and so tired I felt I hadn't slept in days, perhaps not since Charlotte had gone.

'Lord's sake, Shilly, where've you been?' Mrs Peter was in her nightdress and her hair was loose. 'I thought you'd fallen in the grave with her.'

She hadn't worried when Charlotte had been gone night after night, and nor had Mrs Peter helped look for her. No one had helped me but this stranger Mr Williams wanted *me* to help him. My legs gave way and I slumped on the settle.

Mrs Peter put her hand on my forehead though I couldn't feel it there.

'And you're feverish,' she said. 'That's all I need. Another soul in bed. This farm will go to rack and ruin before the month is out.'

She helped me up the stairs then took off my wet things, like my mother would have done. Before I fell asleep I caught sight of something green on the chair. Charlotte's dress.

Charlotte and I were walking on the moor. We came to the marsh near the ford. A pony was caught. I told Charlotte it would die. She took my hand in hers. I thought she was afraid but then she squeezed my hand to comfort me. I woke up.

The next night it was the same. We watched the pony, heard her rasping. She took my hand and squeezed it. I turned to tell her I wasn't afraid, that I'd seen creatures die before, but she was gone. I could still feel her hand in mine and she was squeezing and squeezing. I woke up.

The third night she came again. I felt my hand in hers but she wasn't there. I wanted to pull away but I couldn't move. The only sound was the pony's rasping. I saw the fetch and knew it was her. The pain in my hand was too much to bear and then it wasn't the pony's rasping I could hear but my own because she was going to break my hand she was going to crush my bones she was going to—

I lay sweating and sobbing in the dark, clutching my hand to my breast. It pounded with pain. I lit my candle. In the sputtering flame I caught sight of the back of my hand. There was a red stain spreading across it. The mark of her fingers.

At first light I went to the gorse bush at the end of the path and when I was less trembling I went to the Mowhay. Clouties were still hanging from the thorn tree's branches. Bunches of ragwort lay by the water where we'd left them, for protection when the hay was cut. But now their yellow heads were powdery when I touched them. The magpie's bones were gone. I whistled for St Michael and when he didn't come I remembered he was gone too.

Charlotte had said old wells each had their own strength. But she hadn't told me what the well at Penhale could do and now she was gone and Mr Williams had come to the moor. One passing as one arrived. Did that mean something? Should I help him? But he was a stranger, and he'd laughed at me about the fetch. He wasn't to be trusted.

But he said he wanted to save Matthew.

I was shilly-shallying what to do, wanting help myself. And then there was help. My eyes were opened to a dock leaf beneath the thorn tree. It had been folded and tied with grass. I undid the knots and the leaf opened, tipping pins into my hand. I bent one, as I had seen Charlotte do, and dropped it into the well water.

A big bubble came to the surface and held its shape without breaking. The water shook and another bubble floated up to join the first – two large circles sat on the surface of the water, just as they sat on Mr Williams's face in the form of his spectacles.

Two to beware of, Charlotte had said. *Two to cause harm.*

I dropped a stone into the well to smash the bubbles. It was Vosper's doing somehow, sending Mr Williams to speak to me. I'd have none of it.

THIRTY-TWO

But the well wouldn't let me be. All day my thoughts roved back and forth, sending me back and forth to the gorse bush at the end of the path. I forgot to feed the pigs and I near trampled a chicken by not heeding my feet. It was a bad business. What to do, what to do?

After supper Mrs Peter told John he was still unwell and he had to go to bed. She went up not long after. I let the house grow quiet and the sky darken. Then I eased open the porch door.

The gorse bush at the end of the path had little left to offer me. That was reason enough to go to Vosper's inn. I would take what I needed and go. If Mr Williams should see me then so be it but I wouldn't seek him out.

The few candles made slips of faces loom. I couldn't be certain who else was in the Britannia Inn, who might know me. By the poor fire I saw boots but not their owners, smelt pipe smoke and spirits.

I stumbled to the bar. Vosper saw me and reached for a bottle.

'Run dry already, have you? Thought I'd left plenty to ease your nights.'

The shadows near me moved. An awkward figure appeared from the gloom, moving like his bones hurt him.

'I knew you'd come,' Mr Williams said, but quietly, like only I should hear.

'Would you and the young lady care for a private room, sir?' Vosper said. I could hear the leer in his voice.

Before I could say no, Mr Williams was pushing me behind the bar to the room Vosper used for his own needs. It held a small table with food that looked days old. Boots and rags were lying amongst piles of tattered newspapers. Mr Williams shut the door so we were hidden from the eyes of the bar. He'd brought a candle, which gave the only light, but it was so poor I was forced close to him to see at all. He moved slowly towards the table. Stiff, I thought again, yet he wasn't all that old.

He set the candle on the table and said I should sit. There was a shake in my legs and I was glad of the chair beneath me, though the bottle would have helped me more.

'You needn't be nervous,' Mr Williams said.

'Inns are paths to sin. I don't—'

The door to the bar opened. Vosper came in with two glasses. Porter for Mr Williams and a small beer for me. I didn't meet Vosper's eye but I saw his grin. He'd not given me what he knew I wanted, and his tawdry thoughts were writ clear on his face. At last he was gone, the door shut again.

I reached for the small beer for my thirst was bad. In the poor light I thought I saw Mr Williams's neat moustache twitch as if he was smiling. Though it hurt me to do so I pushed my glass away and sat on my hands. Mr Williams took a good long drink of his porter then wiped his mouth on his sleeve, and I was struck again by his boxy coat. What was he hiding under there – dead game birds from another man's land?

'Why do you want to help Matthew?' I said.

He took another drink and was a long time swallowing, smacking his lips and wiping his mouth with the back of his hand. Enjoying his refreshment, he wanted me to know, as I sat dry-mouthed, watching.

'Why do *you* want to help Matthew?' he said.

'Because he's my friend, and because I know it wasn't him. But he's a stranger to you. Isn't he? You're not from here.'

'No one is a stranger any more.' He picked up one of the newspapers lying on the floor. 'This is from *The Times*, from two days ago. *Wicked*

134

Murder in Cornwall is the headline. And here is the tale. *Little doubt is entertained of Weeks's guilt but what could have induced him to commit such an atrocious deed is still uncertain. Reports claim jealousy was at hand. The deceased was known to favour the advances of other men.*'

'Did you write that? Because what you say about Matthew—'

'I didn't write it.'

'I thought that was what you did.'

He smiled and ran his finger up the side of his glass. He had lied to me. I'd been right not to trust him. I got to my feet.

'You've heard of the new men at Scotland Yard?' he said.

I looked to the door. The farm wasn't far.

'The detectives?' he said. 'You heard Mr Good at the magistrates' hearing. Well Mr Good is a little like a detective. He does a similar job in that he follows a trail of evidence to establish how someone died. That's what a detective does. They look for things.'

'Well I can do that,' I said. I sank back into my seat. Perhaps I was a detective.

'It's more a question of details, the details others overlook. A detective uses them to make the story of a crime, from start to finish.'

'So you're a detective,' I said. And a liar, I thought.

'Of sorts,' Mr Williams said.

'Matthew has no money to pay you.'

'I don't want payment.'

'But then why—?'

'Do you want me to find who killed Charlotte Dymond?'

I nodded.

'Then you must trust me.'

'But you've lied to me – told me you were a newspaperman when you're not.'

'I never claimed to write for the newspapers.'

I opened my mouth to disagree and then saw that he was right. He'd sat with the newspapermen at the magistrates' hearing, that was all. But he was still shifty as an adder, hiding in the moor's green and waiting to bite.

'I see I must convince you,' he said with his snake's mouth. 'Very well. I asked you to trust me so I must give trust in return. Can I trust you, Shilly?'

After a moment I nodded again.

'You must tell no one what I am about to show you. If you do then things may not be well for you. Do you understand me? Young women seem to go missing easily in this part of the world.'

He'd made a plan with Vosper. Would kill me and put me in the river. If I threw the glass at his face then I might have time to run.

I pushed my chair back from the table and took hold of my glass. I tensed myself ready to throw it and fly but he got to the door before me and barred my way. His hands moved. He was going to take whatever weapon he was hiding beneath his coat and I would be in the ground with Charlotte.

He took off his spectacles.

I sat down again.

Then he put his hand to his mouth. He pulled his moustache from his skin and gave it to me. It was light and ticklish in my palm.

Then he pulled his hair from his head and set it on the table. His own hair beneath the false dark was yellow, cut close to his scalp. He used his hands to fluff it like John Peter's chickens fluffed their feathers.

Then he smiled, and everything was changed.

I gave a cry and backed away from the table. Could this be true? Mrs Peter often talked of miracles sent by the Good Lord and now I had witnessed a miracle in the Britannia Inn.

Mr Williams had become a woman.

THIRTY-THREE

I drank my small beer in one swallow but still I was close to falling to the floor.

The yellow-haired woman gave me time to steady myself, letting me look at her for as long as I needed. And I needed a long time. I needed to look at her, she who was now before me.

She.

She smoothing the skin above her lip where her moustache had been. The moustache still in my hand. I closed my fingers over it, so she shouldn't have it back. *Her* fingers now on her lips. Her looking at me.

'So you are quiet sometimes,' she said.

She.

'I hope I've not robbed you of speech permanently, Shilly.' She took a swig of porter and smacked her lips loudly. 'Mime would rather slow us down.'

Two thoughts came to me as I sat dumbly staring. She was perhaps thirty-five years old. She had a small mouth. But were either of these things true? The person before me wasn't the same I had entered the back room with so I couldn't be certain, even now, that what I was seeing was the true self. Perhaps she didn't have a true self. Under that yellow hair and pale face was another body, and beneath that another still.

'Who are you?' I whispered.

'She speaks!' the stranger said.

She rolled her shoulders, stretched her neck and stood. All she'd done was take off her false hair and the moustache and the spectacles, yet it was as if she'd stepped out of the man's body, such was the change in her. The stiffness of Mr Williams was gone. He had been rusty as an old gate. She was water running in a stream. It was a relief to her, I thought, to be rid of her false parts.

'You have a name for me,' she said.

'Mr Williams?' I drank the rest of his porter. *Her* porter. And then I was more my speaking self. 'Why are you dressed as a man?'

'Necessity. I would not choose it.'

Now I understood why Mr Williams's coat was boxy. It was to hide her woman's shape beneath. I wondered at that shape. She was sturdy and strong. Not like Charlotte. Charlotte who was the same all the time I knew her, whose hair stayed long and dark, whose waist was slim.

This woman wasn't Charlotte. She was a liar.

She was becoming Mr Williams again, fixing the false hair back on her head.

'Remember,' she said, 'you must tell no one of this.'

She took a small bottle from her coat and removed the stopper. She placed her finger to the bottle's rim and tipped it, then she rubbed her finger on the skin above her lip. She drew in her top lip as she did this rubbing and she looked like a pony for a moment, like when they make faces. Then she held out her hand to me.

Did she want me to take it? To shake her hand as if we were men?

'The moustache, Shilly. Unless you'd like one for yourself?'

I gave it back but the ticklish feeling stayed in my palm, as if the moustache stayed there still. She pressed the hairy scrap to her face and made as if she was kissing the air, to be sure the moustache stayed where she had put it. There was a laugh in me but it didn't come out as such, only as a gulping, because everything had been made strange, even my own breath and swallow.

'I've turned you into a fish,' she said.

She reached for her spectacles but I stayed her hand. It was cool and soft in mine.

'Who are you, truly?' I said.

She slipped her hand from mine and put on her spectacles. With each false part back in place, Mr Williams returned. It was like the yellow-haired woman had never shown herself. I wanted to see her again but something was between us, thick and clawing as gorse. Her lie.

For a moment neither of us spoke. We only looked at one another. He was giving me the chance to run, to tell the world as I went that Mr Williams was not who he said he was. But what would happen to me if I did? The river, and then the ground.

'You are a strange creature,' I said.

'Not all that strange. There are likely many of us working in this way.' He went to drink from his glass and then remembered I'd had it all.

'I've never heard of any women passing as men.'

'That's because they're successful. You would only hear of a discovery if the disguise were to fail.'

I thought of the men I knew. Were any of them not as they seemed? Their bodies hidden in britches and jackets. Their secrets covered by moustaches and beards. Vosper. Tom Prout. Roe. Any one of them could be something other than they seemed.

'If I help you,' I said, 'will you be paying me?'

'You're quite the mercenary, Shilly. My helping Matthew Weeks is your payment.'

But I couldn't eat his help. I couldn't sleep beneath it.

Mr Williams picked up the candle and stood, his body as stiff as before.

'Why do you move like that when you don't have an affliction?' I said.

'It is part of who Mr Williams was – I mean, who he is. Who I am when I am him.'

'But there's only me here and now I know it to be untrue.'

'But when I am Mr Williams I am always him. It has to be so or I'll forget and show myself to others.'

'You mean Vosper?'

'I mean everyone. I've trusted you, Shilly. You must trust me now. Meet me here tomorrow morning. Eight o'clock. I need you to show me where Charlotte was found.' He was opening the door.

'I can't go back to Penhale.'

In the darkness I couldn't make out what he thought of this. I barely knew how I felt myself. But I knew how it would be at the farm, and I knew my thirst was bad.

'Mrs Peter will turn me onto the moor if she knows I'm trying to free Matthew. Penhale is all I have. If you want my help then you have to help me.' There was my payment.

He waited a moment, his fingers twitching on the candlestick. 'I'll speak to the landlord about a room. It's not the most salubrious of places but there aren't many alternatives when we need to be near the farm and the ford. And you'll be used to poor conditions, I'm sure.'

'Vosper. I don't trust him.'

'All the more reason to be close to him,' Mr Williams said.

And all the more reason to be close to you, I thought.

THIRTY-FOUR

'Left the farm, have you, Shilly?' Vosper said, leading the way up the stairs. The wood creaked so loud I thought the stairs would give way beneath us. 'Wouldn't have thought there was need to, with Matthew in the gaol. You'd be safe in your own bed now.'

We came to a landing. The whitewash was brown and flaking from the walls. The smell of old food, unaired rooms. Two doors facing one another and a third beyond.

'Phillipa won't like it,' he said. 'You know she won't.'

The person that was Mr Williams came up the stairs behind me. 'This is it, yes?'

He opened one of the doors and went inside, and I took it that I should follow. Vosper stepped forward to join us but Mr Williams shut the door before he could come in. I enjoyed the cheated look on Vosper's face but when I looked about me such joy faded for the place was bleak, there could be no denying it.

A straw mattress slung on ropes. A stained blanket. Holes in the window stuffed with rags but still the candle flame jumped.

'You'll sleep here,' Mr Williams said.

'What about you?'

'Across the landing,' he said.

In a better room than this, I thought. The best that Vosper had to offer. Not that that would mean much in the Britannia Inn. Smaller holes in the window, perhaps.

'I'll leave you the light.' He set it on the chair, which swayed even at

141

that little weight, such was the unevenness of its legs. He turned to go.

'Wait,' I said.

And wait he did, but he saw my reaching for his false hair and got away from me.

I stowed my hands in my pockets. 'I only wanted to see—'

'You'll have to be quicker than that, Shilly.'

He opened the door. Vosper was still on the landing, all eager to see what this *gentleman* and I were about in the room.

'We must be out early tomorrow,' Mr Williams said loudly, to me or to Vosper, I didn't know. And then more softly, only to me, he said, 'Be ready when I call.'

The door banged. He was gone and I was shut in, kept where he could find me. Men's heavy steps sounded down the stairs. Vosper might be off to the farm that very minute, telling Mrs Peter I was in a room paid for by a gentleman, and all that that meant.

And what *did* it mean, with this gentleman who wasn't?

I fell asleep to glasses clinking, men shouting. Men who were women shouting. That was the last thought that came to me.

The thought was still with me on waking, with he that made such a thought calling my name through the door.

I found him waiting in the bar. He was wearing his boxy coat and on the bar was a large black bag. There was no sign of Vosper but a man was lying by the cold hearth, his back to us.

'Sleeping it off,' Mr Williams said, nodding at the body on the floor.

I could smell the sleeping man's burning breath even though I was paces away. Terrible, such weakness. I went over and nudged him with my boot. He rolled on to his back but stayed insensible. It was Roe.

'Not a regular customer, so Mr Vosper tells me,' Mr Williams said.

He went behind the bar and rootled in the shelves and drawers. While he was so diverted I slipped a half bottle into my pocket. Vosper and his takings could hang.

'Ah!' said Mr Williams, with wonder in his voice like he had found a great treasure. 'At last, something to imbibe other than alcohol.' But in his hand was only a bit of bread and when he tried it he found it wasn't fit to eat. The chewing seemed to pain him. 'What sort of inn doesn't have a cook?' he said, with sadness in his voice.

'The sort where no one stays,' I said, and we both looked at Roe on the floor.

Mr Williams left the bread on the bar. I took some. The staler it was the longer it would take me to chew, making me feel full for longer. An old trick I'd needed in Blisland. Mrs Peter had fed us so well at the farm that I'd forgotten its uses. But those good meals were gone.

'When you're ready,' Mr Williams called from the door. 'Matthew Weeks waits to be reacquainted with his liberty.'

And that was why I was without better bread and creamy butter, and stew that sometimes had meat. Because Matthew was in the gaol. Because Charlotte was gone. This stranger in their stead, going now to the ford, to that bad place, making me follow. Woe betide me – what had we three done to deserve such things?

I lingered in the doorway, watching Mr Williams walk out across the moor. His boxy back was a black mark in the green. He didn't turn round. He thought I would follow, and that made me angry so I forgot all about being hungry.

I shouted to him to wait, called his name, and I was sure to shout the *Mr* loudest of all. He didn't stop or slow but I caught him easily enough because he kept up his falseness of the stiff hip.

'I think I've hit upon the answer to one mystery, at least,' he said.

'You know who killed Charlotte?' My empty stomach turned over itself and danced.

'Give me a little more time for that, Shilly. Detecting isn't instantaneous. This mystery concerns yourself. Your name, to be precise.'

I took advantage of a sheep hollow to walk a little away from him so he wouldn't see the burning in my cheeks.

143

'I try to be timely,' I said.

'I think you could try a little harder,' he said.

To take him from this kind of shaming talk, which I had heard so often from Mrs Peter that I thought my ears would bleed with it, I asked him when Matthew would go before the judges. That was time that mattered more than my lateness.

'I've made enquiries,' Mr Williams said. 'The circuit judge is keen for the trial to take place during the upcoming session of the assize rather than wait for the next quarter. I'll have to work quickly.'

'You mean *we'll* have to work quickly,' I said.

He glanced at me, shrugged his boxy coat better onto his shoulders, and quickened his pace. But he wouldn't get far without me. The marshes would soon be upon us.

We passed Lanlary Rock, and Roughtor played its old game then of sinking beneath the ground. When we neared the ford the tor showed itself again, rising over the horizon until it was so big it seemed not to be real. I felt it watching me as we walked to the stream. Mr Williams put down his black bag.

'A desolate spot,' he said, and I had to say that yes, it was, for the ford was much changed since I had last been there, when Charlotte was found. The water and the grass on either side weren't the same, though there was nothing different to see. It was the feeling of the place – the skin and bones of it.

'To business, then,' Mr Williams said. He clapped his hands. 'The body—'

But I heard nothing more from Mr Williams, because I saw the fetch.

THIRTY-FIVE

All at once I was cold and the cold hands were at me. I closed my eyes
and tried to say a charm for protection.

'Shilly?'

I opened my eyes. Mr Williams was by my side, his hand on my shoulder.

'Are you quite well?' he said.

'It's . . .'

But there was nothing to say because there was nothing there.
Nothing beyond the pony the fetch had become. She was standing in
the water to drink, looking at me. A thread of water escaped her lips.
There were others in sight. I wished to be like them, able to walk across
the moor and not look back.

'Well, then,' Mr Williams said. 'We'll continue, shall we?'

He spoke with purpose but I could see he was uncertain at my
own uncertainty, and I couldn't tell him of the fetch for he would
only laugh again. We were at different purposes, even as we stood
on the same patch of earth, with the same end. But Mr Williams
was keen to try, and I liked him for that, for Matthew's sake if not
my own.

'Let's begin,' he said. 'I need you to show me where Charlotte was
found and how she was lying.'

I sat down to take off my boots.

'Is that necessary?' he said.

'If I'm getting in the water I'm keeping my boots dry.'

'No,' he said, frowning. 'Show me where she was.'

'But she was in the water. Not in it so she was wet. The water parted round her.'

Mr Williams stared at me. He looked like he would speak but then closed his mouth. He took a little book from his pocket and turned the pages.

'At the magistrates' hearing Vosper said of the body, and I quote, *it was in an old river place*. He called it a pit. This is where he meant, surely.' Mr Williams pointed to the dry part of the river bed, seen when the water was low.

'She was in the river, floating,' I said. 'At first I thought she was tied somehow, to keep her from being carried downstream. But she wasn't. She was just there.'

At the memory of it my thirst worsened. I turned myself from Mr Williams and took the bottle from my pocket. If I was very quick he shouldn't see.

When I had done what I needed I saw that he was peering in the water. The pony was still standing in the stream a few feet away, watching Mr Williams.

'You mean Charlotte was lying on a rock?' he said. 'I can't see anything large enough to support her. Oh, good heavens!'

He stumbled from the bank just in time, for the pony had chosen to clamber out of the stream right in front of him. His feet tangled together and he fell, landing on his back. The pony stood over him, opened her mouth and a great slosh of stream water and spit poured onto Mr Williams' chest. The pony huffed air from her nose, looked around then ambled off to her friends waiting nearby, clipping Mr Williams's leg with one of her hooves as she went. He'd have a real injury now.

I went to help Mr Williams to his feet but it was beyond my strength to keep my laughter inside me.

'Laugh you may, Shilly. You're not the one soaked to the skin in . . . What *is* this? Mucus of some kind?' He put his fingers to his wet breast then smelt them. The look on his face made me laugh even harder.

'It'll dry soon enough and the smell will go,' I told him. 'She must like you, that one.'

146

'Like me? I'll be pleased to remain an enemy of moorland ponies if that's how they show their affection. You seemed to enjoy seeing such an attempt at friendship, Shilly.'

'I can't remember when I last laughed like that. Since Charlotte . . .'

He nodded, and said gently, 'I must ask you a few more questions about how she was found, to be sure the details are quite clear in my mind. Tell me, was her skin discoloured in any way? Was she recognisable about the face?'

'Of course she was.'

'Well, I have to say that means she couldn't have been in the water. Her body would have borne signs. I've followed cases of bodies pulled from the Thames and there's no doubt about their contact with water, I can assure you.'

'She wasn't wet,' I said, 'because she made the water bend round her.'

'You must be mistaken, Shilly. It was a distressing moment, I'm sure. The mind can play tricks when—'

'She was in the water with the water parting round her.'

'That is simply not possible.' There was no smile from him now.

'Charlotte made things do as they didn't ought to. She was . . . She had ways.'

Mr Williams snapped his little book closed and shoved it back inside his coat.

'If what you say is true, then why did Vosper not say so when questioned by the magistrates? He was one of the men who found the body.'

I had no answer for him.

'One of you is lying,' Mr Williams said.

'You talk of lies when you do as you do? You're lying this moment, even as you stand there and call me a liar.'

'That's hardly relevant at this moment, is it? I would ask you to keep your mind on the matter at hand, and I would also ask that you refrain from giving me false information. All you'll do is hasten Matthew Weeks's end. You've already lost one friend and I take it you've no wish to lose another.'

I didn't answer. I thought I would give him the day and then he was on his own. If he wouldn't listen to what I had to tell him then he wasn't going to be any use in saving Matthew anyway, for so much of what had happened was thickety and strange. It was the mark of a hand left in a dream. It was smoke rising from a grave. It was this I knew and could tell. If anyone would listen.

Mr Williams stepped away from me as if I was unhelpful to his thinking. When he had put some five feet between us and averted his eyes from me he said, 'You were here, weren't you, just before she was found?'

'I came at first light. That's when I saw the fetch.'

He waved his hand like he was batting away a fly or a moth. 'Spirits do not concern me. What happened when you returned to the farm?'

'I helped Mrs Peter get the cart to the road. She was going to All Drunkard, to market. When she came back she had the men with her. They started to search. It didn't take them long to find Charlotte.'

'How much time passed between you being here at the ford and the men finding her?'

'I don't know. Those days were . . . difficult. I've tried to forget.'

These words made him look at me once more. He spun on his heel and was all at once enlivened. 'Remember them now, Shilly. It's important.'

More important than the fetch, more important than Charlotte squeezing my hand until it broke.

'Not long,' I said. 'I didn't have time to clean out the pigs before Mrs Peter was back. Then the men went out, I made a few pasties – only one or two and I'm quick with pastry. Then Vosper was in the yard, saying they'd found her.'

Mr Williams made a strange noise then. A kind of tapping sound seemed to come from inside his mouth, but then it was gone and he was speaking again.

'So Mrs Peter goes to All Drunkard and a search party is organised. Word must have spread that men were going to look for Charlotte. There was only a small amount of time between you seeing the ford was empty and the body – Charlotte, I should say – being found here. Tell me, is this spot always so lonely?'

'It's a common path for people crossing the moor.'

'And yet Charlotte had been missing for several days before she was found, with no one, including yourself, seeing hide nor hair of her here. If we disregard the fetch, of course.'

He laughed a little to himself. I kicked a stone into the water.

'And then Charlotte appears,' he said, 'as if from nowhere and while men are searching.'

I heard the tapping sound coming from his mouth again. Like the butter knife catching the butter dish.

'That's what Charlotte did,' I said. 'She slipped about. Disappeared. Then she was there, right where I'd been looking. She did it at the farm all the time.'

'People don't just vanish, Shilly.'

'*She* did, when you put your false hair and eyes back on.'

'I mean, they're always somewhere. The woman you saw is here now, isn't she? And Charlotte must have been somewhere between leaving the farm and being found. Did she have any marks on her, any cuts – beyond the obvious?'

'No.'

'Which means she wasn't touched by foxes or carrion birds, which means she wasn't kept on open moorland.'

'Kept?' I said.

'There was no water damage or signs of animal interference. Think about it, Shilly, if you can.'

I wanted to shove him in the river. See how he liked water damage.

He turned the pages of his little book. 'Three days. Where was she?'

I grabbed his arm and dragged him into the gorse.

'What the—?'

'Shh!' I pointed through the gorse.

People. Twenty at least, coming down to the ford. Men and women in good coats and hats. And leading the way was Vosper.

THIRTY-SIX

'Here's where I found her,' Vosper said, pointing to the dried-out bed below the riverbank. 'This is the spot her head lay.'

'No mention of the body making water bend, I notice,' Mr Williams muttered. 'One might imagine an audience would welcome tales of the supernatural.'

I chose not to say anything in return. We were hiding, after all.

Vosper was carrying a pole. He grasped it with both hands and tried to drive it into the earth but he must have struck moor stone for he couldn't get the pole to stand up. Again and again he stabbed at the ground before finding a clear path. When the pole was standing steady he took a square of black cloth from his pocket, unfolded it and tied it to the pole.

'This flag, ladies and gentlemen, is but a temporary marker for Charlotte Dymond. I'm looking to build a monument that will last. In granite, I hope. But such things are costly, beyond the means of a lowly publican such as myself.'

There was a murmur from the group and the ladies felt in their purses.

'You're the first visitors to this cursed spot,' Vosper said, 'the first to walk in the footsteps of this tragic young woman and the evil man who robbed her of her life.'

'Tell us of the poor child's wounds,' one lady called. She wore the fanciest hat I'd ever seen. Feathers and ribbons galore. The kind of hat Mrs Peter would have called sinful, that Charlotte would have loved.

'Was the girl's head cut from her body?' a tall man said. 'I read in the newspaper it was nearly severed.'

''Tis true, sir,' Vosper said. He gazed at the flag for all the world like it was Charlotte herself.

'How dreadful!' the woman with the feathered hat said, but she said the words not like it really was dreadful, what had happened. She sounded pleased by it.

'Indeed, madam, indeed. Now, if we retrace our steps I can show you the farm where the two lovers lived and where Weeks plotted his terrible crime. Mrs Peter, mistress of Penhale, has agreed to show you the room where Charlotte slept, and there will be a dish of tea for those who want it.'

The group began the climb back up the slope. When they were a fair distance away Mr Williams stepped from the gorse.

'So our landlord is collecting money to record Matthew's guilt in stone.'

'Vosper will keep the money himself,' I said, climbing out of the gorse. 'He doesn't have a charitable bone in his body.'

'Perhaps,' Mr Williams said. 'We'll see what appears here.' He gave the pole a shake. 'Curious, marking the spot in such a way.'

The sight of the black cloth was hateful. It was like keeping the fetch there. I tried to pull the pole from the ground but Vosper had buried it too deep. I asked Mr Williams for help but he ignored me, looking back the way we'd come. Vosper and his followers had almost reached Lanlary Rock.

'Three days,' Mr Williams said. 'Matthew had nowhere to keep her — that's a point in his favour. You'd have found her if she was still at the farm. Heard her, no doubt. She was a spirited creature, from what I've heard.'

I was happy to tell him that Charlotte would indeed have been noisesome if she'd been hidden somewhere at Penhale. And I would have known even without her noise, I thought but didn't say. She would have made me know.

151

'But she had to be somewhere in the time she was missing,' Mr Williams said, 'and she had to be alive, given that the magistrates' hearing made no mention of decomposition.'

'What does that mean?'

He frowned. 'Decomposition?'

When he had explained it to me I wished I hadn't asked. And what came next was no more pleasant. Mr Williams's talk was all the workings of time, and when in time my girl had breathed her last.

'My belief is that she was taken from the moor alive. Then, two things happened, but I can't be sure in which order. One, her captor killed her. Two, he heard about the search party Mrs Peter was bringing from All Drunkard. It's too much of a coincidence that the body appeared just in time to be found. Whoever had the keeping of her wanted her found on the moor rather than wherever it was she'd been held, suggesting the site was incriminating. There aren't many places nearby. If she wasn't kept at the farm then that leaves—'

'Vosper's inn. The old stables at the back.'

A rat ran across the inn's yard as we drew close. Rotten barrels lay about, and a rusted iron bedstead with a leg missing. There were three stables, each with two doors, top and bottom. All were bolted shut.

Mr Williams went to the one furthest from the inn and eased back the bolts. They were stiff and the metal shrieked. The noise was like a patten scraping a slate floor.

Mr Williams dragged the stable door open. Once my eyes grew used to the darkness I could see cobwebs drifting from the ceiling, heavy with dust. Straw white with age. Mould up the walls.

'Nothing's been disturbed,' Mr Williams said.

But it was Vosper who had kept her. I knew it.

I went to the next stable. The bolts slid more easily and my heart leapt. Here there would be signs of Charlotte. But there was only food inside – sacks of flour and salt, joints hanging from the rafters.

152

'Note the dust,' Mr Williams said behind me. 'These items have been arranged like this for some time. Ham in a stable. If I needed any further proof this inn isn't fit to serve food . . .'

I wasn't listening. There was one stable left bolted. One more chance.

The bolts of the last door were slippery in my sweating hands but I would get them open. I would see what Vosper was hiding. He who had taken my girl from me.

Mr Williams watched my efforts, shook his head.

'We've talked much of time, Shilly, and your inability to manage it sufficiently. It's against us now, with Vosper only as far away as the farm.'

Still I scrabbled at the stable door's bolt but it held fast. Some wickedness, surely.

'Vosper has fixed the bolt.'

'And rendered your limbs weakened, too? A mighty mage, the landlord of the Britannia Inn. Come, move yourself.' Mr Williams lifted my hands from the bolt. 'I told you we've no time for this.'

He leant his weight against the door, and used the bolt to lift it a little on its hinges. When he tried the bolt now it moved. The door fell open, hastened by Mr William's weight. But it soon banged against something, even before it was fully ajar.

At first there was nothing to see, just a wall of black. I reached out and my hand struck wood. The stable was packed floor to ceiling with barrels. They were jammed almost to the door. I pulled the stopper from one and a burning smell I knew too well rose up around us.

'I doubt Vosper has a good account with excise men in these parts,' Mr Williams said. He ran his hand across the earthen floor. 'These barrels have been stored here recently. See the fresh marks on the floor.'

'So Charlotte could have been kept here, before the barrels came?'

Mr Williams dusted his hands. 'It's hard to be sure. Without being able to see to the back wall . . .'

'But she could have been.'

'There's the umbrella to consider. If Charlotte really did leave the farm without it, as Mrs Peter says, then she had to get it from somewhere else.'

'Mrs Peter was truthful saying that – I saw Charlotte leave without an umbrella. But she could have made it come to her.'

'From thin air?' Mr Williams said. 'You grant the people of this parish no end of abilities. Bestir yourself, Shilly, and let me close the door.'

'There's always something to be got from nothing,' I said.

'And there's a rational answer to every supposed mystery.' He pushed the bolt home and I winced at the metal's shriek. 'Charlotte made Matthew leave her at the road. She could have called here to get an umbrella, once she realised how bad the weather was. And supposing she did call in, why has our landlord not mentioned it? What does he have to hide?'

'Everything,' I said.

'You're set against him. Why?'

'Because he . . . He has the inn.'

Mr Williams walked towards the inn's back door and I followed his shaking head.

'If simply being a publican is a crime, there isn't enough rope in England to hang all the offenders. No, Shilly, you'll have to do better than that. Let's see what Vosper has to say for himself.'

He opened the door and went inside.

A noise behind me. The shriek of metal again.

I checked the yard. The stables were all bolted. The sound didn't come from them.

It came from her.

THIRTY-SEVEN

I was running up the passage as quickly as my stumbling feet would let me. Mr Williams was seated at the empty bar. I took a high-backed chair by the hearth, needing a moment to stop my hands from shaking.

Thus arranged we waited for Vosper. There was a scarred table by my chair. On it was a dark-coloured bottle. I shook it. Empty as the one in my pocket.

Vosper came in humming a cheerful tune but stopped all at once.

'You caught me out there, sir. Thought I was the only one here. You're wanting a drink?'

I heard the clink of glasses and then drinks being poured.

He was the one that hurt my girl so badly, that kept her locked up and away from me. If not in the stables then somewhere else. It was him. I knew it. My hand was on the empty bottle. I grasped it by the handle so as to make a glass club. I thought of the noise when I smashed Vosper's skull. I raised the bottle.

'Saw you were headed down to the ford this morning,' Vosper said, only to Mr Williams I guessed, for I was still hidden in my turned-away chair. 'Going to see where Charlotte Dymond was found, were you?'

'Indeed I was,' Mr Williams said. 'Idle fancy, really, having heard strange talk on the road. Driver of a coach out All Drunkard way, he told me the girl was oddly placed in the water. Making it run round her. I felt I had to see what the truth of it was.'

So Mr Williams wondered enough to ask Vosper, did he? Couldn't be too certain that what I'd told him was wrong. I felt some satisfaction, though I wouldn't let him see it. I put the bottle back on the table.

'You were there, weren't you,' he asked Vosper, 'when the girl was found? Was my driver right?'

'Oh I don't know about any of that,' Vosper said, lying through his teeth. 'It was a nasty business, however you take it. Weeks will soon meet his maker.'

'And rightly so,' Mr Williams said. 'There's no doubt he did it.'

'None.'

Another lie. More drinks were poured.

'Travelling south, are you?' he asked Mr Williams.

'In the next day or so. Thought I'd look around here first, as I was almost passing.'

'You're not the first to have that idea,' Vosper said.

'I don't doubt it! There's been much talk in the papers. I read that the girl was a flirt, made Weeks jealous.'

After a moment Vosper said, 'I wouldn't know.'

'She was carrying on with everyone. I heard it said in All Drunkard she had her eye on the farm, wanted to bed the son so she could be mistress.'

'I wouldn't listen to anything they say in All Drunkard. If there's nothing else you're wanting I'll be—'

'Been here long, have you? With the inn?'

'Few years now,' Vosper said, but guarded. Mr Williams had made him wary. 'Good drinkers, this side of the moor.'

'And where were you before?'

'Around and about. Nowhere particular. Couldn't help seeing the stiffness in your hip. Military injury, is it?'

I didn't listen to Mr Williams's false answer. That injury wasn't his own. He'd stolen it from someone else. That I already knew.

He was speaking again. 'You've known Weeks a fair while, I gather.'

Vosper made a noise to say yes.

'Is he as bad as they say?' Mr Williams asked.

'He's not to be trusted.'

'You sound as if you've had dealings with him.'

'He lost some of my cattle,' Vosper said. 'Years ago now. Cost me dearly.'

I sat up in my chair. Matthew had never told me of this.

'Weeks always looked out for himself, see,' Vosper said. 'Got no care for others. That's why he killed her. If he couldn't have her then no one could.'

'You farmed then, before turning landlord?'

'For a year or two. The loss of the cattle did for me, and that was Weeks's fault. He was meant to check them but he was idle. They got in to the marsh. He tried to blame the other man Phillipa and I were paying to help him but I knew Weeks was to blame. Phillipa's always been too kind-hearted for her own good. Have you heard about the memorial we're putting up?'

'The other man?'

'Granite, it'll be. Something lasting. We're looking for subscriptions.'

'Who was the man helping Weeks?'

The door opened.

'Speak of the devil,' Vosper said quietly.

It was Tom Prout.

THIRTY-EIGHT

'Glass of your finest,' Tom said, slapping the bar. He sounded like he'd had a few glasses already.

'You mean cheapest,' Vosper mumbled.

A body by my chair, and then, by my ear, 'I need you with me while I speak to Tom,' Mr Williams whispered. 'Come, put him at ease.'

I wasn't sure I'd be much good at that but I did as he asked and took the chair next to Tom. Mr Williams sat a little apart and turned away, as if he was a stranger in the bar, having a drink. Which he was, of course.

'So this is where you are, Shilly!' Tom said. His lip was still swollen and a bad colour. 'Aunt Phillipa's raging at you. Got me doing everything on the farm. Those wretched pigs. When are you coming back?'

'I'm not,' I said. 'Not with Charlotte and Matthew gone.'

Tom took a drink, wincing when the glass pressed his sore lip.

'That's a nasty cut,' Mr Williams said, turning round.

'What of it?' Tom said. He lurched in his chair and slopped his drink.

I thought of Charlotte stamping on the drunkard's hand when we'd come with the eggs. She might have fought the fiend that hurt her.

'Whoever it was had the best of it, I should think,' Mr Williams said.

'He did not!' Tom shouted. 'I gave him a blow right back. Got him clean in the eye, soft fool that he is.'

'Another drink, I think,' Mr Williams said, getting up, giving me a nod.

'Got yourself a gentleman, have you, Shilly?' Tom whispered when he'd gone. 'Now Charlotte's gone you'll look at men.'

'It's not like that. Why were you fighting John Peter?'

'I shouldn't have told you that. Don't say anything to Aunt Phillipa.'

'Why not?' I said.

'Because I wasn't meant to see her any more,' Tom said. 'Mother had said so after Aunt Phillipa started her worrying.'

'You saw Charlotte? When?'

'Promise you won't tell Aunt Phillipa?'

'Only if you tell me what I'm asking. When did you see Charlotte?'

'I . . .'

I got to my feet. 'I had thought to go to the farm this afternoon, and I'm sure Mrs Peter will forgive my leaving when I tell her—'

'Charlotte was going to meet me at Tremail chapel.'

'Is that what you and her were talking about on Sunday?' I said, sitting down again.

'And I can guess why you were going to meet,' Mr Williams said, coming back with a full glass for Tom. 'I've heard all about her.'

Tom grinned. 'She let me—'

'But what about John Peter?' Mr Williams said. 'Why did he hit you?'

Tom took the drink in one swallow. 'John heard me and Charlotte agreeing to meet when I called at the farm. He must have been hiding, in the barn or somewhere, I don't know. But he came to the chapel and we argued. He told me he was going to marry Charlotte and I told him he was a fool for thinking so.'

'She would have married him,' I said. 'She wanted to.'

Tom's grin was gone. 'What?'

'Charlotte was going to marry John Peter. For the farm.'

'You're lying!'

'Or you are,' Mr Williams said. 'Did you really meet Charlotte at the chapel?'

Tom pushed his empty glass towards Mr Williams.

'Get the bottle, Shilly,' Mr Williams said.

I did as he asked, taking a little myself while I was at the bar. The door to the back room was open. Vosper was in there, listening. I tried to tell

Mr Williams but Tom took the bottle from me and was talking again.

'She didn't come to the chapel,' he said, 'but John Peter did.' Tom fingered his sore lip. 'I'd never seen him so angry, didn't know he had that kind of strength.'

'You clearly weren't concerned when Charlotte didn't arrive,' Mr Williams said, 'because you didn't call at the farm until the search party was formed two days later. That strikes me as rather strange when you profess to have cared for her. Perhaps you kept away because you knew all the time where she was.'

'I didn't care for her,' Tom said. 'She let me have my way with her. That's all I wanted. She didn't come to the chapel and I didn't bother to look for her.'

From the back room came a thud then the sound of glass breaking.

We left Tom to the bottle. Mr Williams put some coins on the bar. Vosper came out of the back room to pocket them, keeping his eye on Tom.

'A regular?' Mr Williams asked.

'Too regular,' Vosper said. 'He needs to go back to Tremail.'

Mr Williams went outside and I followed. When we were well beyond the door he held up a hand for me to stop.

'I take it you heard me ask Vosper about the manner in which Charlotte was found?'

'Yes, but he—'

'So you heard him deny your claim that the river parted round her.'

He waited for me to answer. I gave him the smallest of nods, like there was crawlies on my head and I was twitching.

'Well then, now I've done you the service of entertaining your foolish notions long enough to dispel them, I trust you'll put an end to such talk.'

'But Vosper—'

'But nothing, Shilly. There is nothing in this story of yours that has any bearing on my investigations.'

'It's not a story! I know what I saw and I know that Vosper's lying.' But then a thought came to me. One that might help Mr Williams understand.

'Unless he isn't lying. If he didn't see what I saw. If Charlotte meant that only I should see how she truly was in the water.'

But I was talking to myself for Mr Williams was on his way once more, calling to the gorse that I was behind again. Always behind.

'Was Charlotte familiar with Vosper?' he said when I caught him up. 'Was there affection between them?'

'It seemed like Vosper had known her a while. She was different with him than she was with Matthew and John Peter. More . . . familiar.'

'So there could have been relations between them,' he said, 'in the past or since Charlotte had come to Penhale. Vosper was at the funeral to pay his respects, after all.'

'Or to take comfort in seeing her buried because it was him that put her in the ground.' In my bones I knew him to be bad. I thought of him climbing the gallows, the rope lowered over his head.

'There's the problem of the limp,' Mr Williams said.

The vision of Vosper jerking at the end of the rope faded.

'He could have a limp but he keeps it hidden,' I said.

'Shilly, I've seen the man moving and he looks as sound as you or I.'

'But *you're* not sound at this moment,' I said, 'and that's a falsehood. Perhaps Vosper's falsehood is the other way round.'

'Forget Vosper for the moment. I need you to do something, and you're not going to like it.'

He put his hand on my arm to make me stop.

We were at the path to the farm.

THIRTY-NINE

I went first. I couldn't remember if I'd left anything in the gorse bush and I couldn't check with Mr Williams there, though I needed it, with him making me go back to the farm.

I wished the path was twice as long, three times, four – that I would walk it forever, with Mr Williams at my back. But it had never felt so short, and too soon we came to the house. The porch door was open. I crept to it, peered inside, as light on my feet as St Michael had been. Mrs Peter was by the hearth, her head tipped back and her eyes closed. From behind the house came the sound of metal striking stone. I led Mr Williams past the barn and there we found John Peter.

He was thumping his hoe into the weeds of the vegetable plot with no hope of turning the soil. I hailed him. He dropped the hoe and was running at me. His words got caught in his great huffing of breath.

'I thought . . . lost you . . . Shilly, thought you'd gone . . . the moor like Charlotte . . . hurt . . . Mother said . . .' He caught sight of Mr Williams and his words and his running stuttered to a stop.

'This is my friend,' I said. 'He can be your friend too, if you speak to him.'

Mr Williams held out his hand. 'A pleasure to meet the master of Penhale Farm.'

John Peter glanced sideways to me. I nodded. He took Mr Williams's hand and nearly wrenched it off.

I looked to the kitchen's back window. No sign of Mrs Peter. But there would be. Now was the time to find the swiftness Mr Williams kept telling me I lacked.

'My friend wants to ask you some questions,' I told John Peter.

He went back to his hoe and started driving it into the ground again. 'I've got work to do, Shilly-shally. Mother says the farm will go to rack and ruin.'

'Whatever do you mean?' I said. 'Here you are tending the vegetables. You'll soon be right enough.' I fell to pulling the weeds with my hands.

'But I'll have no wife to help me,' he said.

My hands went still. He was looking down at me.

'Ah, but you might,' Mr Williams said. 'There might be someone close now who would marry you and help look after your farm.'

I couldn't speak for dread. I tried not to think about what he was making John Peter believe. Lying again. I was lying too, by not speaking contrary. Mr Williams had set his snakeness on me.

'Shilly would need to be certain of you, John Peter. She would have to be able to trust you.'

'Of course!' he said.

I got to my feet but I didn't look at Mr Williams. 'You'll have a talk with my friend, will you, John Peter?'

He couldn't speak for grinning.

Mr Williams moved closer to him. 'Where were you on Sunday?'

John Peter held the hoe in both hands and twisted it like wringing a chicken's neck. 'You mustn't tell Mother,' he said.

'We won't,' Mr Williams said.

'I went to Tremail, to the chapel. Tom Prout was there. Do you know Tom?' he asked Mr Williams gravely. 'He's a bad man. Mother says he has to help us on the farm but I don't want him here. He drinks, and he wants Charlotte. She told me she wouldn't go about with other men but she lied.'

And for it we were liars, all.

'What happened when you went to the chapel in the afternoon?' Mr Williams said. 'Was Charlotte there?'

He shook his head. 'I split Tom's lip. Did you see it? I got him proper good. Told him she was mine, not his.'

'And then what happened?' I said. 'Where did you go?'

'I was clever then. Cleverer than Tom. I made out I was leaving but I hid instead, in the trees in the churchyard. I waited for her to come.'

'And did she?' Mr Williams said.

'No, she didn't! And then Tom came out of the chapel. He didn't know I was still there, you see, because I was hiding. I followed him. He went home and hid himself away. He didn't want his mother to see the split lip I gave him. I did a good thing, didn't I, Shilly, showing him like that? Because she was mine, no one else's.'

I patted his arm. 'Yes,' I said. 'A good thing.'

His hand closed over my own. 'And now *you're* mine,' he said. 'You'll look after the farm with me and maybe Mother will like that better.'

'Not yet, John,' Mr Williams said. 'You must tell me just a little more.'

I let John Peter hold on to my hand but kept looking to the kitchen window, thinking to see Mrs Peter at any moment.

'What did you do after you followed Tom Prout home?' Mr Williams said. 'Did you go out onto the moor? Did you go to the ford?'

'We'll have sheep on our farm, Shilly. Lots of them. No more cows.'

'That's a good plan,' I said, though it was hard to make such words come. 'And it would be good, too, if you told us where you went after you saw Tom go home.'

'Back to the chapel, of course,' he said. 'To wait for Charlotte. She told Tom she'd meet him there but she lied to him too.' He grinned. 'She didn't come. I waited until it was dark and then I came home across the fields and you were there, Shilly, with Mother and the lantern and then I went to bed. I was in bed such a long time. When I got up, everything was different.'

Mrs Peter's voice rang out from the yard, calling for John Peter.

Before I could hush him he shouted, 'Here, Mother!'

She came round the side of the house but stopped on seeing us.

John Peter stumbled his way to her, telling her I was there, though Mrs Peter could see that herself, plain enough. We had to take our leave, and quickly.

'This way,' I said to Mr Williams. 'Through the fields.'

I didn't look back at Mrs Peter. At what had once been my home. That was gone. Through the fields, back to the inn with Mr Williams was my path now. My steps were slow with the losing of things.

I climbed over the field wall and Mr Williams followed. He was speaking but I found him hard to hear. His voice had become a bee's hum. My feet grew heavier as I walked even though the mud wasn't thick enough to lag them. The heaviness climbed my legs and got hold of my hips. I sank to the ground. It was like the day Charlotte had walked out of the house with Matthew. She was turning me to moor stone again.

FORTY

'Shilly?' Mr Williams said, and all at once every sound was sharply clear. Too sharp. My ears thrummed.

The clink of a bit in a horse's mouth. The steady beat of hooves on the ground.

Roe was riding towards us on the track between the fields, but I was somewhere else. There was water. I could smell the marshes.

I couldn't get up. I couldn't move at all.

'Mr Roe, isn't it?' Mr Williams called, striding over to where the clinking was. 'I'm in need of a butcher.'

Roe pulled up his horse but didn't get down.

'You are a butcher, aren't you?' Mr Williams said. 'Shilly here mentioned you killed Mrs Peter's old pig.'

I was still unable to rise, and Mr Williams did nothing to help me.

'Where's your farm?' Roe said.

'Near All Drunkard,' Mr Williams said.

'Not from around here?'

'Not long arrived, and I'm in need of some help. That's a fine animal you've got there.' He patted the horse's shoulder. 'I heard about the murder, from the girl there.'

Roe looked at me and it was like the ground was a mouth that had opened and was sucking me down its dark, wet throat.

'Weeks will hang for it,' Roe said.

'As he should,' Mr Williams said. 'You saw him on the moor that day, didn't you? With Miss Dymond.'

'Been spilling your guts, girl?' Roe said.

Moor stone in my mouth. Moss spidering my eyes. My ears left untouched so I should still hear them.

'I was at the magistrates' hearing,' Mr Williams said. 'Heard you say you saw them near Lanlary Rock. Whereabouts were you?'

When no answer came, Mr Williams said, 'I'm sorry to pry. I only ask from passing interest, but if you'd rather not say—'

'I was riding. Back to Lanhendra. Halfway between Lanlary Rock and the road.'

'That put you some way from Lanlary Rock, didn't it? By my reckoning the distance from the road to the rock is almost a mile. You must have good eyes, Mr Roe. An important quality for a butcher.'

'Perhaps I was a bit closer, now that I think—'

'And the weather was bad too, wasn't it?'

'Mizzle,' Roe said.

'It was terrible out All Drunkard way. Mist had cleared by the Monday, though, hadn't it?'

Roe grunted.

'Better for riding out here to kill the pig,' Mr Williams said. He gave the horse another pat. 'Heard you say that Weeks collapsed when the pig was stuck.'

'Wretch couldn't face what he'd done.'

'Guilty conscience.'

Another grunt from Roe. 'I had to show him how to do it quickly.'

'Had his own knife, though, Weeks? Could be what he killed her with.'

'Could be,' Roe said.

'I hear they haven't found it – the knife that killed her.'

Roe didn't answer.

'Weeks must have some strength, though, to have cut her neck so badly,' Mr Williams said. 'Quite the brute. You wouldn't think it to look at him.'

Warmth across my throat, like a shawl laid there. Then the warmth getting hot, like the shawl pulled back and forth, rubbing my throat raw. Then the shawl becoming sharp, like a blade. Then the rush of air as my throat opened, like a yawn slipped from my face. Then the blood. Hot in my hands. So much of it. Pouring down my dress, slick up my arms. I could still hear them talking as my breath stopped.

'The girl there's got more strength than Weeks,' Roe said. 'He made a few cuts on the pig's neck but his knife wouldn't go deep enough.'

'Is that so? Well, I'll need a man who knows what he's doing for my old pig.'

'You'll find me at Lanhendra. Mr Carwitham's house.'

'How is Mr Carwitham? Quite recovered, I hope.'

'Not enough to check the stock. I'll have to get on—'

'Of course.'

I coughed up blood and bile and something else. Something hard and coarse. It ripped my mouth as it left me. A bead from her necklace.

I lay curled against the field wall. My dress and hands were bloody and I felt cold air pass through my opened throat.

Mr Williams was standing over me. 'When you're quite recovered, we'll continue.'

'Do you see now what she can do?' I tried to say, though I didn't know if I had body left to make words. I held out the bead I had coughed from myself so that he should take it from my blood-wet hands.

'A stone, Shilly? Kind of you, but there are more than enough hereabouts, should I find myself without one.'

A stone? Why would he not see—?

He was right. My fingers were clutching a small piece of moor stone. My hands and dress were clean of blood. I touched my opened throat. Skin. Smooth and whole.

'Up you get,' he said, offering me his hand.

Somehow my feet remembered what it was to stand but I felt far away from him, far away from that moment in the field. And then we were walking, me leaning on his arm like we were courting, but not like that at all. Like he'd found me in a hedgerow and taken pity on me. And I was all pity for myself. *Shilly-shally, what has become of you?*

He was speaking but to himself. I caught the end of it, and wished I hadn't.

'. . . never have taken her to the inn.'

The empty bottle in my pocket banged against my thigh like a second heartbeat but he was wrong. It wasn't that that left me helpless in the mud, thinking I'd been cut.

'You must believe me,' I said.

'No,' he said sadly. 'That I surely mustn't do.'

I shook him off then. Tottering like a new-born calf I might have been, but I'd totter without his disbelieving arm. He stayed close to me, though, as if waiting for me to fall. When I didn't, he asked me about blades.

'Were the men's shaving razors in place before you left the farm?'

I told him I thought they were. I didn't tell him it seemed so long ago I'd last looked that I couldn't remember where the razors were or what they looked like.

'Then that means it's unlikely one of the razors was the weapon,' Mr Williams said, 'and good Mr Roe has told us something he might not have intended. Matthew's knife was poor. He couldn't have cut Charlotte's neck with it if it wouldn't kill the pig, and I doubt he got hold of another. If he'd bought a better knife locally then someone would have come forward by now.'

'Do you think it was Roe, then?'

Through the fog of my own thinking I heard the strange tapping sound again, coming from Mr Williams's mouth. But then he was speaking and the sound was just his words.

'Roe came to the farm on Sunday evening with no real purpose, it seems to me, other than to tell you and Mrs Peter that he'd seen Matthew on the moor with a woman. The next day he told Matthew to cut an animal's throat when there was no need for Matthew to do so. It was Roe's job, after all. There are different ways to interpret such an action. Perhaps Roe hoped Matthew would reveal his guilt at having cut Charlotte's throat, if Matthew had indeed killed her, or perhaps Roe wanted Matthew to *appear* guilty of something. To those already suspicious, Matthew looked to be unable to face what he'd done. And then Roe was lucky – Matthew had a nosebleed, which left his shirt bloody.'

'But Roe had no dealings with Charlotte,' I said.

'You didn't know she'd had dealings with Tom Prout yet she agreed to meet him at the chapel. Perhaps you didn't know her as well as you thought.'

I was going to tell him that I knew Charlotte best in the world, that Tom Prout was likely lying about Charlotte saying she'd meet him at the chapel, but Mr Williams was speaking again. Always his tongue was going.

'Was John Peter in the house when Roe called?' he said.

'No. Me and Mrs Peter found him outside, not long after Roe left. That's when I saw he had a black eye.'

'John Peter could have got that from fighting Tom Prout, as he claims,' Mr Williams said. 'Then there's the fact he doesn't limp.'

'He was sound on Sunday night,' I agreed. 'And Tom doesn't limp either.'

'But Tom's behaviour is still suspicious. I'm not sure I believe his reasons for not seeking Charlotte before the search party was formed.' The tapping noise again. I was sure it came from his mouth.

We reached another gate. It was tied shut with coils and coils of rope, unopened for years.

'This way will take us back to the road,' I said.

I climbed the gate and swung my leg over the top, dragging the bottom of my dress out of the way to make the going easier, and in doing so I bared my leg below my knee. I readied myself to drop to the other side, but something stopped me. Mr Williams was staring at my bared leg. I stayed where I was, sitting astride the gate. I pulled my dress further up, past my knee. Still he looked. Or rather, she looked. For it was her – the yellow-haired woman who hid beneath Mr Williams. She came towards me, reaching out.

The gate bucked on its hinges with both our weight as we faced one another, then she was scrambling down the other side, and it was Mr Williams's back hurrying away. But I'd seen her want for the flesh of my leg. I'd seen her there.

FORTY-ONE

The rest of the day was questions. Vosper let us use the back room of the inn and Mr Williams asked me about everything that had ever happened at the farm, all the time writing in his little book. I told him about the letter Charlotte had had on the day she went missing. I told him about her going to Boscastle, too.

'She went most Sundays to see her mother.'

Mr Williams looked up from his little book. 'Did you ever go with her?'

'To Boscastle? No. I would have but . . .' She'd never asked me, I realised.

'Then how can you be sure that's where Charlotte went? She could have been meeting other people. Tom Prout, for instance. Arranging to meet at Tremail chapel on Sunday might not have been the first such occasion.'

I opened my mouth but I had no words to answer Mr Williams. How *could* I be sure where Charlotte had gone on Sundays?

He let me stutter and gulp as I had done the night he showed himself to be someone else in that very same room, and then he took pity on me.

'We'll take some refreshment,' he said. 'I've asked a lot of you today, Shilly. It can't be easy, finding that your friend wasn't quite who you thought.'

'I knew her better than anyone,' I said. 'She was mine before she was theirs.'

He looked at me without speaking. Watched me, more like, and I didn't understand why. What was he seeing from behind those thick, false spectacles?

Then he shrugged and said, 'Of course. I meant no offence.'

He got up to call Vosper and I was glad to be free from his questions and his watching. From the whole bad business of it.

Mr Williams came back, followed by Vosper with plates bearing something brown. 'Lamb,' he told Mr Williams.

When he'd gone I sniffed it. 'Rabbit,' I said. 'Old.'

Mr Williams put a scrap in his mouth and chewed with great effort.

'Moorland food too poor for you?' I said, taking a great bite of the rabbit and purposefully eating with my mouth open, making a noise. Mrs Peter used to tell me off for doing so. There'd be no more of that.

Mr Williams opened his mouth likewise and I thought perhaps we had something in common, but then he was putting his fingers in his mouth and rootling around, for all the world like he'd lost something in there. At length he withdrew his fingers and with them three of his teeth.

I dropped my knife.

He set the teeth on the table, rubbed his jaw on one side, and said, 'That's better.'

Taking out his teeth seemed to cause him no bodily pain. He had been drinking, then, to stop the pain, and kept parsley about him to hide the smell of spirits. We had a great deal in common.

'Have you rot?' I said.

He cut another scrap of rabbit and when he chewed now he did so with ease. With relish, almost, despite the toughness of the meat. He swallowed.

'Rot?'

I pointed at the teeth sitting in a little pool of spit. I saw then they weren't bloodied, or bearing any other sign they'd just been torn from his jaw. They were clean, set side by side in what looked to be a piece of bone.

'I take it you haven't encountered dentures before, Shilly?'

I said that I had not, and he told me such things were to stand for his own teeth, which he had lost.

'How did you lose them?' I said.

He sat back in his chair and regarded me.

'I had them knocked out of me,' he said. He took up the dentures and wiped them with a handkerchief, admiring them as he did so, and I admired them too because the teeth were very fine and clean. Much cleaner than my own.

'Because you were dressed like this,' I said, 'as Mr Williams, and someone found you out to be a liar.'

'Oh no.' He fitted the teeth back inside his mouth and took from his pocket a pipe. 'I was without such masculine trappings.'

'Why did he hit you then?'

'Why did *she* hit me?'

Having filled the pipe he put it between his teeth and I heard the pipe chink against the false ones, like chinking good china. That was the noise I had heard that morning. His false teeth. He had moved them with his tongue. When he was thinking. It was a thinking sound.

He lit the pipe's bowl and drew good smoke from it. 'She hit me because a constable was escorting her husband to a nearby cell, a circumstance she blamed on me. And quite rightly, too. But I have a question for you, Shilly.' He tapped the stem of his pipe against his false teeth and again there was the chinking sound. 'What do you think these are made of?'

'Teeth is teeth,' I said, and then I thought what this must mean. 'May God forgive you – are those someone else's teeth in your mouth?'

He laughed at this. 'Fortunately I was spared such privations, having the means at the time to procure ivory replacements. If you haven't heard of dentures, I presume you haven't heard of elephants either.'

I said I hadn't heard that word before, and he told me an elephant was a creature much bigger than a bullock, with horns that grew down its face and were called tusks. It was from these that Mr Williams's false teeth were made. Then he told me that the creature had a nose some three feet long, and that it could suck water up this unlikely body part!

I knew he was making up a tale and I told him so. He laughed, and I told him I didn't like being thought a fool.

'Neither do I,' he said. 'Take this business of where Charlotte was found, your claim that she was in the stream but bore no signs of being wet. That's a tall tale. The elephant, on the other hand, is as real as you or I.'

'It isn't.'

'I can assure you it is.'

'Have you seen one?'

He pursed his lips over his lying teeth. 'No, but that doesn't mean—'

'I saw Charlotte in the stream. You didn't, so you'll have to take my word for how she was found because there's no such thing as an elephant.'

'Shilly, I don't think you quite understand the point I'm making.'

And so he rambled on. I went to the bar, which put an end to the matter of the elephant, and told Vosper he must bring us small beer. Mr Williams and I supped our drinks in silence until he said, 'You didn't seem keen to talk with Mrs Peter today.'

'I've nothing to say to her. She turned her back on Matthew, letting the constables have him.'

'She's afraid.'

'Mrs Peter's not afraid of anything, not with the Lord on her side.'

'Ah yes,' Mr Williams said, 'but she thinks her son killed Charlotte, and that must surely be viewed dimly by our Great Protector, no matter the faith of the mother.'

He was using the end of his knife to push the rabbit bones around his plate but the knife and bones made such a shrieking together that I took his knife away from him. I did it before I had thought whether or not I should. It was only when I saw the surprise on his face that I

175

wondered at my boldness. But by then it was too late. I had done it, and it couldn't be taken back.

'It's a bad sound,' I said, by way of a reason. 'It'll wake the dead.' Those weren't my words but they came from my lips, so I had to own them. They were Charlotte's, truly.

Mr Williams shifted in his chair, to make himself more comfortable or to move away from me, I didn't know. But then he carried on his talking so he must have felt safe enough.

'I was speaking of Mrs Peter.'

'And her believing John to have done away with Charlotte.'

He cleared his throat. 'Yes, well. When she got him inside after he'd appeared in the field, she must have seen blood on his clothes from striking Tom. You said he was upset, not talking sense, and then Charlotte didn't come home. I can see why his mother thought the worst. When Matthew fainted the next day you went to fetch Mrs Peter. You said she was feeding something into the fire.'

'John Peter's shirt?' I said.

'It seems likely.'

The rabbit bone snapped in my hand. I hadn't known I had hold of it. Now it was Mr Williams's turn to take something from me. He laid the broken bones on the little table between us, closer to him than to me.

'And as long as Matthew is facing the gallows,' he said, 'Mrs Peter believes her son is safe.'

'But Matthew will be free soon, won't he?' There was meat juice on my fingers from the bones. I could not say it was gravy for Vosper had no talents for such things. I licked my fingers. Mr Williams watched me over the top of his spectacles.

'I hope that Matthew will indeed soon walk from the gaol,' he said. 'Tomorrow we'll talk to Mr Carwitham. Of the three witnesses who say they saw the couple on the moor, he was the closest to them. If he'll confirm the limping man wasn't Matthew then there's hope for Matthew yet.'

176

'Hope for us all.'

'That's a somewhat larger challenge,' he said. 'One impossible feat at a time, that's my preference.'

We finished our small beer and then the questions returned. Knives and blood and kissing, all the long, long hours until night.

FORTY-TWO

When he went to bed I went to my room. But then I went back down
to the bar.

Vosper was scuttling, making out he was rolling in barrels from the
stables but he was up to no good.

'Going to pay your debts today, Shilly?' he said. 'Your credit's looking
poor.'

I did what I had need of and the room stopped jumping about.

'Why didn't you tell the truth about Charlotte parting the water?' I
said. 'I know you saw it too. You made me look a fool to the magistrates,
and to Mr Williams.'

'You can't be saying such things,' he said.

'Why not if it's the truth?' I said.

'Because people don't like it.' He set a barrel near me and stretched
his back with a groan. 'You know that, having lived with Phillipa. If
you make out you believe, people will come for you. When a farmer's
cow gives blood in its milk, when his daughter's hair falls out, you'll be
the one blamed.'

'Charlotte didn't care about that.'

'She should have,' he said. 'And so should you. I doubt very much
your gentleman friend wants to hear about such things.' He went back
to his barrels.

'You're telling me to lie?' I said.

'I'm just telling you not to say those things. That's not lying, is it?'

'Did you see Charlotte in the water?'

He rubbed his hand across his mouth. 'Say I did. What does it matter? She's dead. You can't undo that, with lies or with the truth, and it makes no difference to Matthew having killed her.'

'You think you know everything, don't you? Well you don't. You can't see what's right under your nose. Him upstairs, he's not what you think he is.'

There was a noise behind me. A floorboard creaking. I didn't need to turn round. I knew who it was.

'It's late, Shilly,' Mr Williams said. His voice was cold. 'We must rise early tomorrow.'

'Nightcap, sir?' Vosper said. 'Got some good stuff I been keeping back. Off the shelf, you could say.'

I took a bottle to the yard. I didn't look back.

But the drink gave me no peace, only made me fumble and cry. The bottle slipped and its precious stuff sloshed into my palms. All at once it changed, turning black and bubbling, boiling. A smell rose up round me. The marsh. I held its darkness in my hands, its power to pull bodies into its depths, and ponies, too, like the one Charlotte and I had found that day. I could feel the ground's sucking strength. It was pulling me in. There was something beneath the cold, clogging surface.

It was waiting for me.

FORTY-THREE

'How do we reach Lanhendra?' Mr Williams said the next morning.

We were seated in the bar. He'd taken the matter of eating into his own hands and on my plate were John Peter's hens' best efforts.

'You cook for yourself, do you?' I said.

He glanced up from his plate, which was chipped in three places. Not good enough for such well-cooked eggs.

'Why?'

'I don't know,' I said.

He started eating again, keeping his false teeth inside his mouth this time for the eggs were soft.

'Do you have servants?' I said.

He dropped his fork on the table, purposefully, I thought, to make a clatter.

'I'm not in need of a milkmaid, Shilly, if that's what you're asking.'

'That's not—'

'And I ask you, again, how do we get to Lanhendra?'

I pushed my plate away though the eggs were good. 'I don't know.'

'You seem rather short of knowledge this morning. And I can guess what's to blame.'

'I know Lanhendra is beyond the ford,' I said quickly.

'But haven't you ever been there? I gathered at the magistrates' hearing that it's not far.'

'Never had reason to. Not on the way to anywhere.'

Mr Williams stared at me a moment, wiped his mouth with a stained napkin he'd found somewhere, then got up and went to the back room. While he was talking to Vosper I quickly finished my eggs, too quick in truth for they nearly choked me, good though they were, and then Mr Williams was leaving by the inn's front door, carrying his black bag. I was to follow, of course. But at least now I was fed.

At the ford I asked Mr Williams to stop.

'We should search the marsh here.'

'The men searched this whole area when the body was found. There's nothing else here.'

'There is. We have to search.'

Something made him stop and look back. The longing in my voice. I wanted him to know my need. For her to know it, and to believe.

'Why?' he said.

I had no answer but the sucking marsh water that had appeared in my hands, and how to tell him that?

'Look around you, Shilly. Nothing but water and peat. Witnesses are what I must attend to. It's they who will help Matthew Weeks avoid the hangman's noose, not your misplaced notions. We must talk to Daniel Carwitham.'

He began walking away.

'We have to search here,' I called.

And he called back to me, without checking his pace, 'I have no time to spare for your muddy diversions, Shilly, and neither does Matthew Weeks. Come,' he said, as if I was a dog called to heel.

We followed the stream. Mr Williams said that when we had walked close to two miles we should cut across the fields and then we'd find the road.

'Did Vosper ask you why you needed that map?' I said.

'I made a generous donation to the memorial fund.'

'You mean his drink fund,' I said.

Mr Williams laughed, and it was Mrs Williams laughing. I was pleased to hear her there.

181

When we left the stream there was room for us to walk side by side. He talked more of elephants, keen to convince me of the truthfulness of his words. I let him prattle on. The walk was pleasant enough without the need to believe him. We were journeying through empty fields, and I wondered if they belonged to Mr Carwitham. The grass was poor, overgrazed. The earth showed through in patches.

We came to the road which was lined with hedges and tall trees on either side, much like at Tremail. After a little way we rounded a bend and then the trees thinned. There were cottages, a figure walking towards us.

'This must be Lanhendra,' Mr Williams said, putting his map away. 'We'll ask this woman which is Carwitham's house.'

The woman was old, older than Mrs Peter, and bent double by the sack slung over her shoulder. Her arms were like sticks of gorse. She'd patched her poor dress many times and the cloth was shiny with age. As we neared her she crumpled to the ground.

'Let me help you,' I said, putting her on her feet again. She clutched at my arm like she feared she'd fall again. She smelt of damp cloth and of stables. Mr Williams stayed a little apart from us. He didn't want to touch the woman, I thought. Was that part of who Mr Williams was, or did the yellow-haired woman feel the same?

'We're looking for the house belonging to Daniel Carwitham,' Mr Williams said.

Without answering him, the woman thanked me, told me I was kindly, and began her slow journey again. But before she'd gone too many steps she said quietly, 'If you must go there, go on a little further. The gate bears the name of the house. It is Gorfenna that you're seeking.'

Gorfenna. The word caught at me. I knew its sound. It was in the language my mother used sometimes when I was young, and in her last sickness. *Gorfenna.*

Mr Williams found the gate. The wood was furred with moss. It bore a sign but the lettering was almost rubbed away.

'This is it,' he said.

A rough path pitted with holes and puddles and weeds stretched from the gate. It was wide enough for a cart but only just, for on each side thick bushes looked keen to reach across and hide the way. At the end stood a row of trees. There was no sign of a house.

'You must let me speak to Mr Carwitham,' Mr Williams said, opening the gate. 'Whatever I say, don't interrupt.'

We reached the trees and the path bent to the left. We followed its curve and found stables and a barn, some sheds. The house was just beyond. It was much bigger than Penhale's farmhouse, with plenty more windows and a finer front door. The bank of trees loomed close. I knew it would be dark inside.

FORTY-FOUR

The door was opened by a housekeeper. Her hair was only half caught in a cap, the strands at her temple greying. I could see the likeness with the woman we'd met on the road. I was about to say so when Mr Williams asked for Mr Carwitham.

'Who shall I say is asking?' the woman said.

'A creditor,' Mr Williams said.

The woman turned on her heel right away, leaving us on the doorstep. I peered inside. The hall had coloured tiles rather than the stone flags at Penhale, and the stairs leading off had a wooden rail at their side. There was finery, but the rail needed cleaning. The tiles too.

'Why did you say you were a creditor?' I said.

But the housekeeper returned then and my question went unanswered.

The housekeeper said Mr Carwitham would be pleased to see this caller if he would step inside. She made to shut the door behind Mr Williams, and so keep me on the doorstep, but I pushed my way in. She looked at me askance but said nothing. There was no arguing with a body once it had crossed the threshold.

She led us down a dark passage and opened a door. It gave on to a long room where a fire was lit. Heavy curtains kept the daylight out. The room smelt of dogs.

Mr Carwitham was seated by the fire. Mr Williams strode over and introduced himself, saying he worked for *The Times* of London.

'*The Times*? But Mrs Hoskin said—'

'Some small confusion, no doubt,' Mr Williams said.

'Ah . . . I . . . Please, sit,' Mr Carwitham said, waving Mr Williams towards a chair on the other side of the fire. Then he saw me.

'I hope things are well at Penhale,' he said. 'Please tell your mistress I'm sorry I haven't helped more since . . . But what are you doing here when Phillipa is so short of hands?'

'The girl is helping me find my way,' Mr Williams said. 'I need a guide as I tour the sites.'

'Sites?'

'My apologies. I should explain the purpose of my visit.'

I slunk into a shadowy corner and tried to disappear.

'As you no doubt know,' Mr Williams said, 'recent events in the vicinity have attracted a great deal of interest at the presses. My editor has sent me to gather material for a substantial story, to appear in instalments in the run up to the trial. There'll be a longer piece once the verdict has been reached.'

'A story?' Mr Carwitham said. 'But surely everything is already known. There's been much in the local papers.'

'My editor is keen to have a more personal sketch of the locale, and of those involved. The rustics in the beer shops, the house the victim lived in. You know the sort of thing, I'm sure.' He took his little book from his bag. 'My apologies for calling without invitation. I saw your stockman yesterday, just by chance, and he said you had recovered your health. I was sorry not to make your acquaintance at the magistrates' hearing.'

'I was indisposed.'

'Of course. But if you wouldn't mind appraising me of some of the specifics of your own involvement with the case.'

'My own? But I—'

'What you witnessed at the ford. You saw the couple, I believe?'

'Yes.'

'And you knew them both, Weeks and Miss Dymond.'

185

'I wouldn't say I knew them. Weeks tended my animals at Penhale Farm. Not ably, I might add. I don't know why Phillipa kept him on.'

I balled my hands to fists.

'And Miss Dymond?'

'I saw her at the farm occasionally, but my dealings were with Weeks.'

'A large number of your animals are kept at Penhale, Shilly tells me.'

'Some of my stock was there,' Mr Carwitham said.

'But no longer?'

'They were harmed. I . . . I don't know how, exactly, but my herd has been reduced as a result.' He cleared his throat. 'Not greatly, you understand, because my stock holding is large. One of the largest this side of the moor.'

'I have heard as much,' Mr Williams said. 'Your animals presumably require more grazing than you have here at Gorfenna.'

'Penhale's land is dryer, and as I was over there so often to help Phillipa, it seemed sensible to keep my stock in such a convenient place. But then they sickened and I . . .'

Was Mr Carwitham going to start scritching? His eyes looked wet but it was hard to see in the ill-lit room. Mr Williams didn't give him a chance to weep as he was on him with more questions.

'And had you met Miss Dymond before you moved your animals to Penhale?'

'It was at Penhale I first met her,' he said.

'I see. So you moved your animals to the farm *before* Miss Dymond went to work for Mrs Peter?'

Mr Carwitham looked for me in the corner, as if I should help him remember. 'It was just after, I think. After the chapel had opened at Tremail. Was she living at the farm then? That was when I asked Phillipa if I could use her land.'

'Mr Roe would have known her longer, perhaps?' Mr Williams said.

'I wouldn't presume to know my workers' acquaintances.'

'And Weeks? When did you first meet him?'

'He'd been at Penhale a number of years,' Mr Carwitham said. 'I couldn't tell you when I first met him.'

'Poor man,' Mr Williams said quietly. 'The gaol is a grim enough place for the halest of men but when a person of Matthew's weak health is imprisoned there . . .'

'He might not be in the gaol long enough to suffer.' Mr Carwitham looked like he would say more but did not.

After a pause, Mr Williams said, 'You doubt his guilt?'

My breath caught in my throat. Mr Carwitham stared at the fire.

'Was Weeks the man you saw on the moor?' Mr Williams asked.

Still Mr Carwitham stared at the fire. He curled and uncurled his fingers.

'You were close to them, weren't you?' Mr Williams said, his voice gentle.

'There was only the stream between us,' Mr Carwitham said, so quiet I could barely hear him.

'Your Mr Roe said as much at the magistrates' hearing. Said you would swear it was Matthew Weeks you saw that day. Would you swear it, Mr Carwitham? The man's life might depend on it.'

At last Mr Carwitham looked at Mr Williams. He moistened his lips, drew breath to speak.

The door burst open.

FORTY-FIVE

A pack of dogs hurled themselves at Mr Carwitham. The room was all tails and barking and their stench. Mr Williams stood in the rush of the creatures, flapping at them with his hat, which only made them bark louder. And then Roe was there. His pursed eyes had opened wide, for once.

Mr Williams and I were out of the door and out of the house and down to the gate while the dogs were still making their leaping fuss. Mr Williams had his hand over his mouth, making sure his moustache was still there, that the dogs hadn't taken it.

We rushed ourselves through the gate, bolted it, and only then stopped to catch our breath.

'I can't abide dogs,' Mr Williams said. 'Horrible lurching things. And the wetness of their mouths. Just look at my coat.'

There was a slick of dog spit across one sleeve, and I could smell the dog tongue on it. The creatures had had a good taste of the cloth. I tucked my smile back inside myself. First the pony, now the dogs. All the moor was grabbing at Mr Williams, trying to ruin his man's clothes, wanting to get to the woman beneath.

'I was sure Mr Carwitham was going to say it wasn't Matthew at the ford,' I said.

Mr Williams was wiping his coat with a handkerchief but it did no good.

'That would have helped Matthew's case greatly,' he said. He sighed and stowed the dirty handkerchief back in his pocket. 'We should go,

188

before Roe tells his master I'm a farmer in need of a butcher.'

We started back the way we'd come, to where the marsh was waiting. I was looking forward, but Mr Williams was looking back, to Mr Carwitham's gloomy sitting room.

'Let us consider Mr Carwitham in a different light than purely as a witness. Was it true what he said, that he first met Charlotte after he'd arranged to move his animals to Penhale?'

'I think so.'

'I'm afraid that's not quite the level of certainty I need, Shilly.'

I pulled a length of grass from the hedge and switched the air with it. The noise was my vexation.

'It's hard to remember. When these things were happening, they were just that – things. Things happened, days passed. We milked the cows, we went to chapel. I didn't know then that I would ever need to think about them so . . . so . . .'

I switched the air more quickly with my grass.

'I believe the word you're looking for is *exactingly*,' he said.

It wasn't, because I didn't know that word, but Mr Williams seemed to think it was my feeling and I let him for it was altogether easier.

'Just take your time in remembering,' he said. 'Go through it out loud. It will help, I promise.'

I thought that switching him with the grass would help more, but I made myself do as he said, and my words were thus.

'I first saw Mr Carwitham at the chapel but I don't know if he saw Charlotte that day. There were lots of people, what with the chapel opening.'

'So we can't believe Carwitham used Mrs Peter's fields purely in order to see Charlotte. His grazing needs appear genuine. Neither he nor his housekeeper were surprised when I claimed to be a creditor. They must be regular callers at Gorfenna.'

That word again. It nagged me like an itch.

'How did you know to say that you were a creditor?' I asked.

'A guess, given the woman we met on the road, and Carwitham

189

using Mrs Peter's fields. A good guess, it seems. He may have been forced to sell his land, or had it taken from him in lieu of debts. But what has caused his losses, I wonder?'

He moved his tongue against his false teeth again and I heard his thinking noise.

'Mr Carwitham blames Matthew for his creatures dying,' I told Mr Williams. 'He said Matthew ruined him because of that. I heard him say so.'

Mr Williams stopped walking. 'How did the animals die?'

He'd asked me so I told him the truth – that their tongues had blackened and fallen out, causing the creatures to lay down and die. That they had been ill-wished.

He shook his head and starting walking again, and talking – his own tongue working very well indeed.

'When we spoke to John Peter yesterday I took the liberty of noting the plants about the farm, which included an abundance of ragwort. Do you deny that there is ragwort on Penhale land?'

I could not deny it. Charlotte and I had used it to protect the Mowhay before it was cut for hay. The weed's yellow heads were everywhere on the farm.

'And ragwort is poisonous to cattle if the creatures should eat it,' he said. 'Do you deny that?'

'Only if it's dried. They won't eat fresh ragwort. It's bitter to them.'

'But can you admit, Shilly, there is a *chance* that Carwitham's bullocks ate ragwort? It grows on the farm – you've admitted that. The animals could have eaten it. You can't be certain they didn't.'

'You can't know for certain that they did eat it,' I said. We were back to the elephant again.

'True. But it's far more likely a possibility than a curse.'

'There's curses everywhere,' I said.

'No, there's ragwort everywhere,' he said. 'No wonder Carwitham blamed Matthew if he was meant to be keeping the bullocks safe and well. It gives Carwitham a motive for saying it was Matthew he saw on the moor with Charlotte, as it does Vosper and Tom Prout, now that I think about it, given the loss of cattle before. So much comes down to cows here, doesn't it? And money, but that's true the world over.'

'I don't think Mrs Peter knows anything about Mr Carwitham having debts,' I said.

'The news will soon be out. That woman we met on the road won't be shy in telling people, not if Carwitham gets rid of her daughter as well.'

We came to the stream and followed it back to the ford. I knew what I had to do when we reached the marsh, whether Mr Williams was willing or no. He was paying me no heed anyway, was talking his thoughts aloud again.

'Surely Carwitham would be more forthright in saying it was Matthew on the moor if he wanted to hide his own crime. Of the three witnesses who claim they saw the couple, Carwitham was the closest. Yet he's the one most reluctant to name the man.'

We'd reached the ford. I tried not to remember Charlotte lying in the water. Her throat. But Vosper I remembered. Vosper making me look at her.

Mr Williams took me from such gloomy thoughts, saying, 'Shilly, you must cross to the other side and be Carwitham.'

'Why must I be Mr Carwitham?'

'Because—Oh no!'

191

FORTY-SIX

A pony crashed out of the gorse in front of Mr Williams, but it was done friendly, her ears pointing forwards. I tried to tell Mr Williams this but he only gave a cry of fear – in his woman's voice.

He raised his hands, as if that would mean anything to the pony, and tried to back away. But the pony wanted to be near him. Nosed him, spoke to him.

'Told you she liked you,' I said. 'I better had be Mr Carwitham. She wants you here.'

I crossed to the other bank, all the time hearing Mr Williams telling the pony to leave him be, to be gone. In the end he turned to violence, which saddened me, for it was only love the pony was showing him. He used his black bag as a weapon and thumped the pony on the backside. She skittered off then with a humphing, but she didn't go far. She was a loyal girl.

'What do you want me to do now that I'm here?' I called from the other side, the Penhale side, where I stood facing him as Mr Carwitham.

'What? Oh yes.' He glanced over his shoulder at the pony. 'Carwitham said there was only the stream between him and the couple.' He checked his little book again. 'And at the magistrates' hearing, Roe reported that Carwitham saw the couple *walking backwards and forwards, though neither spoke*. So how could Carwitham not be sure who they were?'

'There was the mist,' I said. 'The air was very wet with it.'

'Even so,' Mr Williams said. 'Even so.'

I saw what he meant. On his side of the stream there was only ten

192

feet or so of open moor before the gorse and bracken began, where now the pony waited, watching. Even if the couple had kept as close to the gorse as to be pricked by it, and even with the mist, Mr Carwitham could surely not have failed to see who they were.

'And they didn't keep to the gorse,' I said, my thoughts taking sound, as Mr Williams's so often did. 'Constable Rickard told the magistrates there were patten prints and the prints of a lame man all over the place where you're standing. Why would they walk about on such a small patch of ground without going anywhere?'

'They were arguing, perhaps. Turning something over between them. But speculation is no help to anyone. I must ensure we have another means of keeping Matthew from the gallows if Carwitham cannot be relied upon. We'll pay a call on Mary Westlake. Mrs Williams will go.'

He crossed the stream to join me, using the ford's path, and the pony followed but chose to wade through the stream. He waved his arms at her.

'Go away! Go on with you!'

But she stayed where she was, drinking from the stream with great noise.

'She's making ready to soak you again,' I said.

'Then we can't call on Mary Westlake too soon.' He started for the inn.

'There's something we must do first,' I said.

'Not the business of the marsh again. There's no point, Shilly. The area has been searched already.'

'Not properly.'

'And how do you know that?'

'Because she has made me know it.'

'Charlotte? God help me, Shilly.'

I walked to where the long grass marked the water seeping from the earth. Scattered across it were patches of shorter grass that would bear weight because there was likely to be moor stone beneath, though not always. Sometimes the stones had sunk into the dark heart of the moor. I'd be muddy and wet before I went back to the inn but it didn't matter. I had to search the marsh.

'If you must do this,' Mr Williams called, 'make it a useful enterprise. Can you see any prints? The murderer might well have gone that way, thinking to hide their tracks.'

But I wasn't looking for prints.

It was hard keeping out of the water and the sucking mud, and it was a bad place now. I could feel it with every step I took further into the marsh. I looked back. Mr Williams seemed far away. The marsh grew until it was spreading across the whole moor, pulling everything into its dank clutches. The pony I'd seen dying with Charlotte was just the beginning. The one in the river had come to warn me, because another had been caught, its ear poking through the marsh grass where something black was showing. I dropped to my knees and began to sink. My hands closed on the pony's ear and I knew then it wasn't an ear. I pulled. Turfy mud came up with it that was slick and dark and spattered all over me. I pulled harder. There was a thick slopping sound then a stained bonnet came free and fell in my lap where it lay like a stillborn foal.

FORTY-SEVEN

Mr Williams shouted at me to dig. I used a lump of moor stone to
scrape at the slipping soil and all the time shifted my weight so I didn't
linger too long on a foothold and risk sinking. I reached into the cold,
dark ground. My hands closed on her shoes and her pattens. One glove
and then the other. Everything lagged with mud and made strange in
shape.

I carried Charlotte's things across the marsh and laid them at Mr
Williams' feet. He wiped them with a cloth to take away the mud so
that we should see them properly. Mr Williams took up the gloves last.
One of them was filled. Charlotte's hand filled it.

I jumped away and shrieked. The pony watching from the river
bolted.

'Don't touch it!' I said.

He didn't leave it go so I struck the glove from his grasp.

He looked stunned for a moment, and then he struck me across the
face. Not as hard as my father had struck me, but hard enough.

He was surprised by my strength and my return blow caught him
unawares. He fought back, pushing me into the mud, but I twisted and
sent him sprawling into the marsh. It took him like it had been waiting.
Black water oozed from his feet and he began to sink. He didn't see at
first what was happening and kept trying to get hold of me. I stepped
away so he couldn't reach. His struggling only made him sink more
quickly. That was what the marsh liked – a fight.

He was in mud and water up to his knees and then he saw what had

195

befallen him. He screamed. But it was her screaming – Mrs Williams.

What had I done?

I lay on the ground, keeping the shorter grass beneath me and hoping for moor stones just under the surface. I reached out my hands to Mr Williams. He tried to get away from me and sank further.

'Let me help you.' I said it quietly, to calm him. 'You'll go under otherwise.'

He looked me in the eye and knew he had no choice.

I took his hands and pulled, digging my toes into the firm ground at the marsh's edge. I pulled until I thought the bones of my shoulders had come to pieces. At last there was a sound like a sigh as the marsh gave up and Mr Williams flew into my arms.

We lay panting on the ground next to the marsh. I could taste earth and stone, and blood – my own, I thought. My clothes were lagged with mud. My hair stiffening with it.

Mr Williams rolled on to his side and slowly got to his feet. He stood over me but I wasn't afraid. I had shown him what I could do.

'You shouldn't have hit me,' he said. He coughed and shivered.

'You shouldn't have hit *me*,' I said. 'I was saving you.'

'From what – a glove?'

He picked it up, turning to make sure I saw him do it. The glove was still shaped – there was something inside it.

'It's her hand!' I said.

'Both of which were still attached to her when she was found,' he said, tipping the glove and shaking it. 'These ridiculous notions—'

And then he was screaming again.

FORTY-EIGHT

The tongue lay on the ground between us.

Mr Williams's already pale face was now grey.

I nudged the tongue with my boot. The end that should have been at the back of the cow's throat was charred. I knelt beside it. I nudged it again and saw a line across it. I picked up one of Charlotte's pattens and used the metal to poke at the line.

'What's that?' Mr Williams whispered.

'Hair. Tied round it.'

'Hair . . . on an animal's tongue?'

'This isn't done by ragwort,' I said. 'This isn't poisoning. You see now. You believe me.'

He took a deep breath and it was as if he'd decided to be his usual self, such was the change that came over him.

'What I see is a disgusting example of backward beliefs,' he said. 'Who would do this to an animal – cut out its tongue?'

'She burnt them out.'

'Be quiet!' he shouted. 'Let me think. This . . . this *thing*, it could have been on Charlotte's person when her belongings were buried in the marsh.'

'You don't have to bury things in a marsh,' I said. 'They sink.'

He looked like he would strike me again but I didn't care. He had no right to stop me speaking. He'd asked for my help and he was going to have it, like it or not. It was the only way to find the truth.

'Or it could have come from someone else,' he said. 'Whoever put

Charlotte's belongings here. The tongue could have fallen from their clothes, somehow. Been left here unintentionally.'

'Fallen into a glove?' I said.

He used his cloth to pick up the tongue, looking like he would purge his insides. He peered at the hair tied round it. With the mud and the charring it was hard to tell what colour the hair was. It could have been as dark as Charlotte's own. It could have been as light as Tom Prout's.

'It's a charm,' I said.

After a moment he said quietly, 'For what?'

'I don't know. Ill-wishing, or to undo it.'

'Do you think Charlotte meant to punish Mr Carwitham by hurting his animals?'

'No. That was her anger about her mother. She'd come back from Boscastle raging and then the creatures grew sick.' But had she come back from Boscastle that day? Had she been somewhere else?

'Could someone have asked her to harm Mr Carwitham's stock on their behalf?' Mr Williams said. 'Someone who believed in her talents and had a grudge against him?'

'Maybe.'

'And supposing she did somehow remove the tongues from the cows, and I'm not saying she did, would she keep one and use it for some other purpose? What you said before – to undo ill-wishing.'

'She might have done.'

'Of course I believe none of this, Shilly.'

We were both shivering. It was the cold, still-wet mud that clung to our skin and our clothes. The fight was gone from us.

'No sign of the umbrella in the marsh?' he said. 'The necklace would be too small to find, especially if it's broken. But why bury her things like this in the first place?'

'I told you, things sink in a marsh.'

'But whoever killed her chose to dispose of her body and her belongings separately. Why? Her things could surely have been hidden wherever she was being held. It's one thing to get rid of a pair of shoes, quite another to get rid of a body.'

He made me take the tongue from him. It was heavy and the cloth he'd used to touch it stuck to the flesh even though the flesh was burnt dry.

'Throw it back where it came from,' he said. 'Let the marsh have it.'

FORTY-NINE

When we reached the yard Mr Williams said I should go to his room.

'There's a bath,' he said. 'I'll find Vosper to fill it.'

I went first to my own room and laid the tongue on the floor beneath the bed. Whatever it had been used for, it was important. I wasn't going to get rid of it just because Mr Williams told me to.

It took Vosper many sweating and cursing trips up and down the stairs to fill the bath. It didn't seem a common happening at the Britannia Inn. He hadn't had a wash himself for years, far as I could tell. At last the bath was full and he was gone, the door locked behind him and his leering.

Mr Williams busied about, stirring up the fire then going to a large case that stood by the window. He undid his coat and the top buttons of his shirt then reached beneath his clothes. He drew out a small key on a chain, which he used to unlock the case. It made me think of Charlotte's box still in my room at Penhale. How far away the farm seemed at that moment.

'The water will be getting cold,' he said quietly, sitting by the fire to take off his boots.

'Will you get rid of him – Mr Williams, I mean?'

He patted his head. The falseness beneath his hands made him remember who he was at that moment. He took off the short brown hair and fluffed his own cropped yellow beneath. He pulled off his moustache and rubbed his mouth. Enjoying being rid of it, I thought. How to hide the moustache and keep the yellow-haired woman?

She had taken off her things – some of them, at least – so I took off mine in return. I undid my skirt and working shirt. I took off my underthings.

The bath had been placed close to the fire, close to where she sat. But she turned her face away while I undressed. She was the one who was shy.

'You should take off your coat,' I said. 'It's wet.'

She murmured something but I couldn't catch the words.

I got into the bath, let my legs splay so that my knees lifted from the water. I untied my hair and it fell around me. I closed my eyes. I felt her hands enter the water, and let my own rest near the bath's sides. And then our hands caught one another, by chance or intention, on her part or mine, I wasn't certain, but I was certain of the thrum up my arm and down my chest. She didn't pull away. I opened my eyes. She wouldn't look at me. A flush was creeping across her cheek.

A thumping came from the room below, then Vosper cursing. This seemed to wake her from the spell of the room and its warmth and the touch of our hands. I cursed Vosper in return for she was suddenly busy, jugging my bathwater, pouring it into a pail that held my filthy clothes coiled like sloughed adder skins. Still she didn't look at me, only drew the water like it was the most important task she'd ever faced. Her hand on the jug was once more close to mine. If I reached out a little my fingers would touch hers, meaning to this time. Would she like that?

But she moved away, left me unknowing.

'I've brought half the marsh back with me,' I said, washing the mud from my arms and legs.

She was staring into the fire. 'Then I've brought the rest of it.'

Had we brought our fighting back too, caught in the turfy mud that covered us? That we had struck each other wasn't so easily washed away. The fact of it clung on, made me wonder who we were to each other, we who fought, we who had crossed the moor together but were strangers still.

She didn't look when I climbed out and wrapped myself in the clean white cloth she gave me from her case. I sat by the fire, watching her scrub the turfy mud from my dress. I thought how strange it was that she should do that while I sat idle, as if she was the servant and I the mistress. Had she been a servant? Was that why she looked so suited to sitting on the floor and scrubbing dirty clothes? And yet she went about as a gentleman, with people thinking *I* was the one to wash *his* clothes. That other Mr Williams, the one she had watched to see how to be a gentleman. What had she done to him?

Perhaps nothing. Perhaps he was still walking the streets of London, not knowing a woman used his name and his stiff hip. She would take parts of me and use them to deceive others. My lateness. My dislike of inns. When she was me she could go from the moor. She could leave. What a gift she had.

She shook the water from my skirt and wrung it dry. The turfy mud was scum on the surface of the water.

'I'll hang your things in front of the fire,' she said. 'They'll not take long to dry. Then you'll be back to your usual level of dirt, I'd say. You brought no other clothes with you from the farm?'

'I didn't have time,' I said, though it wasn't quite the truth. I'd left little behind.

She reached into the case again and pulled out something beautiful. Dark-blue cloth with white birds that moved like the water at the ford.

'Put this on for now.'

She opened it for me to step into. It was something you wrapped yourself in. It had long sleeves and was like a dress only it did up at the front with a belt made of the same cloth. Mrs Williams tied it for me. I'd never felt such a wonderful thing as the cloth pouring across my skin. It had been a time of wonder, being with her in that room, but that was now to end, for she was opening the door. The warmth vanished in the cold draught snaking in from the landing.

'I'll call you when I'm ready to go to All Drunkard,' she said.

'Can't I wait here, with you? I'll be quiet, I promise. You can tell me about the elephant again, while you wash. I like that story.'

'It's not a story, Shilly.'

'Let me stay.'

She looked like she might, and then something decided her. The fighting, perhaps. Her own uncertainty. Or just me, who I was. I didn't know, but the answer was the same, anyway.

'The elephant will have to wait,' she said.

She closed the door behind me. The landing was dark, as if night had fallen when I knew it was only mid-afternoon.

My room was dark too, and cold. I lay down on the bed and weariness washed over me like sudden rain.

A sound woke me. Close. Soft, sliding into my ear. I fought sleep to wake and catch it.

Shi

A huge hand swiped my belly, knocked my insides out. I stumbled from the bed to get away but where was it?

Shi Shi

All around me. My name. My name hissing from her opened throat.

It was coming from under the bed. Where I'd left the blackened tongue. Mr Williams was right – I should have thrown it back in the marsh. But it was too late now. She had it, was calling me. I had to get out—

Shi Shi Shi

But the door wouldn't open. I dragged on the handle, threw my weight against it, tore my nails on the frame trying to pull it from the wall.

She was beside me. She was breathing on my neck, on my cheek. Her lips sought mine. Her hot, rank breath. She pulled me into the ground with her and marsh water choked me.

FIFTY

The door was flung open.

Vosper looked round wildly, a poker in his hand. He tried to pick me up from the floor but I shied from him and clung to the bed.

'Heard you screaming from the back room,' he said. 'Thought you was being murdered.'

'Shilly?' Mr Williams appeared behind Vosper, one hand fixing his false hair into place.

'Soft as John Peter,' Vosper muttered, going back down the stairs.

Mr Williams stood in the doorway, frowning.

'It was under the bed,' I said. 'The tongue – she spoke with it. Look.'

He did look. There was nothing beneath the bed but dust. And a clutch of empty bottles. He reached in and grabbed one, shook it in my face.

'This is where such notions come from. You've told me enough of the evils of drink – you'd do well to listen to your own proselytising.'

'The tongue was there, I swear it. Vosper took it from me.'

Mr Williams crossed the landing, back to his own room. In the doorway he stopped, and with his back to me, said, 'If you are drunk again in my presence you'll be out on your ear, do you understand?'

'It's not that, I promise.'

He went inside his room but came out again straight away, to throw my clothes at my feet. 'I'll wait for you downstairs.'

He didn't speak until we were well on our way on the All Drunkard road, and then only about practical matters.

'We can't rely on Carwitham's testimony.'

Dark clouds watched us pass beneath. The wind snatched at our clothes. All was not well on the moor while she was restless in her grave. A noise behind me. I spun round. Nothing there. But there would be soon if—

'Are you listening to me, Shilly? If Carwitham won't swear that the man on the moor wasn't Matthew, then we need to show Matthew couldn't have been there. He claims he was with Mary Westlake. We need her to confirm this at the trial.'

His words brought me back to myself, and the work to be done. I saw that he was wrongly dressed.

'You said Mrs Williams would visit Mary.'

'And she will,' he said, patting his black bag.

The houses of All Drunkard came in sight. He told me to wait next to a wall of gorse that spread across the moor. He went round the other side. After a little time a woman appeared, but not the yellow-haired one I would have liked to see.

'This is Mrs Williams,' the woman said.

The figure before me looked barely older than Matthew. Her hair was long red curls. Her thin lips were painted to look fuller than I knew them to be and there was a mole at the right corner of her mouth where there hadn't been one before.

She wore a small black hat. Fur, I thought. Black gloves. A dress of rich purple that was almost black. In mourning for her husband. That might mean she hadn't put Mr Williams in the ground then, for who would wear mourning if they weren't grieving? Unless that was more shamming on her part.

The woman gave me Mr Williams's tall hat to hold, then turned his coat inside out and put it on. The cloth was different on the underside. Mr Williams's coat had been woollen but now it was soft, silky cloth. The woman that was Mrs Williams began to pull at the coat's insides. I saw there were strings sewn into the lining at her hips and one up each

205

sleeve. Two strings looked to run up the back of the coat and come out by the collar. By pulling and tying, her coat lost its boxiness and instead clung to her well-made shape.

'Where did you get such a thing?' I said.

'I made it.'

'You're a seamstress then?'

She smiled. 'Not as such.'

'What does that mean?' I would have something from her, even if it meant asking her questions all day. She'd asked me enough of them.

'I worked in a theatre, making costumes.'

I didn't know what this meant but I guessed it was some other part of someone she'd stolen, stolen so she could be whoever she wanted to be. But such thoughts faded for her coat was so well fitting. I spent a moment looking at her waist.

'I'll need your help with Mary,' she said. She took Mr Williams's hat from me and pressed its top. The hat flattened to the thickness of a slice of bread. 'It won't be like with Carwitham. You must take the lead. I hope we'll have timed our visit so the husband will be out.'

She put the flattened hat in her black bag and began walking again.

'Robert doesn't work far from the house,' I said. 'He might come back.'

'Then you'll have to bite him again, won't you, Shilly?'

FIFTY-ONE

Now that it was me leading I made sure we called at the back door, not like at Mr Carwitham's house, and I told the woman called Mrs Williams to hide herself in the trees in Mary's garden.

Mary answered the door herself. She smiled on seeing me but there were deep lines beneath her eyes.

'Mother said you'd left the farm and gone to Vosper's inn. I told her that couldn't be. I know how much you dislike him.' Her words were running from her mouth and she almost seemed not to hear herself. 'I said, "Mother, Shilly won't spend a night in that place."'

'I've had to, Mary.'

'Why?'

'For Matthew,' Mrs Williams said, coming out from under the trees.

Mary put her hand to her mouth. Her fingers trembled. 'You'd better come in.'

Mary sent her little maid out the front door as we came in the back. She offered us tea but her hands were too trembling to fill the kettle so Mrs Williams said she'd do it. That was part of who she was, this woman newly made in the gorse – the sort to fetch tea in another woman's house. Would she serve sweet things to eat, I wondered, or beware such devilry, as Mrs Peter did? There was much to learn of this one.

Mary and I went into the parlour. It was a fine room. Finer than her mother's parlour at Penhale.

'My friend wants to free Matthew from the gaol,' I said.

'She's a relation of Matthew's?'

'No. She's . . .'

'Why does she want to help him?'

I couldn't answer her.

'Can you trust her?' Mary whispered, glancing at the door.

I couldn't answer that either. What I wanted to say was look at her, Mary. Look at this bright creature come into my life. A stranger. A gift. Her yellow hair hiding. But the words that came to my lips were simpler, those needed quickly. The ones Mrs Williams wanted me to say.

'You can trust me, Mary. I need your help. I know you care for Matthew.'

'He's a good man, would never hurt anyone. The things people have said about him. That he's driven by the Devil, that he tortured her. Wicked things. My mother, too, saying them. And I've not been able to say a word.'

Mary stiffened in her chair as Mrs Williams brought in the tea. So many fine things, and on a tray! There was a teapot, of china I thought, blue flowers at the spout and handle. The cups matched – so light I thought my hard-worn hands would shatter them. There was a little jug for milk. The spoons were polished, might even have been silver, though I had never seen such a thing so couldn't know. The spoons were shining enough to suit the word, at any rate.

Mrs Williams poured and gave Mary a cup. 'Will you tell us what happened on the day Charlotte failed to return to the farm?'

'Shilly, I—'

'Please,' I said. 'For Matthew.'

She held her cup with both hands, keeping it close to her face. 'He did come here. He sat where you're sitting, Shilly, and had tea, from this very pot. It was the last time I saw him before the magistrates' hearing.'

'And your husband didn't see him?' Mrs Williams said.

'I made sure Matthew was gone before Robert came back.'

'Why?'

Mary fussed with the handle of her cup.

'Did Matthew call on you often when Robert was out?' I said.

'He used to. But then Charlotte moved to the farm.' She set her cup on the table and picked at her nails. 'He didn't come to All Drunkard so much after that. After all I'd given him.'

'His fine clothes – they were from you?' I said.

'He deserved them. They made him happy and he didn't have much in life did that.'

'Do you know what prompted Matthew to call on you again the day Charlotte went missing?' Mrs Williams said.

'Something had happened at the farm. He wouldn't say what, only that he didn't care for her any longer. It was because she was after John, of course, but I only learnt that later, after she was dead. All Matthew would say was that he was fighting with everyone and he wanted to leave but he had nowhere to go. Nowhere to go – he kept saying that.'

'He came to you for help,' Mrs Williams said.

'He wanted me to find him a new place. And I would have. Now it's too late.'

'It's not too late to help Matthew,' I said. 'All you need do is tell the truth.'

'What do you mean?'

'At the trial,' Mrs Williams said. 'If you say that Matthew called here then he can't have been the man seen on the moor.'

Mary got up and went to the window. 'I can't.'

'Please, Mary,' I said. 'Matthew will be hanged.'

'Can't you find someone else? There must be someone else.' She plucked at her collar with whitened fingers.

'Do you know if anyone saw him arrive or when he left?' Mrs Williams said. 'Has anyone in All Drunkard said they saw him?'

'No,' she whispered.

'You can save him,' I said.

'Go, both of you.'

'Mary—'

'I want you both to leave this instant. If Robert comes home and finds you . . .'

'Come on, Shilly,' Mrs Williams said, getting to her feet. 'We can do nothing more here.'

As she closed the door behind me Mary whispered, 'Tell Matthew I'm sorry.'

FIFTY-TWO

'You can give Matthew that shameful message,' Mrs Williams said. 'We'll go to the gaol tomorrow.'

The wind had got up and was shaking the trees that lined Mary's yard as we took our leave.

'Even if Mary doesn't think anyone else saw Matthew in All Drunkard,' she said, 'it might be that he met someone on his way to or from the village who can speak at the trial. We have to have something in hand in case Carwitham fails us.'

'Mary might still speak at the trial. If I ask her again, maybe in a day or two.'

'She's like Carwitham, we can't rely on her,' Mrs Williams said. 'If Matthew has a defence counsel then that might be a different matter. He could compel Mary to speak, and seeing Matthew in the courtroom might encourage her to tell the truth. But I still don't know if he'll have anyone to speak for him.'

'But Matthew could speak for himself. He could be his own counsel.'

'The law doesn't allow the accused to speak in court.' She held her hat to her head to save it from being blown away. 'Where has this weather come from? I've never known a place change so quickly.'

'Then couldn't you do the speaking for him?' I said.

'I'm no lawyer, Shilly. I can do much before the trial but during it I have to sit and listen as quietly as anyone else. If only Matthew hadn't told Mrs Peter he'd been to see her daughter. Because he really *was* with Mary, he believed she'd tell the truth. He believed she cared for him.'

'She cares for him more than Charlotte did,' I said.

'But not enough. Robert's favour means more to her. I shouldn't be at all surprised to hear that he's the most generous patron of Vosper's memorial.'

We took the road back to the inn with dusk falling faster than our walking. 'Vosper tells me we can catch the coach to Bodmin from Camelford,' Mrs Williams said, raising her voice to speak over the wind's noise. 'We'll set out early, take Matthew some clothes for the trial.'

'Mrs Peter might have got rid of his things.'

'You'll go and see?'

I didn't want to but I nodded.

'Good,' she said, and then she stumbled. Her black hat was whipped away, vanishing into the gloom. The wind caught her red curls and set them flying around her face like flames. Our skirts were noisy with flapping.

I helped Mrs Williams to her feet. She kept hold of my hand and together we faced the gale and pressed on in the direction of the inn. The wind was screaming. I didn't listen to what it was saying. I didn't let it tear us apart.

'Bad night to be out,' Vosper said when we fell into the bar, banging the door shut behind us.

The quiet of the place made me realise how loud the wind had been. The quiet made my ears hurt.

'But then every night's been bad on the moor since . . .' He caught my look and said quickly, 'Something to eat, Shilly? And for your friend there?'

He hadn't met Mrs Williams, of course. I left them talking about stew, the meat of which was uncertain. My task awaited me outside. Alone.

I wanted badly for some warmth to keep me from the bite of the wind, but all the bottles in the gorse were empty. Besides, hadn't she told me not to drink? I wanted to be better. For her, whoever she might be beneath her false parts. But I couldn't give up everything I was. I took an empty bottle with me down the path. I had made a plan.

The wind was still roaring but I was glad of it now for it hid my footsteps as I slunk to the house. For Matthew's clothes I'd have to go inside, but there was something else I wanted to get for him first. Something Mr Williams would have no faith in but that I thought should be tried, because it was Charlotte who had told me of it. Some wells keep a body from being hanged, that was what she'd said. If only Mrs Peter's was one such well. It would do no harm to try, surely?

Swiftly came a sign that my thinking was right, for as I neared the tumbled walls in the Mowhay the wind dropped. There was great stillness. Even the well's water seemed to flow more gently than I had known it do so before. I dipped the bottle I had brought and found the water warm, when it had no cause to be on such a night, with such a wind. But there it was, all the same. I felt the water's warmth like I'd felt the blood-heat from the horse outside All Drunkard Inn. Her gift to me. One of many, for she had taught me much. She'd taught me that to make a charm strong I had to think of what I wanted while I made it. So I thought of Matthew on the gallows and the rope refusing to knot round his neck, of the hangman being taken ill and dying, of the gaol crumbling to dust. Any of these means, as long as he was kept from the drop.

A rustling nearby – the swish of a thin tail. Through the ferns I saw him, and saw him go again. St Michael.

FIFTY-THREE

I'd never known Mrs Peter lock the porch door. Never even seen a key for it. I lit a candle from the hearth's embers and found Matthew's things heaped in a corner of the parlour. If I was a true friend then I'd take the best of his clothes I could find – his grey jacket with glass buttons, his waistcoat, a good shirt with no mending marks.

I wrapped the bottle of well water in the clothes and balled them to carry, and was about to blow out the candle and be gone, back to the inn, but a selfish thought came to me and held my puff. What was I to wear to the trial? My old working dress was too poor. If I was to be seen in Bodmin with a woman as fine as Mrs Williams then I should have something better. It was only right.

I crept up the stairs, remembering the parts that would give me away. All my trips to the Mowhay with Charlotte had taught me well.

Our room was as I'd left it. St Michael's straw bed still behind the cupboard. Her green dress still lying on the chair. The one she'd worn when she left the house with Matthew. The last time I'd seen her alive.

I took it to the bed and set it out as if she was wearing it, arranged the sleeves and spread the skirt.

'What happened to you?' I whispered to the dress.

I lay down beside her. I slid my arm under her dress as I had slipped it under her shoulders when we'd lain together. My hand closed on something sharp.

I pulled my hand away. Spots of blood on my fingertips. It was

214

beneath her pillow, whatever the sharpness was. I lifted the pillow and there was the magpie's heart, stuck with pins.

That day in the Mowhay – *Tomorrow things will change. His heart.*

Whose heart had she wanted? Not mine.

I left the bird's heart but took the green dress with me. I would look very fine next to Mrs Williams in the courthouse. I would look as fine as Charlotte Dymond.

As I crossed the yard the door to the cold-shed creaked.

I bolted but I wasn't quick enough. A shape darted, had hold of me, was pulling me backwards. I fell. I curled myself small. She would have me now.

'My my, Shilly. What a timid thing you've become.'

Mrs Peter loomed twice as tall as I knew her to be. Her eyes were huge in her old, worn face.

'You scared me, Mrs Peter. I thought you were—'

'What, Shilly? What did you think I was? One of your fetches?'

'You shouldn't mock those things,' I said, getting to my feet.

'You left without a word. No thought for me and John, the farm.'

'I couldn't stay. Not after what you said about Matthew, how you've treated him. How can you think he did it?'

'Because I know it to be true. So does everyone else. There's only the trial to come and then it'll be done.' She moved close to me. 'Penhale is your home, Shilly, but I can't protect you from the rest of the world, from others who seek to take advantage of you. If you will go about with strange men then you deserve what may befall you.' She grabbed my arm. 'Who is he? What were you saying to John?'

I shook her off and was running for the moor like a hare who hears the hounds.

She called after me, 'You leave things be, Shilly!'

I stumbled up the path, Matthew's clothes held tight to my chest and my breath short. I stopped at the road and when I didn't hear her following I reached into the gorse. For shock. For everything, anything. Always the drink.

A full bottle found my hand. I put it to my lips but before a drop passed them I put the stopper back. There had been no full bottles when I came down the path. Or had there been, hiding amongst the terrible empties? Had I left this bottle?

I had become my father.

I let the bottle slide from my hand. It hit the ground with a soft clunk but didn't break. It would be better if I smashed it so as not to be tempted again. But my hands wouldn't do it and neither would my feet. I was weak. I went back to the inn, that den of iniquity. Where I belonged to be.

FIFTY-FOUR

We started early, on foot across the moor to Camelford. It was Mr Williams who walked with me. As we left the inn he caught sight of the bottle in my pocket.

'It's not what you think,' I said.

He shook his head. I said nothing more, knowing he'd view well water to keep a man from hanging as badly as he viewed my drinking spirits.

A coach took us to Bodmin, to an inn called the Barley Sheaf. It was at the top of a hilly street that looked to be full of inns. I'd never been to Bodmin before but knew it to be an important place. The assize court where Matthew would be tried was there, and the gaol, of course. And the asylum. Three places I never wanted to step foot inside, and yet we were going to one that day, and another soon enough after. Would that the asylum kept itself a mystery to me.

The Barley Sheaf was having a spring turnabout. Young girls scrubbed the bird mess off the windows while others weeded flowerpots. The curtains in the bar were being taken down for washing, letting go a haze of dust. A woman with a filthy apron and deep-set marks in her forehead asked Mr Williams to excuse all the toing and froing and the noise.

'It's the assize,' she said. 'We'll have a better sort of person in. You'll not be wanting a room, will you?'

Mr Williams assured her that we wouldn't be stopping, and asked for the quickest way to the gaol. We set off there at once, down the hill of inns. Each one calling me. Each one a test. The bottle of well water clanked in my pocket. I'd drink that if the need worsened, keep myself from hanging.

'Will Matthew's trial be soon?' I asked Mr Williams.

'Too soon, I fear,' he said. 'The assize session is only days away.'

And still we had nothing to keep Matthew from the gallows.

'You must prepare yourself for what you'll see today,' Mr Williams said. 'The gaol is known to be hard on its inmates. It's . . . Well. You'll see soon enough. But you must bear up, for Matthew's sake. We need to know if anyone other than Mary can swear he was in All Drunkard on the day Charlotte went missing.'

The road became flat and we turned onto a small street with not so many people. The tallest walls I'd ever seen loomed over us. They were so towering I faltered. The stone was all I could see. There was a set of gates as big as a house. One gate had a window. A man's face looked out.

'Are you ready for some dramatics?' Mr Williams whispered to me.

'Some what?'

He squared his shoulders and jutted his chin, like he was making ready to fight the man looking out of the window.

'We're here to see a prisoner awaiting trial. Matthew Weeks. I'm a friend, and this,' he said, pushing me to the window, 'this is his sweetheart.'

The man in the window scratched his head. His hair was so thin it barely covered his scalp. Scurfs of skin drifted to his shoulders.

'Sweetheart?' the man said. 'But I thought he did away with her. The newspaper said.'

'Weeks had many such women,' Mr Williams said.

He pressed forward, as if the gates were about to admit us. That was the way to get what you wanted. Make out you already had it. He jabbed a finger in my ribs and I gave a good wail.

'Oh, sir! Let me see my beloved Matthew. They say he'll be hanged and then what will I do?' And tears too – I let my face grow messy from scritching.

'I don't think—'

'Have pity, sir! Have pity on a poor wretch soon to be left all alone in this world.'

'There's rules.'

Another jab in my ribs from Mr Williams.

'Left alone with a child to feed. Oh, how shall I live?'

'Hush, girl,' the gateman said. 'You'll set the dogs off.' He vanished from his window. There was a cranking sound and then the heavy gates were opening.

I thanked him and blessed him and said all sorts of things about his place in Heaven. Mrs Peter could have done no better.

'Now, now, my dear,' Mr Williams said. 'I think that's enough calling on the Lord for one day.'

I kept up my scritching but less wetly now that the gate was open. The man took the bundle of clothes I'd brought for Matthew and had a good rummage in them. The bottle I kept on my person.

''Spose it can't do no harm for you to see him,' the gateman said, 'though it can't do no good either. Keep an eye on her, sir. Don't let Weeks get close. They say he's such a fiend he'd cut another girl to pieces soon as look at her.'

He said he'd take us to where Matthew was being kept. We let him walk ahead so that we could speak in whispers.

'You continue to surprise me, Shilly.'

I wiped my eyes. I had surprised myself.

A row of buildings faced us with a path cutting it in half. Behind this was a second such row. It was like being in a town because the buildings looked like houses. There were carts unloading barrels and crates, sacks of flour. A dog ambled past. Were it not for the quiet that swelled from the stones I should have said the gaol was a very ordinary place.

The gateman led us to a door in the second row of buildings. He lit a lantern and set off down a dark passageway that grew darker still as we went on. There were rush lamps on the walls but they gave a feeble glow and barely showed me where to put my feet. The passage was foul-smelling. It was like when the dead bullocks began to turn.

We passed door after door. Each bore a small glassless window. From some came moans, from others sobs. I pitied every one of the wretched creatures I could hear but not see.

A clang of metal made my heart stop. A hand flailed from the window of the door we were passing. The skin was black with dirt and the nails torn. The hand held a spoon and beat the door as if seeking to bludgeon the wood to death. I couldn't see a face because the arm filled the small window but a voice came from somewhere behind it.

'Bread,' a woman said. 'That's all I took. I took no more than that, I swear it.' The spoon banged the door. 'Only bread. My daughter.'

The gateman gave his lantern to Mr Williams and strode to the cell door. He wrenched the spoon from the hand. He took a large ring of keys from his belt, unlocked the door and disappeared inside. I looked to Mr Williams but he didn't move. His mouth was set in a grim line. The cell was so dark I couldn't see what was happening inside it even if I'd wished to. But I could hear it.

The gateman scat the woman to the floor then beat her with the spoon. She cried out. I buried my face in the sack of Matthew's clothes. There was a tinny rattle as the spoon was cast on the floor. The gateman came out and locked the door behind him. He took the lantern from Mr Williams. There was no more noise from the cell.

There but for the grace of God went I.

We reached the end of the passage. The gateman looked in the window of the last door and gave a loud sniff.

'Here,' he said.

'Thank you,' Mr Williams said. 'Now, my good man, I have some enquiries to make while the girl here speaks with Weeks.'

He pulled a small leather bag from his coat. The jingling coins worked powerfully on the gateman. He bit his bottom lip and pitched forward, eager to see inside the bag.

'I'm sure you know to whom I should make these enquiries,' Mr Williams said. 'You seem a very able person, someone who understands things, yes?' Mr Williams let the bag of coins chink against his palm.

'The chaplain you'll be wanting,' the gateman said. 'Reverend Kendall. He knows all that goes on with Weeks. I'll take you.'

The gateman began to walk back the way we'd come, taking the lantern. Mr Williams followed. He gave me a nod as he passed. I watched them disappear into the darkness.

FIFTY-FIVE

I was alone in the passage, though behind every door was a person. Something was dripping. I touched the wall nearest me. Water streamed down the stone. A breeze came from nowhere and made the rush lamp at Matthew's door flicker.

I put down the sack of clothes and craned to see inside his cell. Another window in the back wall gave some light but the leaded panes were small and cloudy. It took a moment for my eyes to make out the edge of what might have been a bed and some sacking on it.

'Matthew,' I called.

No sound came from within. I tried again. Still no sound or movement. Had the gateman made a mistake? I looked down the passage, thinking to try another door.

Something fell against the other side of the door. I looked in the small window again. Matthew was propping himself against the wood. His neck was twisted strangely. His eyes were sunk back in his skull but he seemed to see me and my heart ached when I saw how that pleased him. He stood and pressed his face close to the square hole. There was dried blood around his nose and mouth.

'Matthew, what have they done to you?'

But then he disappeared again. I did my best to look in the too small window and saw him slumped on the floor, his eyes closed. Now was the time to give him the well's protection. I took the bottle from my coat, unstoppered it and wedged my arm through the little window. It was a bad angle but I did my best to pour the water.

Matthew's noise of sudden waking told me I'd got at least some part of him wet.

He was back on his feet and at the window. I saw now that there was dried blood on his shirt front as well as on his face.

'Mary,' he whispered.

'It's Shilly. I've come to see how you are.' The words sounded foolish to my own ears.

'Mary,' he said again.

'It's Shilly. From the farm.'

He rolled his head to and fro against the door. 'Why won't she come?' he said.

I put my hand to the door in the hope that comfort would travel through the wood.

'Mary can't come,' I said. 'But she wishes you well. I saw her yesterday. Had tea, like you did when you went to call on her.'

'She said she'd help me,' he whispered.

'I know. She told me you went to see her, on the day Charlotte went missing. Did you see anyone else in All Drunkard that day?'

'I saw Mary. I was at her house. She'll tell you.'

'Did you see anyone on your way there, or on your way back to the farm?'

'I was there. Mary, tell them. Tell them I didn't do it. I didn't cut Charlotte. I would never . . .' Then came only sobs.

'What about a song, Matthew?'

I sang the lines he'd so often sung on the farm. *Sweet maidens all, pray hear this tale.* He started to sing too and my heart was glad but then my gladness was gone for it was a wretched, sad song. His voice faded and mine wouldn't come.

'Will you be there, Shilly?' He sounded more like his old self and I thought perhaps I'd get some sense from him.

'At the trial? Yes. I think they'll make me speak again.'

'When they hang me.'

223

'Don't say such a thing,' I said. 'We're going to get you out.'

'Reverend Kendall has told me how it will be. He sits with me most days. He wants me to confess so that I'll be forgiven before . . . I'll have a service all of my own that morning. He says I'll sit in a black pew and look at my coffin and prayers will be said for me. And then I'll walk out to the wall and they'll put the cap over my head and then the rope and then it will be over.'

'Matthew, don't . . . don't.'

He fell again. Fresh blood streamed from his nose.

A noise at the other end of the passage. Footsteps. Coming towards me from the darkness.

FIFTY-SIX

I shrank against the wet wall. My breath came hard and fast.

Someone cleared their throat. There was more light. Mr Williams stood before me but the man with him wasn't the man from the gate.

'This is the Reverend Kendall,' Mr Williams said. 'He's been ministering to Weeks.'

'You should be ministering to his stomach,' I said. 'He's near starved.'

Kendall peered in the cell window. He didn't seem surprised to see Matthew lying on the floor.

'The warders do their best but he refuses to eat. His crime weighs heavy and until he confesses—'

'You've been a great help, Reverend,' Mr Williams said. 'The girl has brought clothes for Weeks to wear at the assize. I trust you'll ensure he has them on the day, that they don't find their way out of the gaol on the backs of others?'

The reverend smiled and patted the sack. 'Have no fear. He'll be wearing them.'

'Good. If you would be so kind as to light our way back, we won't trespass further on your time.'

'You may take the light,' the reverend said. 'I need no such flame when God is with me.'

He took a key from deep within his black clothes and opened the lock on Matthew's door.

Mr Williams inclined his head to me that we should leave. We made our way back down the passage. The reverend's voice followed us.

'Come now, Matthew. Up you get. Let us pray . . .'

We came in sight of the open door and the daylight made my eyes stream. I was almost glad to see the gateman who saw us safely back to the street, but in truth I was low in spirit after seeing Matthew so wretched, and it wasn't daylight alone that set me scritching. My steps were slow with the bad business of it all. There seemed no hope left, and I had nothing to drink away the pain of knowing it to be so.

Mr Williams took my arm and pulled me along the street. I waited for him to chide me about my timekeeping, and was ready to sit down and weep for the rest of my days, Shilly-shallying to the end.

But instead he said, 'I have good news to share once we're away from here,' and my limbs once more moved with purpose, all the long toil back to the Barley Sheaf.

There we took a table by the window overlooking the street, out of the way of the cleaning girls and the dust. Before he would tell me his news, Mr Williams made me say what had passed between Matthew and myself. I told him of Matthew's fainting and the way his thoughts rove about.

'This doesn't bode well for the trial,' he said. 'The jury will think his weakness confirms his guilt – that he can't bear to hear the evidence.'

'He might get well before then. If the reverend would only feed him.'

'There isn't time, Shilly. The assize sessions are nearly upon us.'

'The trial can't be held if he's ill though, can it? It wouldn't be right. He can barely stand.'

'The jury will hold Matthew up themselves if they have to.'

A moan escaped my lips and I put my head on the table for the badness of this. Mr Williams chided my free expression of pain, then leant his face close to mine for whispering, his moustache tickling my cheek.

'But here is something to give us heart, Shilly. The reverend informed me of work being undertaken before the trial. There has been much coming and going to the gaol, it seems, and Matthew is to have a defence counsel. A Mr Slade.'

From slumping in my chair like the black cat insensible by the fire, this news raised me up with gladness. Hope, at last!

'But this creates another mystery,' Mr Williams said. 'Who is paying for Mr Slade's services? They won't come cheaply.'

'Did the reverend not tell you?'

'He claims not to know. One thing is certain, though, Shilly. Someone else is looking out for Matthew Weeks besides us.'

A shout went up that the coach to Camelford was ready to leave, and we were soon on our way back to the moor. This time we weren't alone, for joining us in the jouncing of the coach were two men, and a woman with a newspaper. These helpful bodies kept Mr Williams and I close together for our continuing talk. I was near as breath to the yellow-haired woman.

'Could it be Mrs Peter?' I said.

'Paying for Slade? Unlikely. Think how keen she's been to find evidence against Matthew. She wouldn't give him a chance to escape the gallows at the final hour, not if she still fears for John Peter.'

'Mary, then?'

'A way to clear her conscience for not defending Matthew publicly? Perhaps. But would she have the money?'

'Only if Robert paid,' I said, and Mr Williams made a scornful noise.

'Does Matthew have any family living?' he asked.

'His mother. Some brothers and sisters. But since his father died they've not been well off. His mother's a charwoman.'

'Not much chance his family could afford a defence counsel, then,' Mr Williams said. 'And I doubt they'd pay for it even if they could. Reverend Kendall told me no one but lawyers and clerks have been to the gaol to see Matthew.'

'His family must have heard about the murder, though, that Matthew is to be tried.'

'Oh indeed,' Mr Williams said, nodding in the direction of the newspaper the woman in the coach was reading. 'News appears to travel as swiftly on Bodmin Moor as it does in London.'

We went on for a time in silence. I was thinking of Matthew covered in his own blood in the gaol. Mr Williams was staring at the floor of the coach. What he was thinking of I couldn't guess, but that he was thinking of *something* I was sure, for the tapping sound came, that of his tongue against his false teeth. I readied myself for some dreadful task he'd give me.

'The limping man . . .' he said. 'The limp will doubtless be part of the prosecution's case. It's the factor each witness cites for identifying Matthew as the man on the moor.'

'There's more to a person than whether or not they're lame.'

'But that's what we must pursue, Shilly, for the men have seen the limp and stopped looking for anything else. We must see beyond it. See what's really there.'

'How? What is there to see?'

'That I don't yet know, but Constable Rickard might be of help to us.'

It was my turn to make a scornful noise, so loud the other passengers found cause to stare at me.

'I share your scepticism, Shilly,' Mr Williams said in a hushed voice, 'but we must work with what we have. Rickard told the magistrates that he and Vosper found prints between Lanlary Rock and the ford, and at the place the body was discovered.' He was fussing with his false moustache, pulling one of the ends. 'The limping man's prints are distinctive. We might find one or two to examine, though Sunday's rain won't have helped, nor all the other feet tramping across the sites. And with Rickard pressing Matthew's boot in to the prints—wait. Wait a moment.'

His moustache had come away from his face on one side but he hadn't noticed. I pressed it back on to his skin though my want was to pull it off and throw it out the window.

'What are you . . . ?' He put his hand to his face. 'Oh, I see.' Then he was back to tapping his tongue against his teeth, back to thinking. And then his thought came, and with it a great gasp, such that I feared he'd swallow his false teeth and choke.

'We *can* check the prints,' he said. 'Vosper made drawings of them before Rickard pushed Matthew's boot into the print.'

'Will Vosper let you see them?'

'He will if he's got nothing to hide.'

But Vosper was always hiding something.

FIFTY-SEVEN

When we got back to the inn Vosper was unloading crates and barrels from a cart. Another man was helping him, one I didn't know. Vosper was cursing him.

'I told you never to come before dark,' he said.

'But I had to be rid of them,' the man said. 'There's talk they'll be round tonight.'

Vosper saw us and silenced him with a cuff round the ear.

'You took it, didn't you?' I said.

'Took what?'

'You know what. It was under my bed. Creeping about when an honest soul is trying to sleep, taking what isn't yours.'

'You're a fine one to talk!' he said.

I went inside, leaving Mr Williams to speak to him. A pair of liars.

The bar was full of strangers. I'd never seen so many people in it. I heard Charlotte's name and talk of the ford. They'd been down there that afternoon, Vosper leading the way again, Mrs Peter serving more tea at Penhale.

Vosper and Mr Williams came in and eased their way to the back room where Vosper kicked the piles of newspapers and shoved the furniture about.

'I haven't time to be finding bits of paper. I've got customers.'

'I'm sure you'll have even more once the stone memorial goes up,' Mr Williams said. He laid a sovereign on the table.

Vosper grinned. 'I'll find them drawings for you.' He started rootling again. 'I'd forgotten all about them. Make a nice little show for the customers. They'll like seeing Weeks's prints, could go looking for them on the way to the ford. Pretend they're constables. I could ask Rickard to come on the walks. He'd like that. Would he want paying, though? Ah!' He held up a large piece of paper, thick-looking and yellow, folded. 'Now be careful with this, sir. I'll be getting use out of it for years to come.'

A voice in the bar called for the landlord. Vosper made to leave but Mr Williams stopped him.

'One more moment of your time. We visited the gaol today. Weeks was in a poor way.'

'The gaol isn't known for its kindness,' Vosper said. 'I wouldn't wish a spell inside it on anyone.'

'It was your words that put Matthew there,' I said.

'Not mine alone,' Vosper said. 'And Weeks deserves to die. Charlotte didn't, for all her sins. I owe her justice.'

'Because you had relations with her?' Mr Williams said.

Vosper laughed. 'Not quite,' he said.

The call from the bar came again and Vosper scurried off.

'Sound of foot,' Mr Williams murmured, watching him go.

I opened up the paper. It was heavily marked with mud but there were two shapes – two boot prints, drawn in pencil. The narrower end of each was at the bottom of the page. This I took to be the heel. The shape was pinched in the middle and then wider at the top for the toe of the boot. They were set at an angle to show which was right and which left. But the drawings weren't the same. The left one was missing the toe and the right one had the toe shaded.

I pointed to the shaded part. 'Why have they made it like this?'

'To show the right print is heavier than the left,' Mr Williams said. 'To show the limp.'

'Then the drawings are wrong,' I said.

'But Vosper said he copied them from what he saw on the ground.'

'They might have been on the ground,' I said, 'but they're not Matthew's. They're the wrong way round. Matthew was lame on his right leg so he put his weight on his left. The toe should be missing on the right print because his right toe turned up.'

'Then this is it!' Mr Williams said, staring at the paper, his eyes wide. 'This is the evidence that could save Matthew. It proves he wasn't the man on the moor. I'll give it to his counsel tomorrow and then my work will be done.' He looked up from the paper at last. 'You should come to see Slade with me. This is your discovery, Shilly. It's you who has saved Matthew Weeks from the gallows, and through logic, facts. No bending of rivers or tongues bound in hair.'

We were standing close together. He put his hand on my shoulder. I stared up into his face. Her face.

'This is how crimes are solved.'

I thought he would move away then, do some writing in his little book. Talk to Vosper. But he didn't. We stayed like that. His hand on my shoulder. My flesh warming beneath her touch.

FIFTY-EIGHT

Mr Williams woke me the next morning by shouting up the stairs on the matter of time, again, and my poor keeping of it. I would be Shilly-shally to the grave. But my end was not yet come, for that morning it was time to go back to Bodmin.

He was waiting outside, studying the paper bearing the prints. He looked me up and down. The yellow-haired woman beneath the moustache liked what she saw.

'It was Charlotte's,' I said, smoothing the front of the green dress.

'Well, it's yours now,' Mr Williams said, setting off. 'Slade's taken lodgings close to the gaol. Reverend Kendall gave me the address.'

But something was troubling me as we crossed the moor. It sat squarely on the joy I should have felt at finding a way to save Matthew.

'What do you think Vosper meant when he said "not quite"?' I said.

'When?'

'Yesterday in the back room, when you asked him if he'd had relations with Charlotte.'

'That he'd wanted relations and she hadn't? That she'd wanted him and he spurned her? Either way it suggests some feeling expressed between them.'

'Charlotte would never have wanted him,' I said. 'He can't be trusted. Do you believe his drawings are what he says they are, that of the prints he found on the moor?'

'It's precisely because Vosper let us have the prints that we can trust them,' Mr Williams said. 'He doesn't appear to know they contradict the course of events that everyone else has accepted. He copied what he found and believes it implicates Matthew.'

Once again Mr Williams believed Vosper. I walked on with force in my steps, enjoying the feeling of the ground being marked by my feet. I pictured Vosper's face beneath me, his mouth crushed by my heels.

We were a mile or so from Bodmin when our coach was slowed by others on the road. Many were walking but there were full wagons, carts and gigs too. There was shouting and hailing and even singing when we passed one well-laden wagon. I heard bottles clinking together.

'Why are all these people on the road?' I said.

'Getting to town early for the trial tomorrow. And for the hanging they're sure will follow.'

So the day was almost upon us. The day we would see Matthew freed.

We reached Slade's lodgings around noon. He was staying above a dressmaker's shop on the road behind the gaol. The buildings there cowered from the gaol's huge walls. I thought of Matthew behind those walls and hoped he was in better health than when I'd last seen him.

Mr Williams knocked and a woman answered. She led us through the shop to stairs at the back. The lower floor was crammed with cloth, such colours and patterns I'd never seen. I was glad to be wearing Charlotte's fine dress.

Mr Williams took great notice of the cloth. He asked the dressmaker about her trade. Where did she buy her twill? Had she had a shortage of gabardine in the last few months? It was the woman beneath Mr Williams who was asking, she who made her changing clothes.

There were pins a plenty. When the dressmaker and Mr Williams went up the stairs I slipped a cushion studded with them into my pocket. Charlotte had used them at the well to learn of things to come. I would try and do the same. To have some notion of what might befall me, to not be running to catch up with what life decided for me – that would be a gift worth having.

Off the landing at the top of the stairs was a small sitting room, where a man was seated at a table piled with papers. The man shook Mr Williams's hand with great vigour.

'I trust we're not disturbing you,' Mr Williams said.

'Not at all. I have to pay a call shortly.' He took out a watch. 'But until then, you have my attention.'

He invited us to sit. I let Mr Williams take the chair nearest him.

'What can I do for you?' the man said.

He was thin and stretched. I had the sense that before we came in he'd been jumping around the room and now he was holding himself in check. He was like the black cat waiting to leap.

'It's more a case of what I can do for you, Mr Slade,' Mr Williams said. 'You are, I believe, the defence counsel for Matthew Weeks who is accused of murdering Charlotte Dymond.'

'I am. Not that I'll do much good for the poor wretch,' he said, leaning back in his chair. His fingers were ink-stained. He drummed them on the table. 'What's your interest in the matter?'

'I'm a friend of Weeks.'

Mr Slade frowned and a smile played at the corners of his mouth. 'I wasn't aware my client was so well connected.'

'I have a professional interest in the case,' Mr Williams said. 'You've heard of the new men at Scotland Yard?'

'Of course. They're long overdue. You wish to join them?'

'I've encountered difficulties in my attempts to date.'

'Difficulties?'

'Reluctance, you might call it.' Mr Williams picked at his gloves. 'I believe that my petition to join the force would be helped by documentation of some kind. Something to guarantee my credibility. A letter of reference, say, from a professional person, should my detection services prove useful.'

So that was why he wanted to free Matthew. For his own ends.

FIFTY-NINE

A noise like that made by John Peter's chickens came out of my mouth. Slade looked at me as if remembering I was in the room. Mr Williams stared at his boots. He cared only for himself. And why should I have been surprised? He didn't know Matthew. He wasn't helping out of a sense of rightness to free an innocent man. I had been used to help Mr Williams get what he wanted and soon he would have no more need for me. I was like a carthorse only good for the knacker's yard.

'And your companion?' Slade asked Mr Williams.

'The girl lived with Weeks at Penhale Farm,' Mr Williams said without looking at me, as if in his thoughts he had already left me behind.

'She spoke at the magistrates' hearing? I have her testimony, I think.' Slade shifted the papers on his desk and pulled out a smudged sheet. 'Ah! The one who spoke of spirits and so incensed Mr Lethbridge.'

'I know what I saw,' I said.

'None of that matters now,' Mr Williams said quickly. He drew his chair closer to Slade's desk, turning away from me as he did so. 'I've reviewed the evidence against Weeks, talking to witnesses, examining the scene of the crime. I've had to disregard much local superstition, which has slowed my progress.'

'There's been talk here in town,' Slade said. 'The body floated above the water, a drayman told me, and a woman selling game pies said the girl was able to fly. That's where she went when she disappeared – she flew to the top of Roughtor!'

He laughed. Mr Williams smiled a little but he was nervous, I could tell.

He feared Mr Slade believed such tales. Did Slade believe them? I would try him, show Mr Williams I wasn't the only one who saw the world that way. He would get the letter he wanted, and I would have something for myself.

'There was the tongue,' I said.

Both turned to look at me, as I knew they would.

'Shilly!' Mr Williams hissed.

'In the marsh. We found her missing clothes—'

'Did you find the umbrella?' Slade asked.

'No,' Mr Williams said. 'I can't work out where she got it. I've considered Vosper's inn, as it's the only place close to Lanlary Rock, but there's no evidence she was kept there, and I can't find a motive for the landlord to kill the girl.'

'But there was a cow's tongue stowed in one of her gloves,' I said loudly. 'Vosper believes in such things. He's said as much to me. Make him come to the courtroom and tell the truth.'

'Is she right?' Slade asked Mr Williams.

After a moment Mr Williams nodded. 'In part. The tongue was there. But it means nothing. Merely some barbaric local practice,' he said, looking at me. Then to Slade, 'I've concentrated on the material facts of the case – motives, witnesses. I had hoped to find a strong alibi for Weeks from Mary Westlake, but she has proved to be unhelpful. Daniel Carwitham, too.'

'Ah yes, the inscrutable Mr Carwitham,' Mr Slade said. 'He gives me great trouble.'

'I'm still unsure what he'll say at the trial,' Mr Williams said.

'If Carwitham does swear it was Weeks he saw then I fear there won't be any doubt in the jury's minds. I've called Mary Westlake as a witness. She might admit Weeks was with her if pressed.'

'Mary will tell the truth,' I said. 'I know she will.'

'It would certainly help Weeks's case if she did,' Slade said to Mr Williams. 'To speak frankly, I fear the opposition has much on their side.'

'Don't give up hope yet,' Mr Williams said.

'Why? What have you discovered?' He grinned. 'Besides the tongue.'

Mr Williams turned to me. 'You should say, Shilly. It's you who saw the truth yesterday.'

His words made me feel bad for telling Slade about the tongue and so shaming Mr Williams, but the tongue was part of the truth too. Matthew, I thought. Remember Matthew ill in the gaol and the gallows waiting. If the boot prints got him safely away from such an end then I must tell Slade about them. The tongues and the bending of the water would still be true but I would keep those truths for myself.

'Is this some sort of dumb show?' Slade whispered to Mr Williams. 'Is she waiting for a spirit guide?' He took his watch from his pocket again.

I took a deep breath and in a rush told him of Matthew's limp, how he tilted when we walked together, that it was his right leg that was weak.

Mr Williams showed Slade the drawings and explained to him the shaded parts.

'So these can't be representations of Weeks's prints,' Slade said.

'Which means they weren't his prints found on the moor,' Mr Williams said.

'Which means—'

'He wasn't the man seen with her,' I said.

'Well, well,' Slade said. 'You might have just saved a man from the gallows, and saved me a failure in the courthouse. For that I owe you much indeed.'

'The letter of recommendation will be sufficient,' Mr Williams said.

'And for your friend?' Slade began tossing his papers about to find a clean sheet.

Before I could speak Mr Williams said, 'Shilly has no need of letters.'

'Fine, fine,' Slade said. 'Now, tell me, my good man, what name should I put?'

Mr Williams lifted his thick spectacles from his nose and peeled his moustache from his lip. Then he took his false hair from his head and ran a hand through his yellow hair to fluff it. And there she was.

SIXTY

Slade laughed and dropped his pen. 'I see now what your *difficulties* have been. I admire your strategy.'

He kept looking at her. I wanted him to stop, and at last he did because he remembered the call he had to pay. He grabbed his hat and coat and stick, knocking over his chair as he did so. He didn't stop his rushing to pick it up.

'My appointment – it's of importance to Weeks's case,' Slade said. 'I shouldn't keep him waiting.' As if it was our fault Slade had forgotten.

She reached out towards the blank paper Slade had been about to write on. Her hand hovered above the page like a bird held by the wind.

'I'll see to the letter this afternoon,' Slade said. 'I promise.'

He gathered the papers on his desk and wedged them in his coat pocket. In his haste he tore some.

She slowly withdrew her hand from the empty page that should have been her letter.

'Who are you going to meet?' she asked. She put on her false hair and moustache, the spectacles. Mr Williams had returned.

'Thomas Good,' Slade said.

'The coroner?'

'I have some questions for him about the state of the body.' Slade was opening the door and halfway down the stairs in a single movement, such was his pace. 'Why don't you come with me?' he called up.

'Afterwards I'll stand you dinner. A small token of my thanks.'

Mr Williams said he would be delighted. Would he take his false teeth out in front of Slade, I wondered?

Mr Good was in town for the trial, and Slade had agreed to meet him at the Barley Sheaf. As we toiled back up the hill, Mr Williams told Slade all about our findings out and our toings and froings across the moor. In return, Slade told Mr Williams of his talks with Matthew at the gaol.

'Seems not to understand my purpose,' he said. 'I'm not certain he even realises he'll be tried.'

'Tell me,' Mr Williams said, 'who is paying your fee?'

'That I don't know. It's been settled anonymously.'

'Any speculation as to the likely benefactor?'

'Mrs Peter. Weeks had lived at Penhale a long time. They were close.'

Clearly Slade had never met Mrs Peter. He knew nothing.

Mr Good was already seated when we arrived, a plate of chops in front of him. Slade introduced Mr Williams to him as someone who was helping build the case. I wasn't introduced but Mr Good remembered me from the magistrates' hearing.

'The fetch girl,' he said.

'Charlotte's friend,' I said.

'Thank you for meeting me,' Slade said.

'I've met with Mr Cockburn for the prosecution,' Mr Good said. 'I owe the defence the same opportunity.'

Slade took the roll of paper from his coat and begged some ink from the man at the bar, then he turned to Mr Good. 'Tell me of the cut.'

With some sadness, Mr Good pushed away his plate of half-eaten chops. 'The wound was deeper at the back part of the neck than on the right side.' He showed on himself where the worst of it was. 'This leads me to believe the wound commenced there, at the back of the neck.'

'So she was attacked from the front,' Mr Williams said.

'I think it likely.'

She would have seen them coming for her. My poor girl.

'To attack from behind and make the cut in that way,' Mr Good said, 'it would have been too cumbersome. If the assailant were behind her, he would have made the cut in the front part of her neck, reaching around for purchase.'

'Where was she found?' I said.

This was my chance to prove to Mr Williams what I'd seen at the ford that day.

'She was by the river,' Mr Good said. 'In a dried-out part of it – a kind of pit.'

'Thank you,' Mr Williams said, 'you've been most—'

I hadn't finished. 'But the men had moved her, hadn't they, by the time you got there?'

Mr Good tilted his head back to take me in, as if I was a body newly found.

'I gather she'd been moved a little from where she was found, yes, simply to make it easier for me to examine her. But nothing significant. I checked with the man who looked to be in charge. The publican. I forget his name.'

'Vosper,' I said.

'He said they'd rolled her away from the water before I arrived. But she hadn't been in the river. That was clear to see.'

'There were no signs that the body had been in the water?' Mr Williams asked Mr Good.

'None at all,' Mr Good said. 'She was perfectly dry. Strangely so, in fact.'

'What do you mean?' Slade said.

Mr Good idly fussed at a gravy stain on his cuff. 'She was warm to the touch. Not the warmth a live body has. She was hot, but she'd cooled by the time I got her in the barn so I thought no more of it. Some strange feature of the ground by the ford, no doubt. A thermal spring or some such. Turf cutters had disturbed the ground in all sorts of ways.'

241

There was more talk of knives and cuts and blood, and then Mr Good took his leave, letting Slade pay for his chops and wine. While the men said their farewells, Mr Williams spoke to me in a low voice.

'You see, Shilly, there can be no truth in your assertions. A man of science has disproved them. Charlotte Dymond was found *by* the river. She didn't float on top of it or make the water bend around her. She lay on the ground. I'm sorry if you can't accept that fact but it's the truth.'

'And what of her body's heat? How do you make sense of that? You can't, and nor can your man of science.'

'As Mr Good said, a spring or some such. I've seen the turf cutters' marks for myself.'

'And the tongue in the marsh?' I said.

'Superstition. Nothing to concern us.'

'What concerns me is my own dinner,' Slade said, taking his seat beside Mr Williams. 'I've bought the coroner's chops, now will you let me buy yours?'

'That's very kind of you,' Mr Williams said.

'Elephant,' I said.

'Shilly . . .'

'I don't think they're on the menu,' Slade said, and laughed at his own joke.

I took no notice of him. He didn't matter, nor did the other people looking at us, for I was raising my voice. I would shout if I had to. I got to my feet.

'Elephant, elephant, elephant.'

'Shilly, sit down.'

'I believe you,' I said. 'If you say such a creature is real then it must be so. You've learning of things that *I* haven't, and I have my knowing of things that *you* don't have. If I believe you, why won't you believe me?'

He had no answer for me, only shook his head.

A woman was coming over to the table, the one tasked with cleaning last time we'd called at the inn. I thought she would tell me to quieten my noise but instead she told Mr Williams she had a room for him, if he still had need of one.

'We're not going back to the moor?' I asked him.

'With the trial tomorrow it makes more sense to stay here tonight. Now sit down!' he hissed.

I said I would rather try and see Matthew. 'Will you come with me?'

'There's little point seeing Weeks now,' Slade said. 'Best leave him to rest before tomorrow's ordeal. But if you feel the need for some fresh air, then by all means take your leave.'

'Don't go far, Shilly. Mr Slade will want to prepare for your testimony.'

'That won't be necessary,' Slade said.

'You're not calling Shilly as a witness?'

'And risk her talking of fetches again? Or elephants, for that matter! Besides, she has nothing material to add to the case. She saw Weeks and the girl leave the house together, then she saw Weeks come back alone. Mrs Peter can provide that information.'

'But Mrs Peter will lie!' I said.

'And I will force her to tell the truth,' Slade said.

I had no faith he would, but Mr Williams seemed to have stopped caring about Matthew's fate. All he wanted was for Slade to write his precious letter. He was asking about it when I slipped outside.

SIXTY-ONE

I went to the gaol but the gateman wouldn't admit me. Matthew wasn't to have visitors. Reverend Kendall's orders. I walked the streets instead, speaking to no one, barely looking where I was going.

When I came back to myself I was in some pleasant and living place with grass and a bench, and that was good for my spirits were low, caused by many things. Slade was one of them, saying I couldn't give my evidence and help Matthew, and all because I'd told the truth. I tried to tell myself that Matthew didn't need me in the chair for witnesses, because the well water would save him, and if that failed then there were the boot prints, and I *had* helped with that evidence. Mr Williams had said so, but at the thought of him I felt more wretched still. And then a burst of black and white swooped by.

The magpie settled in the tree nearest to my bench and looked at me. I asked how his wife and children were and he chirped to say *well, thank you*, and *how are you, Shilly? How are you, Shilly?*

I am sore and lost and hurting, Mr Magpie, I said in my head, and he dipped his own head and said how sorry he was. *Sorry sorry sorry.* And then he was gone – away in his hurry of feathers and flying and freedom. I thought of the magpie Charlotte had torn open for the still beating heart. It should have been a wretched thing to think of but it made me feel better because I felt close to her again in that moment. Close to the living, breathing Charlotte. Not the cold, lost one who called me from her opened throat.

* * *

When I went back to the Barley Sheaf it was late. Mr Williams wasn't in the bar. I asked for him and was told he'd taken a room upstairs. I found the door and when I knocked it was Mrs Williams who opened it.

'Where am I to sleep?' I said.

'I asked for an extra blanket,' she said, 'so that you shouldn't feel the floor too keenly.'

That was something, at least, and it was cleaner than the stuff Vosper kept on his beds. My thirst was bad but I couldn't go down to the bar for I had no money, and I didn't want to be in front of the magistrates myself for thieving.

'Did Slade write your letter?'

She rootled through her black bag. 'He will,' she said. 'Once the trial is over. You'll turn around while I undress, Shilly.'

She waited for me to do so. Then I looked, of course. She couldn't seal up my eyes as Charlotte had done.

She undid her close-fitting purple dress and stepped from it, and I saw that the dress was as cleverly fashioned as her two-sided coat for it had padding sewn inside to make her shape look something it wasn't. The dress had given her curves above and below her waist but her true body was scrawny. She wasn't much more than skin and bone, but if I had had to say how Mrs Williams was built I should have said something very different. It was like Mr Williams's stiff way of walking – her other selves that let her real self pass unseen, let her travel where she pleased. To come and go. To go – that was the thing.

Now she wore nothing but a thin shift that lay close to her skin.

'I told you not to look.'

I said nothing. I wouldn't say sorry for I felt there was no wrongness in looking. Nor would I look away.

'If you must look,' she said, her voice uncertain. She turned a circle, slowly, shyly, and came back to face me. She was still wearing Mrs Williams's long, red curls.

'Take it off,' I said. 'Her hair.'

245

She did and her yellow hair was glorious beneath.

I moved closer to her, with each step fearing she would say no, that I mustn't. But she didn't speak or move away, just kept her eyes on mine. No smile but no warning either.

I was by her side. I put my hand to her cheek, her beautiful pale cheek. She closed her eyes and leant into my hand. I stroked her temple, the curve of her ear. Her lips parted and she made a small sound. I kissed her, lightly, to see what she would do. Her arms wrapped round me, her sharp hips pressed into mine. We were close as moor stone.

'You did this with . . . with her?' She spoke the words into my neck.

'You know I did.'

She drew away from me, kept her gaze from mine. I felt her trembling in my arms.

'Don't be afraid,' I said, twining my fingers in her close-cropped hair.

'But Charlotte . . . Did you—?'

I pulled her face closer to mine, to take her words away. 'She's gone.'

And then she was kissing me.

When I was certain she was asleep I dressed again, leaving my feet bare. Her coat was on the floor. I picked it up as gently as I could. In the pocket was the leather bag she'd used to bribe the gateman at the gaol. I eased open the string. The coins chinked. I waited but the sound didn't cause her to stir.

Downstairs, a man was still pouring. He took my money and gave me what I needed. I went outside, to the stables, and felt the world come right again.

Back through the bar, up the stairs to the door of our room, so light on my feet I was flying. I could fly to the top of Roughtor. But I stopped flying to listen, to be certain she was still asleep. Take care, Shilly, my girl. There was no sound. I eased open the door.

A sudden light as the candle flared and then her face in pieces in the shadows.

'I can smell it on you,' she said.

I began to say *what are you talking about, of course I haven't* . . . But my words dried up. She spoke the truth. It was who I was. Who I had been for a long time.

'Was it for my money that you . . . ? No. Don't answer.'

She blew out the candle and drew the blanket over her. I climbed in beside her. If I could only hold her, have her warm me. It had been so cold since Charlotte had died.

'No,' she said. 'Not like this. I won't have you like this.'

And she kicked me to the floor.

SIXTY-TWO

When I woke, Mrs Williams was already dressed, wearing her purple mourning, which made her body other than I had known it in the night. She was looking out of the window, and I became aware of voices in the street below. When I got up to join her she moved away.

'I'll meet you downstairs,' she said, without looking at me. 'Don't keep me waiting.'

So that was how it would be between us. She thought I had spoilt things, because of my weakness. But she was going to leave the moor as soon as Matthew was free. That had always been her thinking so there had never been anything to spoil, and that was her doing. Her fault. All of it her fault.

I looked out of the window. The street was packed with bodies.

We joined their pushing and shoving. The courthouse drew everyone to it. When we reached it, I could see why.

It wasn't as large as parts of the gaol had seemed but the courthouse was large in a different way. It was granite-built, the stone filed smooth, not like the rough stones that made moor houses. There were long windows set high above the ground. I couldn't look inside but people could look out at me.

There was hardly room to turn round in the crowds but when I caught sight of a familiar bustling shape I fought my way towards it. There were still ways to help Matthew, even if I couldn't speak to the judge in the courtroom.

It was John Peter who saw me first. He hauled me close to him, freed me from the tangle of arms and legs.

'Shilly-shally! When are you coming home?'

'Put her down, John,' his mother said. 'Shilly has decided to make her own way.'

Vosper was there, carrying a basket of food. They'd come for a picnic.

'I hear you went to see Matthew,' she said. 'Did he confess?'

'No.'

Her face fell. 'It won't make a difference.' She rummaged in the basket. 'I've brought plenty. Will you take something?'

'Matthew's in a bad way,' I said.

'Is he indeed?'

'He's that weak he can barely stand. Fainted while I was with him. He didn't seem to know who I was.'

Her hand in the basket stilled. She looked like she would speak.

'All the years he lived under your roof,' I said, 'keeping the farm going. You can't tell me he doesn't mean anything to you. You can't tell me you want him to suffer.'

'He's brought it on himself,' Vosper said.

Mrs Peter wrapped a pasty in a cloth and pressed it into my hands. 'I don't want you to starve,' she said. 'And when all this is over, if you want to come home—'

There was shouting by the steps. The courtroom was open.

I let the crowd stream by. Mrs Peter, John and Vosper went up the steps, and then Mrs Williams found me.

'Did you soften Mrs Peter at all?' she said.

'Her heart's hard as moor stone.' And yours too, I thought.

'No matter. Slade has the prints.'

And Matthew had the protection of the well. Two ways to keep him safe.

We were halfway up the steps when the crowd surged and became a heap. A woman screamed. There were cries of 'someone has fallen'.

Blue-clad constables rushed to help the woman to her feet. Still people pushed to get inside. Mrs Williams and I were rushed through large double doors and past the unfortunate woman who was laid out on a bench, her hat squashed against her head.

We fought our way to seats, the courtroom packed tight and roaring. Above us was a gallery. The people seated there pounded the floorboards and thumped the struts holding it up. I caught sight of Reverend Kendall near the door. On my other side were the newspapermen, pencils in their hands. How would they write the story this time?

The noise dropped. All eyes turned to the front of the room. Men with papers scurried in, followed by a gentleman in a rich red coat and old-fashioned, long white curls. It made me think of sheep. I guessed him to be the judge. He moved slowly to a large chair with a fancy back and put a device next to him that looked like a hunt master's horn.

Then two more gentlemen came in, not quite as well dressed as the first. The men wore the same sheep hair but navy coats rather than the judge's red. One was Slade. The second man was older. He had sandy hair and a sharp nose.

Then the air in the room changed. The crowd became as silent as if they'd all ceased breathing. I couldn't see what it was that made them so but I could hear it. The slow clank of metal as one foot was dragged forward then another. It was the noise of Charlotte's pattens. But it wasn't Charlotte coming now. It was Matthew, his feet in chains.

SIXTY-THREE

There was a hiss from all corners of the room. Mrs Williams, too, caught her breath. She muttered something but I couldn't catch the words.

Matthew was in a poor state – more terrible than I'd feared. The constables at his side looked to be holding him up rather than stopping him running away. His limp was worsened by the chains at his feet. The newspapermen were delighted, squinting between him and their little books.

The constables set Matthew in a box that looked like a pulpit, and took away their supporting arms. He swayed as if he would fall. His face was yellowed sickly. The blood I'd seen on him in the gaol had been cleaned but his pallor spoke of more nosebleeds since. At least his clothes were in good order. He was wearing the things I'd taken to the gaol, looking as fine as his poxed skin and twisted features allowed. I hoped the newspapermen would see the jacket's glass buttons in the low light. Matthew would like that.

The judge cleared his throat and looked at Matthew for the first time. He seemed unmoved by the signs of Matthew's ill health. I wondered if all prisoners appeared as he did.

'Matthew Weeks,' the judge said in an almost shouting voice, 'you are charged with the murder of Charlotte Dymond. How do you plead?'

Matthew didn't seem to know how to answer. Perhaps his time in the darkness of the gaol had closed up his mouth.

Slade whispered to Matthew who then croaked, 'Not guilty.' His words set free a storm of noise.

The judge shouted, 'Order! Order!' but it took time for quiet to return. Then the judge picked up the device he'd brought in with him and put it against his ear. It was some kind of funnel with a handle.

Mrs Williams groaned.

'Mr Slade,' the judge said, 'tell your client to speak up. I didn't catch his plea.'

'Of course, Your Honour,' Slade said. He told Matthew to speak again. I was heartened that this time Matthew was stronger in voice, as if he believed himself to be not guilty.

The judge said the jury was to be sworn in. Gentlemen trooped into the courtroom and took the rows of chairs next to the judge. They were all high hats and watch chains.

'Why are there no women?' I said.

Mrs Williams was looking in her little book. 'For the same reasons there aren't any women in the detective force. Men don't think us capable. But things will change, Shilly. Mark my words.'

One of the jurymen looked familiar. It was Mr Lethbridge, the magistrate.

'Look,' I said.

The little book fell from Mrs Williams's hand when she saw him. 'Hardly a figure unconnected with the case,' she said.

One of the jurymen seated behind Mr Lethbridge raised his hand to someone in the crowd. Reverend Kendall returned the juryman's wave with a nod.

'Some relation?' I asked Mrs Williams.

'Probably,' she said with bitterness.

While the jurymen took it in turns to swear an oath on the Bible, Mrs Williams was muttering to herself.

'What is it? I said.

'A bad start,' she said. 'They will have taken against Matthew already.'

'Why? They've only just come in.'

She pointed at Matthew. 'Because of his appearance.'

'He can't help the way he looks,' I said.

'It's not just his face, Shilly. As you say, that can't be helped. But what could have been avoided was making Matthew look like an upstart, someone who doesn't know his place. Didn't you hear the noise people made when he came in?'

'Because he looks so ill.'

'That's not why they hissed,' Mrs Williams said. 'They hissed because of his clothes. You've made him look like someone else, not a farm servant. People don't like that – not the people watching, not the judge, and certainly not the jurors. Why on earth did you give him those ridiculous clothes?'

'Because he likes to look smart!' I said. I felt tears coming. *You've failed him*, said a voice in my head. 'I thought he'd be pleased to wear his best things today. He wouldn't have liked to look like a farm servant. I thought . . .'

'He would have been better off in muddy corduroys and a stained shirt.'

'Why didn't you tell me?' I near wailed.

'Because I thought you wouldn't need telling! But clearly I was wrong. The fault is mine. What's done is done. But remember this, Shilly. Everyone and everything has their allotted station in life. It's one thing to change one's dress and demeanour to uncover deceit and crime, it's quite another to do so when one's own self is at risk. People – all people, regardless of their class – like things set firm. They don't take well to unquantifiables.'

'And you?' I said. 'What's your station in life?'

'Hush.' She looked around to see that no one was listening. 'We must concentrate on the matter at hand, and the hopes we still have. Slade has the boot prints. It's up to him now.'

Something was happening at the front of the room. The sandy-haired man who'd entered with Slade stood. Quiet returned.

'Alexander Cockburn,' Mrs Williams whispered, 'for the prosecution.'

The trial had begun.

SIXTY-FOUR

'Your Honour, gentlemen of the jury, today we will hear an all too familiar story, that of a jealous man exacting revenge on the woman who spurned him.'

Cockburn stood with his hands hooked onto his dark coat. His voice was full of certainty even though everything he said was a lie.

'But despite the familiarity of the story,' he went on, 'we must not refrain from examining the details of the case and holding them to scrutiny. When a man's life hangs in the balance, as does that of the prisoner, Matthew Weeks, we must be certain of our judgement before we release a man's soul to face the judgement of the Almighty. Examination of these details will show clearly and without a doubt that Weeks did wilfully murder Charlotte Dymond. Let us begin with an important witness in the case. Call Mrs Phillipa Peter, mistress of Penhale Farm.'

Mrs Peter took the seat next to the judge. This set her close to Matthew in his box but she didn't look at him. It broke my heart to see how he turned to her, seemed to lean towards her as if for comfort. He would find none there.

The judge pressed his funnel to his ear and Mrs Peter listed everyone who lived at the farm up to the day Charlotte went missing. She called John Peter the head of the house and said he was 'responsible for the running of the farm'. Matthew was John Peter's servant, his boy, 'who saw only to the most menial of tasks'. I was her 'little maid', and Charlotte was 'the flirt' who made men 'mad with jealousy'.

254

She said everything she'd said at the magistrates' hearing, about Charlotte and Matthew setting out together, Roe coming to say he saw Matthew on the moor with a woman . . . The whole sorry tale. Mr Lethbridge on the jury bench nodded all the while as if to say yes, it was just as he remembered.

When Mrs Peter spoke of Matthew's stockings being covered in turfy mud, Cockburn asked her to cease her prattle, and he called to one of the men standing by the door.

'Bring in the stockings belonging to the prisoner.'

So that was why I hadn't been able to find them. Mrs Peter had kept them back from washing, hidden them to use against Matthew. Such cunning she had in her. Such cruelty. I didn't know her at all. At that moment in the courtroom she was a stranger to me.

The stockings must have been waiting ready because no sooner had the door to the courtroom opened than in they were carried. The man bearing them made his way to the jury.

'The prisoner has confirmed that he was wearing these stockings on the day in question,' Cockburn said.

'Thin evidence, this,' Mrs Williams muttered. 'Your mistress could have covered the stockings with mud herself between Matthew coming back and her giving them to Rickard.'

Mrs Peter looked delighted to see the stockings again. 'There now, see,' she said, pointing. 'See how dirty they are? That's from him going across the moor with her.'

'And there was blood on his shirt, I believe?' Cockburn said.

'Awash with it, he was!'

Cockburn called for Matthew's shirt to be brought in. So Mrs Peter had kept that too. Of course she had, the deceitful woman.

A scurrying man went back and forth before the jury, holding the stained shirt for them to see as if it was a lamb at market. Cockburn told the men that it was Charlotte's blood, from Matthew having killed her. Mrs Peter was only too pleased to agree with Cockburn, and he let her rattle on until she'd said all she wanted on the matter of mud and stockings, shirts and blood, then he thanked her and sat down. Slade stood.

'Now things will be interesting,' Mrs Williams said.

I hoped that she was right.

SIXTY-FIVE

'Mrs Peter,' Slade said. 'Please tell me what the weather was like in the days before the deceased disappeared.'

'It was very dirty, sir.'

'And what effect would you say this had on the ground?'

'Well, it made it bad going. The turfy mud was wet.'

'Stop, stop,' the judge said. He waved his ear funnel about. 'I cannot understand this rustic speech.'

Mrs Peter began again but much louder. 'The turfy mud was wet!'

Being able to hear her words seemed no greater help to the judge. But then Slade spoke up. Because he was from Cornwall, he said he would act as explainer for the judge to tell him what Mrs Peter meant when she said words like 'turfy mud', meaning peat. I had thought everyone knew that. Mrs Williams lifted her eyes to the roof as if better help would come from there.

Slade began his questioning of Mrs Peter once more. 'You have stated that the weather had left the moor muddy in the days before the deceased disappeared. Presumably you would not claim that Penhale Farm and Roughtor Ford were subject to different weather than that experienced at All Drunkard – that's the local name for All Worthy, Your Honour – which is but a few miles from those places? That the farm and the ford did not languish under their own special rain cloud?'

There was laughing in the gallery above me.

'Of course not, sir,' Mrs Peter said. ''Tis all the same on the moor.'

'So if the turfy mud was wet at the farm and the ford then it would

257

have been wet at All Drunkard too, and on the moorland that runs between the farm and All Drunkard, isn't that correct, Mrs Peter?'

'Well, I . . . I suppose so, sir, yes. But—'

'Weeks's blue stockings that he was wearing on the day in question, we have seen that they are muddy.'

'Like he'd been rolling around in it at the ford.'

'But Mrs Peter,' Slade said, turning over the stockings, 'you have just told this court that the moor was muddy from your farm to All Drunkard, which is where the prisoner states he went. How can you be sure that this mud is from the ford and not from the path to All Drunkard?'

'Because I know he went to the ford,' Mrs Peter said.

'How do you know?' Slade asked.

'Because he killed her! And because Mr Carwitham saw them at the ford together. He'll tell you, sir. Mr Carwitham is a gentleman farmer much respected in our parish.'

Slade held up his hand. He was a fool to think that enough to stop Mrs Peter's mouth.

'My good woman,' Slade said. 'We will come to the other witnesses in due course but I would like to take this opportunity to inform the jury that the witness to whom Mrs Peter refers, Mr Daniel Carwitham, has not, to date, confirmed in person that he saw Weeks at the ford with the deceased. But to return to the matter at hand. There is no means of ascertaining that the mud found on the prisoner's clothes came from the ford rather than the journey to All Drunkard, which he claims he made. Which brings us to the matter of the blood on his shirt, Mrs Peter, which you have already discussed with my friend, Mr Cockburn.'

''Tis Charlotte Dymond's blood, sir. From where he cut her throat.'

'When did you find the bloodied shirt?'

'The day after she didn't come back,' Mrs Peter said.

'And am I correct in saying that you had a visitor at the farm on that day, a Mr . . .' He checked his papers. 'Mr Roe? He came to butcher one of your pigs.'

'That's right, sir. Mr Carwitham sent him to us. A most kind man is Mr Carwitham.'

'Yes,' Slade said, giving her a faint smile. 'And would you tell us what happened when Mr Roe came to kill the pig.'

'Well, he killed it and cut it up for me.'

'And did Weeks help him?'

'He tried but his knife was too poor.'

'His knife was too poor to kill the pig,' Slade said slowly. 'And what happened after Weeks tried to kill the pig?'

She shifted in her seat and looked at the judge.

'Mrs Peter?' Slade said.

'He . . . he fainted,' she said quietly.

'Speak up!' shouted the judge.

'He fainted,' she said again.

'He fainted,' Slade said. 'Matthew Weeks was found lying on the floor beneath an animal letting blood, isn't that right? And isn't it also true that the prisoner suffered a nosebleed shortly after he fainted?'

Mrs Peter nodded but only after a moment had passed.

'So, this shirt that you claim bears the blood of the deceased was found the day *after* the prisoner returned home without her, and *after* he had lain beneath a bleeding animal, following which he had a nosebleed. Is that correct, Mrs Peter?'

Mrs Peter twisted her mouth and refused to answer until the judge shouted at her. Then she said 'yes' but so quiet the judge had to shout at her a second time.

'Thank you, Mrs Peter,' Slade said. He went to sit down.

But she hadn't finished.

'That is the shirt he was wearing on the day he killed her,' she cried, 'I know it. He had blood on him when he came back without her. And the mud – I know it was from the ford, I know it!'

259

The judge shouted at Mrs Peter to leave her chair and at last she was gone.

'Those last words will linger in the minds of the jury,' Mrs Williams said, slumping in her seat. 'Let's hope the fact your mistress was the first to speak will mean other testimony has a more lasting impression. I wonder how much of the proceedings the judge can even hear.'

The next witness was Mr Good. Cockburn stood to question him and I saw this was the way of a trial. First the prosecution and then the defence, and then they had their turns again.

'Would you be so kind as to tell us, Mr Good, in what direction was the cut made on the deceased's body?' Cockburn said.

'It appears to have been made from left to right around the neck – that's the deceased's left to right – due to the depth of the wound on the left-hand side.'

'So that would lead us to believe the murderer was right-handed, is that correct?'

'Yes. A right-handed person would likely pull the instrument around the neck towards them, once they'd made the first incision. It would be too awkward to make a cut that progressed in that direction with the left hand.'

Cockburn turned to the jury and spent a moment slashing the air in front of him to show how the cut in Charlotte's neck was made.

Then there was confusion. Slade was asked to say if the prisoner was right- or left-handed. Matthew looked to have fallen into some kind of waking sleep. His eyes were open but he didn't hear when he was spoken to. Slade told him what was wanted. The whole courtroom leant forward to catch his answer.

Matthew said he was right-handed.

SIXTY-SIX

There was a burst of noise from the crowd. I just about heard Mrs Williams say that nearly everyone in that courtroom was likely to be right-handed, that didn't mean they'd cut Charlotte Dymond's neck. I hoped the jurymen thought similar.

'When the cut was made there would have been a large quantity of blood,' Slade said, having his turn now with Mr Good. 'If the prisoner did kill the deceased then he would, in all likelihood, have been heavily marked with her blood.'

'That is correct,' Mr Good said.

'So, if we work on the assumption the deceased was killed on the day she failed to return to the farm, then we must look at the accused's clothes. His bloodied shirt was not discovered by his mistress until the following day and there are two other potential causes for the blood.' Slade showed the jury the shirt again. 'And what little blood there is. See here, gentlemen, the small amounts on the collar and on the side here. Not as much as one would expect to flow from all of Charlotte Dymond's veins. But the coroner doesn't believe she was killed on the day she failed to return to the farm, do you, Mr Good?'

'That I don't,' Mr Good said. 'I firmly believe the girl was killed shortly before the body was discovered. That is, two days after her disappearance.'

'And if you're right in that belief, then we have no bloodied clothes to connect with the prisoner at all. We have evidence from several witnesses who saw Matthew Weeks as he journeyed to Plymouth in the days following the disappearance of the deceased, and from the constable who apprehended him in the port. All of them report that Matthew Weeks had no blood on his clothing. He did not take a spare shirt with him when he left Penhale Farm, and is not known to have bought or borrowed any once he was on his way. Gentlemen, there simply isn't enough blood to connect Weeks with this crime.'

Next was Tom Prout, all cocky-sprawling in the chair. He didn't have much to say apart from that Charlotte was meant to meet him at the chapel and she didn't come.

After him was Roe, who told Cockburn what he'd told the magistrates, that he saw Matthew on the moor with a woman. That he'd known Matthew by his limp. That there wasn't a doubt in his mind. Then Slade stood. He made Roe admit that he wasn't close to the couple, and that the weather was poor for seeing well across the moor, just as Mr Williams had when we saw Roe in the fields. But Roe didn't waver.

'There wasn't a doubt in my mind,' he said again. 'It was Weeks.' And he was allowed to go.

Vosper followed Roe to the seat by the judge. Cockburn made him repeat that he too had seen a man and a woman on the moor and that the man limped. Then Slade asked Vosper where he'd been when he saw the couple, just as he had asked Roe.

'I was coming out of my establishment,' Vosper said, 'that's the Britannia Inn. I was close to the road when I saw them and they were not a hundred paces from me. I admit the weather was poor but I could see enough to know the man was limping, as Weeks does.'

'Beyond the limp,' Slade said, 'was there anything else about the man you saw that suggested it was indeed Matthew Weeks?'

Vosper scratched his stubbled cheek. 'Well, he had on a fine coat, as Weeks was wont to wear.'

'Did you see his face?'

'Like I said, he was walking away from me, towards Lanlary Rock, though what he and she were wanting with it on a dirty day like that I don't know. Well, I suppose I do now. He was wanting to do away with her, wasn't he?'

Slade wasn't quick enough to stop Vosper before he'd said his last words. Mrs Williams pressed her hands into her eyes.

'Why didn't Slade ask Vosper about the boot prints?' I said, but she only shook her head.

It was nastily hot in the courtroom by that time. The pasty Mrs Peter had forced on me had gone greasy. My throat burnt and I was dizzy with lack of drink. I'd have taken any kind – sinful or otherwise.

'Will they stop for crib?' I asked Mrs Williams, and then had to tell her that crib meant eating that wasn't a meal proper, as if I was Slade and she the judge not understanding.

'I doubt it,' she said. 'The law requires the judge to hold the trial in a single day, wherever possible. There can't be too many witnesses left, and he's clearly keen to get through them, the pace things are running.'

It didn't seem quick to me. The trial felt like the longest day of my life.

Next were two girls I didn't know. They were silly, fluttering things from Lezant parish, where Matthew's family were from, and they had known him as a boy. He'd called to see them on his way to Plymouth. They told the court he was tired and thirsty when he arrived, and that they hadn't known he was coming. They gave him something to drink and let him rest in their kitchen. They asked him where he was going but he wouldn't tell them. He left after an hour or so. The younger of the two was wide-eyed as a calf.

'He sang to us,' she said. 'He sang "Sweet Maidens All". He couldn't have come to Lezant from doing away with that woman like people say he did. His singing was so beautiful and he was so soft with us, even though he was tired.'

She knew him as I knew him, that girl, whoever she was. It wasn't all against him.

Then came the call for Mr Robert Westlake.

'What can they want Robert for?' I asked Mrs Williams.

'No . . .' She slumped in her seat. 'She's done for him. The selfish creature. I should have hauled her here myself.'

'What is it?' I said.

'Mary has refused to come.'

SIXTY-SEVEN

Robert was as smartly tucked and brushed as I'd ever seen him.

'Mr Westlake,' the judge said, 'I understand that you are here on behalf of your wife, Mrs Mary Westlake, who has been called as witness for the prosecution and the defence but who is unwell, I gather.'

Robert coughed into the hat he was holding. 'She is, sir, yes. She's barely left the house since Weeks made his accusations. Suffered great distress. We both have.'

'Indeed. Mr Cockburn, your witness.'

Cockburn rose and stood close to Robert in the manner of a friend. 'Mr Westlake, as you are aware, the prisoner has claimed that, rather than walking on the moor with the deceased on the date in question, he was in fact, and I quote, "taking a dish of tea" with *your* wife in *your* house in All worthy. Mr Westlake, will you please tell the court if the version of events claimed by the prisoner is true?'

Robert's hands tightened around his hat. He looked at Matthew and spoke to him rather than to Cockburn.

'It is not true,' he said. 'My wife is a respectable woman, and the fact I have had to come here today to confirm this . . .'

'I'm sorry to question you on such an indelicate matter,' Cockburn said. Robert dropped his gaze to the floor. 'But could you confirm for the court where your wife was on the afternoon in question.'

'We attended the morning service at Tremail Chapel, as we do every Sunday, and then we returned home for dinner a little past midday. Following this we spent the afternoon together in quiet contemplation of the Bible, as is our common practice on Sundays.'

'I see,' Cockburn said. 'So you were at home with your wife all afternoon. Did anyone call at the house during that time?'

'No. No one called at the house. No one at all.'

'So you had no visitors. Thank you, Mr Westlake. You've been most helpful.'

Cockburn sat down and Slade stood.

'Mr Westlake, can you please tell the court your occupation.'

'I don't see that has any relevance to Weeks's murder trial.'

'You must answer the question,' the judge said.

Slade folded his arms across his chest and swayed back and forth on his feet.

'I'm clerk for a solicitor in All Worthy,' Robert said. 'For Mr Simon Arnold.'

'And how long have you worked for Mr Arnold?'

'Eighteen years.'

'Eighteen years, my my. So you know your employer well, I would imagine. You are close.'

'I wouldn't say that.'

'No?' said Slade. 'I've heard it said that Simon Arnold considers you a member of the family. You're like a son to him, I gather. Am I correct in stating that his place of business is his house in All Drunkard – sorry, All Worthy – and that this is where you work?'

'Yes.'

'I see. Now, Mr Westlake, I remind you that you have taken an oath to tell the court the truth, and that a man's life hangs in the balance. I put it to you that on the afternoon in question you were not at home with your wife, as you claim, but were in fact at the house of your employer, helping him prepare some documents in connection with a land dispute. Isn't that correct?'

Robert dug his fingers in to the top of his hat. 'It is not. I was at home with my wife, as I have stated. No one called.'

'He who works on a Sunday is not an upstanding Methodist, is he, Mr Westlake, so I must charge you with backsliding as well as lying.'

'Your Honour, I—'

'I put it to you, Mr Westlake, that you were not at home and therefore cannot claim to know for certain that Matthew Weeks did not call on your wife.'

'I was at home. My employer has confirmed to Mr Cockburn that I was not at his house that afternoon. Mr Cockburn has a letter, signed by Mr Arnold. If you'll just look at that.'

'I have looked at it, Mr Westlake, but it simply states that you were not at your employer's house. It gives no sense of where you actually were. If you were not at Mr Arnold's house but were at your own house instead, as you claim, then I would ask you to find someone to confirm that you were there. Someone other than your wife, of course. But you've been unable to do so because it was your maid's half day, wasn't it? And you have stated, under oath, that you had no callers. So you have no one to confirm that you were at home on the afternoon in question.'

'But you have no one to confirm that I wasn't there, other than Weeks.'

Mr Slade turned on his heel. 'No further questions, Your Honour.'

Constable Rickard was called.

'They'll have to ask *him* about the prints,' I said.

'Yes,' Mrs Williams said faintly. She was pulling at a loose thread on her glove. There was a shake in her fingers. I stopped it by taking her hand into my own, and I willed my certainty to find its way into her heart, for the boot prints would let Slade show, once and for all, that it wasn't Matthew on the moor with Charlotte.

Cockburn got to his feet but instead of speaking to Rickard ready-seated by the judge, Cockburn spoke to the judge himself. 'Your Honour, the prosecution has no questions to put to the constable.'

'Counsel for the defence?' said the judge.

Slade stood. 'The defence has no questions for Constable Rickard,' he said.

'No!' Mrs Williams cried. People turned to look.

'Quiet in the court!' the judge shouted. Slade didn't turn round but he must have heard Mrs Williams, he must have done.

Rickard looked uncertain about what he should do until one of the scurrying men herded him out of the chair and then out of the door.

'Call the last witness,' the judge was saying but I was barely listening. How would the jury hear about the boot prints now if no one asked Constable Rickard about them?

'Call Mr Daniel Carwitham of Lanhendra.'

It was Matthew's last chance.

SIXTY-EIGHT

Mr Carwitham looked well-to-do in a smart black coat. He set his hat on his lap and leant his cane against his chair. Then he was looking at me, or at least it felt as if he was, until Cockburn stood to question him.

'Mr Carwitham, your proxy Mr Roe gave evidence to the magistrates that you saw a man and a woman walking together near Roughtor Ford on the day in question. Your description of the couple matches those given by Mr Roe and Mr Vosper. Quoting your testimony to the magistrates, you have stated, "the man was lame and the woman carried an umbrella". Is this correct?'

'It is.'

'And could you confirm for the jury, please, that the man you saw was the prisoner, Matthew Weeks?'

'I believe it to be the same man.'

He didn't look at Matthew when he spoke. Matthew himself hadn't looked at anything but his feet for some time.

'Can you be a little firmer, sir?' Cockburn said. 'Was it the same man – yes or no?'

Mr Carwitham neither moved nor blinked. 'I believe it to be the same man.'

And he would say nothing else to Cockburn.

Slade had his turn. 'Mr Carwitham, you had met the prisoner and the deceased on a number of occasions prior to the date in question, is that correct?'

'I had dealings with them both at Penhale.'

'So you would be able to recognise Matthew Weeks at close quarters.'

'The weather was poor that day,' Mr Carwitham said. 'The mist.'

Still he was rigid in the chair. What a cold man he was, to feel nothing when his words could send a man to his death.

'But surely you would have been able to see if it *wasn't* Weeks,' Slade said. 'He has, one must admit, a very particular set of features.'

'The mist. It was—'

'Mr Carwitham, can you at least confirm to the court that you have doubts that the man you saw was Matthew Weeks?'

'I believe it to be the same man,' Mr Carwitham said again.

Slade's shoulders slumped. 'No further questions, Your Honour.'

Mr Carwitham didn't get up from the chair but the judge didn't notice. He began to address the court.

'That concludes the witness testimony. We will now move to—'

'I will swear it!' Mr Carwitham cried.

The court broke into noise. People got to their feet.

'Silence!' the judge shouted.

Mr Carwitham was pale and his face looked to be slick with sweat. Cockburn danced about in front of him.

'Repeat yourself, sir!' Cockburn said. 'For God's sake repeat yourself!'

'I swear it,' Mr Carwitham said over the noise. 'I swear the man I saw was the prisoner, beyond all doubt. I swear it.'

Then everything fell to madness. Cockburn cried out in delight at the same moment Mr Carwitham slid from his chair to the floor as if he was a leaf caught in the wind. The scurrying men rushed to him and everyone in front of me stood up again so I couldn't see what was happening. The judge shouted for order but none came. All around me was noise and heat and the creeping of evening.

Someone took my hand. I guessed it was Mrs Williams. I think perhaps I cried.

SIXTY-NINE

Mr Carwitham was carried insensible from the courtroom. We had to stay seated and sweating for the speeches. I wished I could have been carried out insensible.

Cockburn and Slade talked of what the witnesses had said. Each man made the testimony suit their own tale but neither gave a good answer to the question of who had taken Charlotte from me. Slade had done a fair job of showing a different way of looking at the bloodied shirt and such, but he hadn't done enough. Mrs Williams and I had given him the boot prints and he hadn't used them.

The judge began his own speech and went on for some time. At last he asked the jurymen to leave the courtroom so they could do their deciding. Then he eased himself from his chair and left by a different door. Cockburn and Slade went with him. Matthew stayed in his box, the two blue constables at his side.

'How long until the jury come back?' I asked Mrs Williams.

'Each trial is different, but something tells me they won't be long in this case. I don't think the trial will have done much to change the opinion the jury had when they arrived this morning. We might as well stay here and wait.'

Most people had the same idea for very few left the room. Some got up and stretched, some moved to talk to friends. I watched Reverend Kendall go to Matthew's box. Matthew bent to listen to him, the first time he'd moved in hours.

'Why did no one mention the boot prints?' I said.

'My guess is that the prosecution didn't need to,' Mrs Williams said. 'By the time Rickard was called they felt they'd made a strong enough case. Using the boot prints as evidence was always going to be a risk.'

'Because of Rickard himself.'

'Constables can do more harm than good.'

If Rickard had been within reach at that moment then I would have struck him so hard that Bodmin Moor would never have been troubled with his constabling again. Mrs Williams felt the same. I could see it in the tight way she held herself, how her fingers gripped her little book. She wouldn't speak her raging but I could feel it, because I'd been with her and felt her heart beat beneath her skin. I had that, at least.

'It's Slade's fault too,' I said. 'He didn't even *try* to use the prints.'

'Because Cockburn didn't. Cockburn didn't mention them at all, even that they existed let alone that they didn't show what people had supposed them to. The prints weren't used as evidence against Matthew so Slade had no cause to retaliate. Do you see? Slade couldn't use them to defend because they weren't used to prosecute. I had assumed Cockburn would use the prints, risky as they were, because other parts of their case were so weak. The bloodstains, Carwitham's reluctance . . .' Mrs Williams was gripping her little book with both hands and staring at it as if she thought it would move. 'But I was wrong,' she whispered.

'It wasn't you up there, though, was it?' I said. 'Slade's a fool.'

I tore into my cold, greasy pasty. All at once I was starving though I felt sick with worry about what the jurymen would say when they came back. I broke off a piece of pasty and gave it to Mrs Williams.

'Don't judge Slade too harshly,' she said. 'He had a hard task, given the cause of death certified at the inquest.' She took a bite of the pasty and made a face.

'It's past its best,' I said.

'Aren't we all?' she said sadly.

The jury came back and then came the judge, with Cockburn and

Slade after him. It was half past ten at night. The jury had been gone for only half an hour.

'Time enough to take refreshment and confirm they agree with each other,' Mrs Williams said. 'I see they've let everyone in.'

The witnesses were crowding the doorway. I caught sight of Mrs Peter pushing to the front. John Peter and Vosper craned their necks behind her.

The judge asked if the jury had reached their verdict. A burly man with thinning white hair stood. Mrs Williams had told me he was the foreman.

'We have, Your Honour,' the foreman said.

Then the judge told Matthew to stand. He got to his feet but had to hold on to the front of his box to stay upright. The constables stood ready to brace him if he fell.

'What say you?' the judge said to the foreman.

I held my breath. I thought of the well in the Mowhay and hoped its power really was to save people from hanging. Mrs Williams's hands were clasped as if in prayer.

'We are all of the opinion,' the foreman said, 'that the prisoner is guilty.'

Mrs Williams's clasped hands fell into her lap, and I felt the drop of them as thunder. The world was shaking with the foreman's words, and no amount of drink could cease the dreadful pitching. We had failed him.

And what of Matthew? He didn't move or make a sound. I wondered if he understood what the foreman said, if he'd even heard.

Things moved very fast then. The judge put on a cap of black cloth and turned to face Matthew.

'Matthew Weeks, the jury have come to the conclusion that you are guilty of the offence with which you are charged. There is no hope for you in this world and my earnest entreaty is for you to endeavour to obtain mercy from the Almighty, which man cannot grant, by turning, in your final hours, to the gaol chaplain, the Reverend Kendall.'

There was movement by the door. Kendall sidled towards Matthew's box. Still Matthew gave no sign he understood what was happening.

'You shall be taken from here to the place from whence you came,' the judge said, 'and be hanged by the neck until you are dead. Your body will be buried in the precincts of the prison. May the Lord—'

Matthew fell backwards in his box.

SEVENTY

The constables couldn't revive him. Everyone was saying he was dead from shock but I knew the truth of it. The well water had taken Matthew before he could be led to the gallows.

But then a shout went up that he was alive though in a dead faint. The gaol's warders helped the constables lift him from the box, Reverend Kendall directing them. Matthew was eased to the floor. He was having another nosebleed.

'They'll keep him alive so they can kill him,' Mrs Williams said.

The people crowded in the doorway were told to move aside. I couldn't see Mrs Peter or John but Vosper was there. The warders and constables carrying Matthew passed very close to him. People were trying to leave and others were trying to look at Matthew. All was confusion and in the middle of it Vosper slammed his fist against Matthew's skull. There was nothing Mrs Williams and I could do but watch. I couldn't even cry.

At last it was over and Matthew was carried out. The judge, Cockburn and Slade had already gone. Those left were gathering their belongings and making their way to the door. Mrs Williams and I slowly did the same, though I lacked the will to even move my limbs.

'What about your letter from Slade?' I said. 'Will you go and ask him for it?'

'It doesn't matter,' she said. 'I didn't save Matthew. I won't try again.'

'Then what happens now?'

'We must find somewhere to sleep, I suppose.'

That wasn't what I was asking, but it was as good an answer as any we would have that night.

'And then tomorrow,' Mrs Williams said, 'I feel I should be there, for the . . . event. I owe it to Matthew, having failed to clear his name.'

'Then I should go too,' I said.

'It won't be pleasant.'

'I don't want Matthew to be without a friend. Perhaps he'll know I'm there. It might give him some comfort.'

And the well water. It might still keep him from the noose.

We passed through the door and into the night air. People were going to their lodgings, if they had some, or seeking ground to sleep on. I knew I wouldn't sleep. I wanted time to think over everything that had been said even though I knew there was little use doing so. Matthew hadn't killed Charlotte but he was to be hanged. That was all there was to know. Then I heard a familiar voice.

'Poor Mr Carwitham,' Mrs Peter said.

I made out the shapes of John Peter and Vosper beside her. They were seated against the wall of the courthouse, having the last of their picnic. I made Mrs Williams stop. We listened from the steps.

'Quite overcome, he was,' Mrs Peter was saying. 'They carried him out as they carried Matthew. Mr Carwitham much more dignified, of course.'

Vosper gave a snort. He was standing apart from her and John Peter, looking out over the town. John Peter trilled a song to himself. *Such pretty words he sang to me, beneath the budding hawthorn tree.*

I would never hear Matthew sing again.

'And to think that none of her family came,' Mrs Peter said. 'That tells you all you need to know, doesn't it?'

Vosper made a noise again but this time it wasn't a snort. More like a cough.

'What – were they here?' Mrs Peter asked him. 'A woman from Boscastle told me the family hadn't come.'

I stepped into sight. There was no need to hide any more.

'You?' I said to Vosper.

'Shilly!' John Peter charged over and got his arms around me.

'Humphrey Vosper, you're never a relation of Charlotte Dymond!' Mrs Peter said.

Still he looked out over the town.

'That's what you meant when you said "not quite", isn't it?' I eased myself from John Peter's arms. 'When Mr Williams asked if you'd had relations with her.'

'Humphrey, why did you never say?' Mrs Peter said.

'Would you?' he said. 'Her being like she was, like her mother before her. Who would own a farm girl born out of wedlock?'

'But you're telling us now,' I said. 'Why?'

'Because it's done.' He started to walk away.

'Did she know?' I called after him.

He faltered. 'No,' he said. 'Her mother asked that I keep it from her.' And then he was gone, out of reach of the few lamps lit.

'Humphrey a relation of Charlotte Dymond,' Mrs Peter said. 'May the Lord preserve us.' She gathered up the picnic things and handed them to John Peter. 'Have you a place to stay, Shilly?'

'We'll find somewhere.'

'We?' Mrs Peter straightened up.

Mrs Williams appeared beside me.

Mrs Peter looked her up and down, then turned away. 'Come, John. Help Mother with the basket.'

They set off after Vosper, but before they had gone too far Mrs Peter called back.

'The field down the way. That's where most are staying.'

'You should go with your mistress,' Mrs Williams said.

'She's not my mistress any more. I can come with you, back to the Barley Sheaf.'

'No.' She took a step back from me and looked at her gloves. 'Go to the field, Shilly. Be with your own people.'

'But—'

'I'll be there, when they hang him.'

Then she left me in the gloom of the courthouse's walls. I was alone. And Matthew was to die.

SEVENTY-ONE

What choice did I have but to follow Mrs Peter?

But when I came to the field I went my own way, weaving between the many fires that made the air sweet with burning gorse. Shadows were singing and dancing. Some were so drunk they were rolling on the ground. There were fights too. Proper wrestling in one corner, drunk raging in another. I tripped on a bottle and went sprawling. I picked it up and shook it. There was no Mrs Williams to chide me and even if she did see me searching for drink, she would soon be gone so what did it matter? The bottle was empty. My arms were empty. I lay down by a fire but the flames gave no warmth. There was no warmth left in the world.

When I woke the sight that greeted me was Vosper. He was crossing the field, carrying a fat stone jug. I followed him past the slumped bodies, the bodies stirring, and everywhere the black marks of burnt-out fires.

He led me to Mrs Peter, and on seeing her I wondered again at my choices in life, wondered if I had any to make of my own, for surely I would always be searching for a master or mistress. My path had brought me back to one again, without my choosing it. The world was full of Mrs Peters paying and Shilly-shallys earning. This Mrs Peter was standing in the Penhale cart. Blankets and sacking were piled at her feet. I stayed out of sight, round the cart's back end. A choice of a kind.

Vosper eased the jug to the ground. It was heavy and made a clinking sound.

'What on earth have you got there?' Mrs Peter asked him.

Vosper knocked the jug with his foot to make it clink again. 'Donations, for the memorial. People want to give, though they've not got much themselves. We'll soon have enough for quarried moor stone. No gateposts for the girl.'

'Have you decided on the lettering?' Mrs Peter asked him.

'Not yet. Robert wants to word it, and he's got the best letters. Gave me a pound yesterday. We'll have a ceremony, shall we, when it's in place?'

'Mr Lethbridge might come and say some words, if it's for quarried stone. Now, we must get ready.' She patted a hunch of blanket in the cart that I took to be John Peter. 'Come on, my dear.'

'They say he's confessed,' Vosper said.

'At last!' Mrs Peter said. 'Praise the Lord.'

'He can't have,' I said.

They turned and saw me.

'Lord's sake, Shilly – creeping like that!' Mrs Peter put her hand to her breast, as if to be sure her heart was still beating. 'You see now, the jury was right to find him guilty. If only Matthew had confessed sooner. He could have saved us a day in a hot courtroom, and saved poor Mr Carwitham such suffering. What a selfish creature Matthew is.'

John Peter unwrapped his head from his blanket.

'Oh my sweet boy!' she said. 'There won't be a scrap of doubt now. Everyone will know Matthew did it.' She fell to kissing John Peter's face.

'There's nothing you can do for Weeks,' Vosper told me. 'Have done with your scritching.'

'Matthew didn't do it. He didn't do it, Mrs Peter!'

'Shilly, when will you see what's clear to the rest of the world?' Mrs Peter said. 'And get up off that wet ground. I can't have you coming back to the farm with a cold. There's too much work waiting for you. Get up and come to the gaol.' She glowered down at me from the cart, her hands on her hips, her eyes narrowed. 'And that will be the end of Charlotte Dymond and Matthew Weeks.'

I walked to the gaol as if in a dream. Past inns and kiddlywinks, past shopfronts and stalls, past barrow boys and flower girls, past dogs snapping, children scritching. Past it all I floated until the gaol rose up before me and my legs went stiff as oak branches. John Peter half-carried me the last part of the way and I let him for I knew I'd be trampled by the crowd if I didn't. But part of me would have been gladly crushed.

We didn't need to go inside the gaol to see the deed done. The gallows were on top of the outside wall, giving a good view. The dangling rope framed by the beams that supported it. So little, really, to kill a man.

Crowds had gathered early, meaning we were too late to get a place by the wall like Mrs Peter wanted. Vosper cooled her rage by saying that at least she wouldn't have to strain her neck to see.

There was a shout. People pointed. There were bodies on the gallows. The crowd pushed forwards. Vosper, Mrs Peter and John were lost in the press. I felt a hand take mine. Mrs Williams, appearing from nowhere like the fetch.

On the gallows a man pulled a black hood over his face. A second man was led out. A limping man. A singing man.

The hooded man put the noose round Matthew's neck. The crowd was buzzing like flies on a dead cow. The well water – now was the time for it to work. Now the walls must crumble. Now Matthew must grow wings, fly to the top of Roughtor. Now, please God, something—

The others on the gallows stepped back. They bowed their heads. Mrs Williams kept hold of my hand.

Then there was nothing. No noise from the crowd. No movement on the gallows. A bird flew overhead.

Then Matthew dropped. His body jerked, his legs trying to run on air. I thought it was good his limp was gone, at last. And then he was still. The well water hadn't saved him.

A hand took my other hand. A hot hand, the palm rough as gorse.

SEVENTY-TWO

The crowd cheered. Women screamed. I might have been one of them. Mrs Williams bowed her head.

When this other hand squeezed it hurt but I didn't cry out. I didn't look at her but I knew she was there. When she tried to breathe the air bubbled from her opened neck. I could smell her old blood, the turfy mud.

I stood between Mrs Williams and that other. I didn't move. The other squeezed my hand again and I felt a small bone pop. Still I didn't move, I couldn't. I'd failed Matthew and I'd failed her. The wrong man was hanging from the gallows above Bodmin Gaol and all that rattled through my poor head were the words we sang at the end of the hay-cutting.

I have ee! I have ee! I have ee!
What have ee? What have ee? What have ee?
A neck! A neck! A neck!

Then the words in my head grew too loud to bear and all the while she squeezed my hand and sought to break me.

I was on the ground. My arms were tight around myself. It took Mrs Williams some moments to ease me from my own grip. She tried to take my right hand. I cried out in pain. The harm was real.

'You're in shock,' she said.

Then she gasped and drew a handkerchief from her coat. She pressed

283

it to my face and when she drew it away there was blood. She gave me the handkerchief to press to my nose.

'Come, lean against this.'

She tried to lead me to a low wall but I wouldn't let her touch me. My head was light and my hand was throbbing. I reached the wall and fell against it with relief. I forced myself to look at the gallows. Matthew was still there, alone.

'Why don't they take him down?'

'The law requires them to leave the body for an hour and a minute after hanging. No one must touch it in that time. Don't look at him,' she murmured. 'He'll be at peace.'

'No he won't! And neither will she!' I was shouting but no one cared. There were plenty of soft souls wandering the streets of Bodmin that day.

Mrs Williams looked like she was going to put her arm around me but thought better of it when I flinched.

'Have you read the confession?' I said.

'It's not his.'

'Tell me what it says.'

'It can't do any good. And I very much doubt he wrote it anyway. Well, we know he wouldn't have written it himself, don't we. He couldn't write.'

'And he couldn't have checked what was written for him before making his mark.'

'If indeed he ever saw the confession, or knew of its existence,' Mrs Williams said.

'This is Kendall's doing, and the lie will be written in stone on Vosper's memorial.'

'Does moor stone wear away, like sandstone?' she said. 'Perhaps in time the weather will undo the lie.'

'Moor stone lasts forever.'

We didn't speak on the journey back to Vosper's. It wasn't just because the coach to Camelford had other passengers, because the silence stayed when it was only the two of us, on foot across the moor. We didn't speak because there was too much between us unspoken. Matthew's body on the gallows, and what came before it – the night we'd spent together.

We reached Vosper's late in the afternoon. I felt we'd been gone years. The place was deserted but sounds drifted from the room behind the bar. Vosper. He was singing. I would take his tunes from him. Stop his mouth for good. But Mrs Williams was going up the stairs. To ready her case. To leave.

I followed her, grabbed her by the hand, harder than I meant to. She cried out, but not in pain of the body. Some other kind of pain that had been there between us all the way back to the inn.

'We can't help the way we are,' I said, meaning many things. Fetches, love, and so much else besides.

'You and I are not the same, Shilly.'

'If you would stay you'd see.'

She wouldn't look at me.

'I'm sorry for taking your money,' I said. 'I would give it back to you, if I had it. If you were to stay a little longer I could try—'

'It's not the money.' She slipped from my grip, put distance between us. 'What will you do now?' she said, as if we were newly met. As if she didn't care what the answer was.

'I . . . I suppose I'll find another farm. Mrs Peter thinks I'll go back to Penhale, back to how things were before.'

'Perhaps that's for the best. I know you tried to help me, in your own way, to save Matthew. For that I must thank you.'

'In my own way?'

'We'll say goodbye now. Take care, Shilly.'

'No, wait—' I reached out for her again but she was closing the door against me. The last I saw of her, her hand was over her mouth, as if she didn't trust herself to speak.

SEVENTY-THREE

I went out to the yard, then to the road. The path to the farm was in sight. The other way, across the moor, who knew what waited for me there? Surely Mrs Williams wasn't the only one who could change herself, who could leave people behind. Charlotte had been right. The life we had – it wasn't enough. I wouldn't go back to how things were before. I couldn't.

And yet, and yet.

Charlotte had sought to change her life, to ask for something more, and she was gone. Matthew, too, for wanting more than others believed him worth. I was no different to either of them. Well, I was. I was a coward, for I was walking down the path to Penhale. I was walking back to Mrs Peter and everything I already knew.

My feet took me to the Mowhay. The ground inside the ruined walls was hard and cracked. The thorn tree was smaller than I remembered. The scraps of cloth tied to its spindly branches were faded and grey.

I'd believed in Charlotte – told everyone I could about her strengths, about the things that had happened since her death, and what good had it done? If I hadn't been so keen to tell everyone about the fetch and the wretched tongue I would have been called as a witness at the trial and spoken of the things Mrs Williams knew were important. Boot prints. Bloodstains. Perhaps I could have saved Matthew.

It was my fault.

I forgot the pain of my broken hand and lunged at the thorn tree. I clawed the branches to strip them of their rags and then I went for the tree itself but the supple wood would only bend, not break. I pulled a stone from the ruined wall and attacked the tree. I slashed the trunk and pounded the branches. Then I fell to the walls and dragged out the stones to take every trace of the holy well from the field. I was sobbing and shouting and my hands were bleeding.

And then I saw it.

Something white was showing. A scrap, hidden in the wall. I reached in and drew out the paper. There was writing. I couldn't read it but I knew what it was.

I'd found Charlotte's letter.

SEVENTY-FOUR

I was running and panting and I had to go faster, had to get to the inn before she left. Had to see her, one last time. One last try.

My thoughts were running even faster than my legs, and the one that ran the fastest was that Charlotte had left the letter in the place most important to her. She'd left it for me to find.

I ran across the road. I didn't slow on reaching the inn's front door but hared inside.

'That desperate for a drink, Shilly?'

It was Vosper, behind the bar. No sign of Mr or Mrs Williams in the front room, only a few old men back beetling the corners.

I raced up the stairs and flung open the door to Mrs Williams's room.

She was there – standing by the bed. My breath flooded back into my body.

'I thought you might have gone.'

I was shaking as I tried to take the letter from my pocket and my right hand wouldn't do as I willed. Charlotte had broken it, I remembered.

'Shilly, whatever's the matter? You're bleeding. Did Mrs Peter hurt you?'

At last I got the letter free. 'It's the stones – the well. But the letter, look. You must read it to me. Tell me what it says. Why did she go across the moor that day?'

Mrs Williams took the paper from me but didn't open it. My blood had smeared it.

'Vosper's taking me to Altarnun,' she said. 'I'm catching the carrier to Jamaica Inn.'

Her chest of belongings was closed. Her coat was laid ready on top of it.

'You can't go,' I said, 'not yet.'

'I must, Shilly. It's over.'

'Please – just wait. I found the letter at the well, the old well, in Mrs Peter's Mowhay field. It was where Charlotte . . . It was a special place for her. I found the letter hidden in the wall. She must have left it for me to find.'

'You think it's the letter Charlotte had on the day she went missing?'

She eyed me warily. In my head I was screaming at her. At last she changed her mind, and unfolded the paper.

She tilted it this way and that. I leant close to her.

'The hand is poor,' she said, 'and you're in my light, Shilly.' She went to the window and began to read. '*My dear Charlotte. I hope you will like this gift. It is made by my own hand. I remember you have a liking for nice things. You must not come back to us no more. Your mother does not want it. She says she will kill you if you come back to us again.*' Mrs Williams' voice faltered and she turned to look at me.

'Is there more?' I said.

She nodded.

'Then for heaven's sake read it!'

'*You must not come back. You have plenty years now not to have need of your mother and she says she cannot bear the shame of you in the village. I am sorry to say this to you. I hope you are well. May God bless you and forgive you.* There's a signature but I can't make it out. No date either.'

'The village must be Boscastle,' I said.

'Well, this could be the truth of the matter, finally.' Mrs Williams sat next to me on the bed. 'I take it you don't have postal deliveries out here in the wilderness?'

I didn't know what she meant.

'Postmen,' she said. 'Do men call with letters, wearing red uniforms?'

'No.'

'So how would a letter reach the farm?'

'The person writing it would give it to someone who was bringing something else. Like the carrier. He takes things everywhere. That's how Charlotte used to go to Boscastle, in his cart.'

'Did anyone call at the farm with something for Charlotte? Think, Shilly.'

'She'd been at the farm for months before she died. Many people came.'

'But had you ever seen her with a letter before the one that came on that Sunday?'

'No, but she could have kept it in her box if it came before then. She always kept her box locked. But when I saw her with the letter on that Sunday I had the feeling it had only just come and she hadn't read it yet. And she could read. Her mother taught her.'

'And you said she was upset that Matthew took the letter from her, even though *he* wouldn't have been able to read it. I think you're right, Shilly. Why would she be upset with him unless she hadn't read the contents herself yet? Now, who could have given it to her?'

It was hard with Mrs Williams looking at me with such eagerness, her teeth making her strange thinking noise.

'It must have been Tom Prout,' I said. 'He came to the farm after chapel and before Charlotte and Matthew left. I only saw her with the letter once Tom had gone.'

'But how did he come by it? And there's still the matter of the gift the letter mentions. Did you see Charlotte with anything besides the letter?'

'She had a new bonnet. A smart one, in red silk. The one I found in the marsh.'

'When did you first see it?'

'After Tom had been. When she chased Matthew up the stairs she had it.'

Mrs Williams looked at the letter again. '*I hope you will like this gift. It is made by my own hand.*'

I felt a creeping across the back of my head as if someone was marching their fingers through my hair. It was the feeling of a memory rising to the surface and breaking free.

'Charlotte told me – her aunt, she makes hats.'

'Then the bonnet and the letter must be from her.'

SEVENTY-FIVE

'Sir,' Vosper called through the door. 'I have the cart ready.'

Mrs Williams rushed to open the door. Vosper nearly fell over, such was his shock on seeing her.

'I . . . this is Mr Williams's room,' he said. 'Isn't it?'

'It is, and it's my room too,' she said. 'Mrs Williams. Delighted to see you again.'

She held out her hand. He took it, slowly.

'You were here the other evening, and at the courthouse,' he said.

'I was indeed. Now, my good man. I have some questions to ask you.'

Vosper scratched his belly. 'If it's about the bed sheets I told your husband they'd been washed.'

'It's about something much more serious,' she said.

'Mrs Williams, no!' I said.

She spun to face me.

'You can't trust him,' I said. I lowered my voice. 'He's related to the family, it could be him that did it. We're not safe here.'

Mrs Williams gave me a broad smile. She took from her pocket something that gleamed. A knife. Small and cruelly curved.

'His relations are exactly what I need to ask him about,' she said. She pointed the knife at Vosper and then at the chair. 'Would you care to sit?'

He staggered, as if she'd already cut him, and then made for the door. But she was quicker than him and put her knife to the back of his neck. He froze.

'Don't mistake me,' she said. 'I will use it.' And to show him she spoke the truth a bead of blood appeared at the knife's tip. I willed her to drive the blade deep. To finish him.

She made him go to the chair and sit down, all the time keeping the knife against his skin.

'I didn't know the excise employed ladies,' he said.

'The inn's supply lines are not my concern,' she said, and Vosper sat more easily in the chair. 'Was a bonnet left here for Charlotte just before she disappeared?' she asked him.

'And why do you want to know?' he said.

'Who brought the hat – the aunt herself?'

He gave a low laugh. 'She'd not come out here. Sent it with the carrier to Camelford, knowing it would find its way to me. One of my regulars brought it on.'

'Who?' Mrs Williams asked.

'A man who helps keep the Britannia Inn well stocked. You saw him in the yard.'

'When did the bonnet arrive?'

'The night before she went out with Weeks. My helpful regular usually comes after sunset, if he does as he's told. I gave the hat to Tom the next day. He came in for a drink after chapel, said he was going to the farm to see her. Said all sorts of things,' he muttered.

'And you didn't like that,' Mrs Williams said.

'I didn't. It wasn't the first time I'd heard the like said about her but we had an understanding, she and I.'

'But you said she didn't know you were related,' I said.

'Because it was the truth.' He leant back in his chair and looked at his boots. 'I knew her as a child in Boscastle, before she was put out to work. She remembered me, just about. Knew I was from the same village, didn't know we shared blood. I haven't had much to do with the family since I left. They're none too keen on beer shops. Her mother thinks the family's better than we are, even though she had that carry-on that left her with the girl.' He gave a low laugh. 'No word from them in years and then the aunt sent that hat and the letter, and a note telling me to give both to Charlotte.'

'Did you read the letter?' I asked him.

'I didn't want to know what they had to say to her.'

I felt the creeping across the back of my head again but fainter than when I'd remembered that Charlotte's aunt made hats. Instead of fingers marching through my hair, this time there was only the sense that a hand caught it, and was gone.

'I thought maybe I wouldn't tell Charlotte about the hat,' Vosper said, 'didn't want to upset her, but it seemed a waste not to give it to her. She liked her fine clothes, didn't she? You were a friend to her, Shilly. More than I was. For that I'm grateful. I've tried to show you, with the drink. But why are you asking about the letter now, anyway? What did it say?'

'That Charlotte would be killed if she went to Boscastle again.' The words were foul-tasting in my mouth.

This didn't shock him. He merely shook his head and returned to staring at his boots. I couldn't look at him. I moved to the window. The tattered remains of a brown curtain hung limply to one side. It must have borne a pattern once. Shapes were faintly present on the cloth. One of them moved. A moth crawled across the folds, searching for the light. I felt the creep of trapped memory again.

'Was it her family?' Mrs Williams asked Vosper.

'That killed her? It was Weeks that killed her. Her family liked to threaten but they didn't care enough to risk acting on it. Probably thought if they frightened her then she'd do what they wanted. Not that she had time to prove she would heed them. She went missing right after the letter came.'

The moth was trapped in the curtain's folds. I laid my hurt hand close to it, trying not to feel the curtain's grimy fur. The moth climbed on to my finger. I held it to my face.

'But maybe she did have time to cross her family,' Mrs Williams said. 'She set out right after she got the letter, refusing to let anyone go with her. What if she was going to Boscastle and was met on the way by one of the family – someone checking she would do as she was told? The letter could have been a test, and Charlotte failed it.'

'But I've told you,' Vosper said, 'they wouldn't risk a hanging if they were caught.'

'Perhaps they didn't need to risk their own necks,' Mrs Williams said. 'Because someone from the family was here already. Someone in easy reach of Penhale. Someone who could see if Charlotte went out that afternoon in the direction of Boscastle.'

Now the moth was free of the curtain I could see its colours. It was golden. Its wings caught the feeble light from the dirty window and shone. There was something I had to do. I was being tested like Charlotte.

'You think I did it?' Vosper said. 'Well, well. So that's why you're here. Fancy yourself a constable do you, Shilly, and you've found someone foolish enough to help you.' He laughed. 'You're right, I was close to the farm and I did see her go out on the moor that day. But I saw her with a man who limped, as did two other people. How do you account for that?'

'I can't,' Mrs Williams said. She sat on the bed.

'I'm not part of that family any more,' Vosper said. 'They're ashamed of me like they was ashamed of the girl. Even if they'd asked me to hurt her, I wouldn't have done it. Risk my neck to do their bidding when they'd cast me out? Not likely.'

The moth fluttered from my finger and settled above my breast.

'I told the truth to the magistrates and to the judge,' Vosper said. 'It was Weeks I saw. There's no one else it could have been.'

SEVENTY-SIX

He stood up. Mrs Williams didn't tell him to sit down again. The knife dangled in her hand.

Vosper gave her one of his leeriest smiles. 'Well, my dear, now you've asked me your questions and I've told you my answers, can I interest you in a drink? Given that your husband seems to have taken himself off somewhere and won't be wanting to start for Altarnun, we could have a private talk in my room.'

'I'll still be wanting your services,' she said.

'We'd best be going, then, if you want to reach Jamaica tonight. I'll be downstairs, when you and Shilly have finished your constabling.'

He laughed as he left us and I was glad to be rid of him, he who had shared blood with my girl and never helped her, when all she wanted was her family.

The room was all gloom and dirt. Mrs Williams and I were as still as the old chair. The only movement was the moth at my breast. Its wings twitched. My scalp twitched with it. My thoughts were dark and sucking as the marsh but within them something was writhing. Something important.

'Do you believe Vosper?' I said.

Mrs Williams stood. 'I think we'll have to. He doesn't have a motive. He doesn't have a limp.' She turned to look at me. 'And even if he had both, what would it matter? Matthew's dead.'

'I was so sure it was Vosper. I've always felt him to be wicked.'

'And therein lies the problem, Shilly. You felt Vosper was guilty but you didn't know it.'

'I knew it in my bones.'

'But that's not the same as knowing it in fact. You have your own reasons to dislike Vosper.'

'I don't know what you're talking about.'

'Oh, I think you do. Vosper has kept you well supplied, hasn't he?'

I looked out of the window but of course the panes were too dirty to see.

'You loathe your dependency,' she said, coming to stand close behind me. Her breath was warm on my neck. 'But you can't admit it, not even to yourself, so you direct it on to Vosper. He's a publican who gives you what you so badly need and therefore you despise him, when it should be yourself you despise.'

'We can't all change like you can!' I shouted, and it felt good to shout, to force her to listen. 'God knows I've tried, and so did Charlotte. Some people are cursed with one way of living and who are you to judge us?'

She tossed the knife on the bed and moved away from my shouting because she didn't care.

'I must go. And so should you. We have nothing left to discuss. I'll see you to the door.'

She herded me down the stairs as if I was a cow being driven to summer pasture. As if I was something she had to be rid of. And at that moment I wanted to go. To be far away from her who made me feel so low about myself. My thoughts were dark and wretched, but as she pushed me through the inn's back door, there was some light in the darkness. Sunlight, the yard dripping with it.

I'd forgotten there could be beautiful days. I'd forgotten, too, the moth at my breast. In the bright sun the moth lost its golden colour and looked white as it fluttered away. And then I remembered.

The white butterfly I saw on the day Charlotte was found.

I didn't faint but I came close. Mrs Williams got hold of me. I couldn't find my words. The moth disappeared in the sun's glare.

297

Mrs Williams muttered something about drink but she was wrong.

'There was a white butterfly,' I spluttered. 'It settled on his riding crop. The moth made me remember. He knew what her aunt said in the letter so he must have seen her.'

'Who did?'

'Mr Carwitham.'

SEVENTY-SEVEN

I was running and gabbling. She caught me by the arm.

'What are you talking about?'

I made myself slow down. I had to get it right.

'On the day Charlotte was found the men came to Penhale before going to search. Mr Carwitham was there. He was by the kitchen window. Mrs Peter was talking to him about Charlotte, about how her family hadn't brought her up right.'

I could hear Mrs Peter's words as if she was next to me. I could see Mr Carwitham on his horse as if I was standing by the window.

'He told Mrs Peter that sometimes home is a dangerous place. He was talking about Charlotte's home – he must have been.'

'But how could he have known that?'

'If he saw Charlotte after she got the letter.'

'Not necessarily,' Mrs Williams said. 'Carwitham could have found the letter somewhere.'

'No, he couldn't. It was hidden in the wall, remember. And the only person who would have known to put it there was Charlotte. Mr Carwitham was the man on the moor.'

'But this doesn't necessarily make him a murderer. And there's still the question of the wretched limp. Carwitham is perfectly sound.'

'We must go to Lanhendra,' I said. I knew Mrs Williams would follow.

We took the path we'd so often taken – to Lanlary Rock and down to the ford. I barely saw them as we passed and twice came close to straying into the marshes, but we were almost there – almost knowing what had been done to my poor girl.

Through the empty fields belonging to Mr Carwitham and onto the road and at last the cottages of Lanhendra came into sight. We hurried on to the gate bearing the name Gorfenna and took the path up to the house.

A hand grabbed my collar and hauled me backwards. Mrs Williams shoved me into one of the sheds and pulled the door almost closed behind her.

'What is it?' I said.

In the thin shaft of light left by the door I saw her put a finger to her lips. I squinted into the yard. Roe was coming up the path towards us.

I staggered from the door. My feet caught one another and sent me sprawling into the scraps of straw beneath me.

Roe's footsteps came closer. I held my breath. Had he seen us before we got inside? He was close by the door.

And then he was walking on, his steps growing quieter. He hadn't stopped. I let out my breath. Mrs Williams slumped against the wall.

I pushed myself to my feet and something small rolled under my hand. Then it was gone beneath the straw. I ran my hands across the floor and caught hold of it again. I went to the door and eased it wider to better see.

'Careful,' Mrs Williams hissed. 'We need to be on our guard.'

But then she saw what I was holding. The red bead caught the light as I turned it this way and that.

'So this is where she was kept,' Mrs Williams said.

SEVENTY-EIGHT

She urged me to wait, to take care. I didn't heed her. I couldn't. Some frenzy was on me to find Carwitham. I wrenched open the front door.

The hall and stairs. The passage behind them. I had no plan, no thought as to what I'd do when I found him. Another door that opened when I pushed. A hearth, a table.

'If you're looking for work you'll find none here.'

A woman's voice, bringing me to my senses. I was in a kitchen.

'Everyone's been let go.'

It was the housekeeper, Mrs Hoskin. She was rattling a poker in the grate.

'I'm not here for work,' I said. She didn't remember me from before. Or she was too drunk. I could smell the spirits on her breath.

She frowned and came towards me, still holding the poker. 'Then what do you want? Does he owe you money?'

I backed away but came up against a chair piled with torn and filthy cloth. And then I saw the rest of the kitchen was likewise dirty. The room smelt of old meat. There were muddy boot marks on the slate flags. Cobwebs hung from the ceiling, heavy with flies and dust.

The housekeeper shrugged. 'It's too much for me but he doesn't care.'

She returned the poker to its place by the grate and sat at the table. There was a bottle of cloudy liquid at her elbow and a glass within reach. The woman cast a sly glance at me then filled the glass. It was her weakness, not mine. I wasn't that person any more.

'What do you want, then,' she said, 'if not work?'

I thought of the old woman on the road when we had come to see Carwitham before.

'Your mother. I've seen her, on the moor. That's why I'm here. She told me to come in and speak to you.'

The housekeeper fell to scritching. 'Cast out, she is, as I will be soon. He sold the fields quiet enough, and then the stock were lost, but the house'll be noticed. He can't hide that.'

'Is your master out on the moor?'

'He's not been out there since his leg took bad. I'd almost pity him if he hadn't let my mother go.'

I sank into a chair. 'How was Carwitham lamed?'

'Why should I tell you? And what do you want here anyway? I don't believe my mother would've asked a stranger to come in to see me.'

'Would this help loosen your tongue?'

Mrs Williams stood in the doorway, holding her small leather bag. She squeezed it and there was the sound of coins clinking. The housekeeper smiled.

Mrs Williams joined us at the table, sitting across from the housekeeper and me. She set the bag of money in the middle.

'He came off his horse,' the housekeeper said. 'Threw him, he told me.'

'When?' Mrs Williams asked.

I caught a sound from deep within the house. A bell was ringing. The housekeeper gave no sign of having heard it.

'Can't remember exactly,' she said.

Mrs Williams pulled the money bag a little out of the housekeeper's reach.

'Well perhaps if I think about it,' the housekeeper said. 'It was two weeks ago, or thereabouts. I know it was a Sunday, at any rate, because I'd roasted a chicken. He always has a chicken on a Sunday but he wasn't back to eat it so it was drying out. I remember thinking that, about the drying meat.'

'What time did he come back?'

'It was late, I know that. I'd started to worry because the weather was dirty. When his horse was at the gate without him I knew something

302

was wrong. That animal knows its way back, you see, but it was all sweating and muddy up the legs. When I saw that I told Mr Roe to go and look for the master.'

'And did he find him?' Mrs Williams said.

'The master came back first so they must have missed each other. It was dark by that time. Close to nine o'clock, I shouldn't wonder.'

The bell rang again, this time with more fury.

'And what state was Mr Carwitham in when you saw him?' Mrs Williams said. 'If you did see him on his return?'

'He made such a noise coming in to the house I couldn't have missed him.'

The bell had stopped ringing.

'And?' Mrs Williams said.

'He was in a poor way. As muddy as his horse, all up his legs, and he was cold, you could see that to look at him. His teeth was chattering and he was pale as milk. When he asked me to help him up the stairs I knew his leg was bad. He could barely walk. That's when he told me the horse had thrown him.'

'Did you ask if he'd seen Roe?'

'Of course I did. By that time I was wondering if he'd met with an accident as well. But Mr Carwitham was muttering, not really speaking. It was the shock of the pain, in his leg. He wasn't himself.'

'What did he say?'

'Oh I don't know.'

Mrs Williams' hand closed over the money bag. The housekeeper fussed with the shawl about her shoulders.

'It wasn't anything,' the housekeeper said, 'not real words. He was hurt. I couldn't make out—'

'That's enough, Mrs Hoskin,' Carwitham said.

SEVENTY-NINE

He was standing in a doorway at the rear of the kitchen, wrapped in what looked to be an old horse blanket and clutching a bell. He closed the door behind him, locked it and pocketed the key. The housekeeper's mouth quivered. She stood, keeping her eyes on him, then quick as you like snatched the money bag and ran out the door we'd come in by.

Carwitham followed her. He closed the door and leant against it, barring our way. He let the bell drop to the floor. It made a hollow clang against the slate.

I'd seen him since Charlotte had disappeared. How had I failed to see he was lame?

He'd been clever.

When the searchers had gathered at Penhale he didn't get down from his horse. When we came to Lanhendra he stayed seated. By the trial he looked to be sound – but he'd had the cane he always used, because he was a gentleman.

Mrs Williams reached for the pocket of her coat but Carwitham saw it. He fumbled with the horse blanket and when he threw it off I saw what he'd been holding underneath. The long nose of a shotgun gleamed in his shaking hands.

'Don't make me hurt you,' he said, aiming the gun at each of us in turn.

'Why did you do it?' I said.

'I don't want to hurt anyone,' he said. 'I didn't want to . . . I didn't mean . . .'

'But you did hurt someone,' I said. 'You hurt Charlotte very badly. You took her from me. I loved her, I—'

Saying her name called her. I knew she was in the room, that she was by my side. I could feel the air escaping from her cut neck as she tried to speak.

Shi Shi

I gave a little cry and curled up on the chair.

'Shilly?' Mrs Williams said.

'What is it?' Carwitham took a step towards me. The shotgun dipped to the floor. 'Is it . . . her?'

'She won't rest,' I sobbed, 'because of what you did, because Matthew was hanged for it.'

Carwitham dropped to his knees. Tears streamed down his face but he made no sound of scritching. His mouth gaped and his breath was shallow. Mrs Williams was moving towards him. He gathered the shotgun into his arms again.

'She's here now?' he said, his voice a croak.

I nodded. He looked around the room. I could feel her close to me. I could taste her blood.

'Where are you?' he cried.

Mrs Williams was once more creeping.

'Stay there!' he shouted, pointing the gun at her until she shifted back.

But when I got to my feet he didn't shout. Charlotte was still by my side. We stood over him. She reached for his face but couldn't touch it. I took her hand in mine.

'She's here, beside you,' I said.

Carwitham's breathing grew shallower and again he looked about him. 'Where is she? When I saw her green dress in the courtroom I was sure she'd come. I've feared it ever since . . . But then I saw it was only you. I'm sorry. Tell her I'm sorry.'

I sank to the floor in front of him.

'Get away from him, Shilly!' Mrs Williams said.

My face was inches from Carwitham's.

'You must tell us what you did to her,' I said. 'That's all she wants.'

He opened and closed his mouth. I could hear the grinding of his teeth. I willed his words to come. But it was Mrs Williams who spoke.

'You paid Matthew Weeks's defence, didn't you?'

EIGHTY

Carwitham's eyes rolled in his head. 'That poor boy. I tried to save him, my love. Doesn't that take some of the blood from my hands?'

'The only person on the moor that day was you,' Mrs Williams said. 'And you knew Vosper had seen you after your fall, when you were limping.'

'Isaac said there was no other way. We had to say it was the boy. I didn't want to but Isaac knew what to do. He's a good man.'

'Isaac?' Mrs Williams said.

'Roe,' I said.

I felt Charlotte drop to the floor beside me. She pressed her dirty face close to Carwitham's but he saw nothing. Again he searched the air for traces of her, like some creature seeking a scent. The shotgun lay in his lap.

'Isaac helped you, didn't he?' I said. 'He came to Penhale that night to make us doubt Matthew. Was it Isaac that hurt her?'

'No, no,' Carwitham moaned. 'Isaac's a good man. He says I'm safe now the boy's dead. Isaac's given his own money for the memorial. Safe now. Safe.'

His head dipped, as if he was falling asleep. Charlotte clawed at his hair, tried to drag his head up. I felt her spite, felt her anger at her powerless limbs.

Mrs Williams was moving towards Carwitham again and this time he didn't notice. She was going to take the shotgun but I didn't want her to – not yet. Not until he'd said what I needed him to say.

I yanked on Carwitham's wrist to stir him. He shuddered to wakefulness and looked at me. 'You are safe now,' I said. 'Matthew's dead. No one can hurt you. You can tell us why you did it.'

'It'll be written in stone soon. *Charlotte Dymond, wilfully murdered by Matthew Weeks.*'

I felt Charlotte pull on my hand like a dog on a chain.

'Shilly!' Mrs Williams hissed. 'What are you doing?'

I went for Carwitham again. 'Charlotte's listening. You must tell her what she wants to hear.'

'Safe,' he muttered. 'Safe to tell you. Your mistress was so good to let me use the field. She didn't ask why I needed it. She'd give me anything I asked for. Said blood was what mattered, not money.'

'Is there anyone who isn't related to Mrs Peter in this blasted place?' Mrs Williams said under her breath.

'But Phillipa didn't know she gave me more than just land,' Carwitham said. 'She let me see you, my love. Whenever I wanted. And then you started coming to see me, but only if the weather was poor. When the sun shone you went to your other place. I prayed for it to rain every Sunday, for the wind to howl and keep you coming to me.' He fell to sobbing, tucking his chin into his chest.

I eased up his head and pressed my face close to him. His eyes were darting, the whites broken with red streaks.

And then he lunged at me.

I heard Mrs Williams shout, thinking he was going for the gun, but he pressed his lips to mine. I turned my face away and he slumped into a heap.

'No, you won't let me kiss you any more, will you? I forget, I forget. You want to be mistress of Gorfenna before you'll let me kiss you. But you can't be. I told you. I can't marry someone like you.' He gave a little laugh – a strange, shrill sound. 'That you would have thought so!'

'You lied to her?' I said.

He was smiling, shaking his head. 'I never said . . . you didn't listen . . .' Then his smile was gone. 'But you took the few things I had left anyway, didn't you, you bitch.'

He was on his knees. The shotgun clattered out of his lap. I backed away but he crawled towards me. I let go of Charlotte's hand but I could feel she was still there. Wisps of smoke coiled from the corners of the room.

'You took my best stock, made them suffer. I didn't understand at first but Isaac knew. He knew it was you.'

He stopped crawling and tucked his head into his chest again, whimpering.

'Shilly, please,' Mrs Williams said. 'There's nothing more to be learnt here.'

I slapped his face and he looked up, startled.

'Charlotte wants you to say it, Carwitham. She's here, listening. If you say what you did then you'll see her, and you want that, don't you?'

He ground his teeth again. 'You've ill-wished me, girl, haven't you? Made me like this.'

'You found her by Lanlary Rock,' I said. My voice was thin, my mouth dry.

He hunched himself into my lap. Smoke was building all around us.

'The adder helped me,' he said. 'Like a gift from God it spooked the horse. I've never been a praying man but I thanked the Almighty for sending me that creature.'

Mrs Williams was once more edging her way round the table towards Carwitham. His eyes were fixed on me.

'I begged you to help me, told you I'd been foolish. But *you* were the fool because you believed me.'

The magpie's heart stuck with pins. A charm to win back his love. She must have thought it had worked.

Carwitham was still prattling away. 'It was God that sent the adder, wasn't it? So that means it was the right thing, asking you to help me back to the house, and you seemed only too willing.' He stroked my

309

cheek. 'And then I kept you safe, here, where I could look at you. Where no one else could touch you. You didn't like that, my love, did you? Shut away and screaming. I couldn't have all that noise while I decided what to do with you. But I took too long. People were going to look for you. I had to make you quiet.' His face fluttered between smiling and fearfulness. He was a stream that didn't know which way to run.

'I made Isaac come with me to the ford. We took your things. I . . . I couldn't bear to have them so close, all the time . . . Your face . . . But then we had to wait, hiding like rogues in the gorse because the girl was there.' His voice hardened. 'That girl. You kept asking for her. Well I gave you back to her. I put your things in the marsh, and the charm to stop you. Used your own wickedness against you. I liked that very much. A lesson for you, my love. But even then you didn't listen. The marsh wouldn't take you. You didn't sink, just slithered from it like the snake you are. Tempting a man and then biting him. The Devil moved you to the water. No hand of man could have done that. And when I saw you in the river, how you made the water part . . . I was afraid, my love. I was afraid of you then, even when you were dead.'

'Which of you cut her?' I said.

Her hands were round his neck. The smoke had thickened to a cloud above us. I couldn't breathe. The room was darkening.

'I couldn't . . . Isaac's is the steadier hand.'

He sat up. He looked around him, his eyes darting, flicking, settling on nothing. It was as if I'd vanished. And I knew why.

'My love?' he said.

Mrs Williams gathered me up and helped me slip past Carwitham. He had no care of us now. She opened the door and bundled me into the passage. Behind her I saw Carwitham turn but he wasn't looking at us. The door closed.

I couldn't make my legs work. They'd turned to water.

'Come on, Shilly, please!'

Mrs Williams dragged me down the passage. I could see the front door, the light promising escape through its panes. And then a shadow blocked it.

Roe.

Mrs Williams cried out. I slipped from her arms to the floor.

'What the devil are you doing here?' he said.

There was a scream from the kitchen. Roe rushed past us down the passage.

Now my legs returned to life. My breath was fire in my lungs. I grabbed Mrs Williams's hand and we ran.

We were just past the shed when the shot rang out. Birds scattered from the trees.

EIGHTY-ONE

We ran to the gate. I wrenched it open and my fingers caught the worn letters on the sign. *Gorfenna*. I knew then what the word meant in the old tongue. *To end*.

Mrs Williams went through and I followed but then I saw Roe at the top of the path. He dropped to his knees and covered his face.

Mrs Williams grabbed my arm, dragged me away from the sight of him, him that had taken my girl from me. I hoped he never knew one moment's happiness in the rest of his days, and I hoped those days were many so that he should long be wretched.

We ran up the road, crossed the fields and were on the moor again, running from that house, from the men in it. From the work of their hands.

Running, running, and the stream came in sight. Only when we reached the ford did we let ourselves catch our breath, our thoughts, and only then because we were past running.

It was Mrs Williams who spoke first, her breath ragged over her words. 'When you told Carwitham that Charlotte was there, that she was in the room, you saw her, didn't you?'

'Does it matter? Carwitham believed me.'

'Yes, but . . . Did you see her?'

'It's not about seeing. You've never seen the elephant and yet you believe it's real. I knew Charlotte was there. I could feel her – her sorrow, her anger. You can choose whether or not to believe me. I know what I believe. Not that it means anything now. You're leaving. Matthew's dead and everyone thinks he did it.'

Vosper's black flag was still standing, though the ponies had nibbled it ragged. Soon the stone memorial would go in its place and for all I knew it would remain there for hundreds of years, bearing its lie long after my bones had become dust.

'At least the umbrella makes sense now,' she said.

'Does it?'

'Given that we know who Charlotte met on the moor it's quite simple to work out. For all his recent poverty, Daniel Carwitham was a gentleman. He would have ridden with an umbrella tucked in to his boot, I would imagine, and given it to Charlotte to use.'

An umbrella tucked in a boot. Just as Mrs Peter had kept hers in the porch at Penhale. Had the answer been there all along, if only I'd seen it? Surely that was too ordinary for Charlotte Dymond.

'Charlotte could have conjured it herself,' I said. 'There's always something to be got from nothing.'

Mrs Williams looked like she would speak but thought better of it.

'We can't know for certain, can we?' I said. 'We must each decide for ourselves what to believe.'

'That we must,' she said. 'Come, let's leave this dreary place.'

We walked on, reaching Lanlary Rock. A friend on the moor. I would have need of it now, alone as I was.

'So you'll go to Jamaica Inn,' I said, 'and then to London?'

'To Jamaica, certainly. From there, who knows?'

'Then we must say goodbye again, Mrs Williams. This really will be the last time.'

'You'll have to learn all my names, if we're to work together.'

I nearly fell over my own feet, had to lean against Lanlary Rock to keep myself standing.

'What you can "feel", Shilly, I don't claim to understand it, and I won't say I want to, either. But it was you who got the truth from Carwitham in the end.'

'I . . . I'd want paying.'

'That can be arranged.'

'And I can't be someone I'm not. I won't. You'll have to have me as I am.'

'We'll be working together as equals, Shilly. Each using our own . . . talents.'

'Only working?'

She folded her arms across her chest. 'Will you come with me?'

Strands of her long hair moved this way and that in the breeze, as Charlotte's had once done. My first love lay beneath the ground. I had a choice but I was blind as I tried to make it because the creature before me kept changing. She was always able to get away.

'Who are you?' I said.

She turned away. 'I asked you once if you trusted me. If you still do, if I haven't betrayed that gift of trust, then come with me.'

'How can I trust you when I don't know who you are?'

'Trust has to be earned,' she said. 'I understand that. I didn't trust you. Not at first.'

'But I did everything you asked.'

'And why was that?'

'Because I wanted to find out who had hurt Charlotte.'

'I had to be sure that was the reason. You see, Shilly, I had to rule you out before I could trust you.'

'You . . . you thought I'd done it? That I'd *killed* her?' I felt as if she'd dashed my head against Lanlary Rock.

'I had to consider it. You loved Charlotte – that I never doubted. But look what love can become when it's not returned. Look at Mary, and Roe for that matter. You had to face Charlotte having relations with others. Did you reach a point of crisis? There's no one to account for your movements on the afternoon Charlotte went missing, and you were at the ford shortly before she was found. You gave Mrs Peter Matthew's muddy stockings, and you could have made sure she found a bloodied shirt that belonged to him. How did you know to search for

Charlotte's lost things in the marsh? And I'm sure you won't deny that you tried very hard to prejudice me against Vosper.'

I saw how she'd seen it, saw myself swinging from the gallows.

'But it was a man seen on the moor,' I said.

'Such things are not impossible. I've shown you that.'

'Then what made you believe I didn't do it?'

'Your faith. After Matthew was hanged you still wanted to find out what had really happened. If you'd been guilty then you would have rested easy after the execution, like Carwitham thinking he was safe. But you didn't. You came to me with the letter.'

'So until today you still thought I did it?'

'*Could* have done it.'

I should have felt revulsion. I should have walked away. But I stayed where I was and the warmth of relief flooded through me like the spirits I'd first stolen from my father all those years ago. She didn't believe I'd hurt my poor girl.

'You're wrong,' I said.

'What do you mean?'

'Charlotte did love me. Carwitham said she asked for me. It was me she wanted.'

'Of course,' she murmured.

'It doesn't matter. None of it matters.'

'Something like that does,' she said.

'Yes.'

'So?'

'So I'll come with you,' I said. 'If you tell me who you truly are.'

After a moment she nodded. 'A fair bargain.'

She took a cloth from her pocket and wiped away the mole by her mouth, the red paint on her lips. She put her hands to the back of her head and after some fumbling lifted off her long red hair and let it fall to the ground. She ran her hand through her own close-cropped yellow hair, making it stand in tufts.

'What's your name?' I asked the yellow-haired woman.

'Anna. I am Anna Drake.' She seemed to find the words difficult to say, as if she didn't say them often. They could have been another lie for all I knew. 'And what should I call you?' she said.

'Charlotte.'

A look of uncertainty crossed her face. 'That's your true name?'

I nodded.

'Why didn't you say so before?'

'It's been so long since anyone called me that, I'd almost forgotten. And at the farm it was only ever her name. I'd rather she kept it. I'm Shilly now more than I'm Charlotte.'

And then I whispered so that only she should hear – not the moor stone, not the marshes, and not the ponies.

'All the Charlottes are gone.'

AUTHOR'S NOTE

Falling Creatures is a work of fiction with a factual story at its heart – a story that resists a neat telling.

Charlotte Dymond did live at Penhale Farm. Matthew Weeks was tried and convicted for her murder. The memorial still stands on the banks of Roughtor Ford, and the story continues to fascinate those in the local area and others further afield who come to know of it. I believe the reason for its endurance is the many gaps in our knowledge of the case, the important elements that can't be reconciled. The confidence of the cause of death as it appeared on Charlotte's death certificate, and was subsequently reiterated on the memorial, is undermined by the paucity of evidence used to convict Matthew. The facts present more questions than they answer.

The reason we know what we do about the story is largely down to historian Pat Munn. Her exhaustive research is documented in her book *The Charlotte Dymond Murder* (first published by Bodmin Books in 1978 and reissued by Bodmin Town Museum in 2010), and this work informs much of *Falling Creatures*. Some of Munn's conjectures I have pursued, others I've ignored, and a few more have taken on a life of their own in the writing of this book. Anyone wishing to know more about the murder of Charlotte Dymond, and the ways in which this novel interacts with the evidence, should read Pat Munn's book.

They should also visit the Shire Hall in Bodmin. Now a Tourist Information Centre, this building was originally the courthouse in which Matthew's trial was held. A permanent exhibition allows visitors to watch and listen to a re-enactment of parts of the trial and to review the evidence themselves. For a novelist writing about an event that took place over a hundred and fifty years ago, this is an unusual boon. I've visited the Shire Hall on a number of occasions and benefitted from the knowledge of the helpful staff who answered my questions as I tried to fit the pieces together.

As those familiar with the story will no doubt be aware, I have taken a number of liberties with the documented facts, including changing some of the key dates and shortening the timeframe between events. I have also changed the names of some of those connected with the case, invented new participants and done away with others completely.

A large number of documents relating to the trial are in the public domain, including – amazingly – the brief prepared for the prosecution, now held in the Cornwall Record Office in Truro. There was also extensive coverage in local and national newspapers. *Falling Creatures* uses quotations and details from some of these documents, particularly in the depiction of the trial.

In Mrs Peter's evidence, given in the brief to the prosecution, she makes a reference to having asked 'my little maid' to fetch in some washing after Charlotte had gone missing. In Cornwall a 'maid' is a young woman in a general sense rather than a domestic servant, and in the context of fetching in washing the woman in question would be a farm worker like Charlotte. But Charlotte was the only woman employed at the farm at that time. In her book Pat Munn suggests this reference is probably a mistake by the person transcribing Mrs Peter's evidence, but the effect of such an error is a powerful one: for a heartbeat of history there was someone else with Charlotte at the farm. In that moment I glimpsed Shilly.

A number of other books inform the novel: A. K. Hamilton Jenkin's *Cornwall and the Cornish* and *The Story of Cornwall*, Judith Flanders' magisterial *The Invention of Murder*, and *Imposters: Six Kinds of Liar* by Sarah Burton.

ACKNOWLEDGEMENTS

I am grateful to my agent, Sam Copeland at Rogers, Coleridge and White, for his unfailing commitment to this novel. Thanks, too, to my editor Sophie Robinson and everyone at Allison & Busby for their enthusiasm and support.

An early extract of *Falling Creatures* appeared in issue 106 of *New Welsh Review* under its previous title *Something Black Was Showing*. My thanks to editor Gwen Davies for featuring the piece, and for her support over the years.

I was lucky enough to be awarded a scholarship for a week's stay at Gladstone's Library in 2015 when I was editing the novel, and benefitted greatly from the peace that fills the library's reading rooms. Thanks to the Warden of Gladstone's, Peter Francis, and Dr Louisa Yates, Director of Collections and Research, for the opportunity.

Thanks to my readers: Katy Birch, Caroline Oakley, Hannah Ormerod and Jem Poster. And thanks to Calista Williams for deploying her expert research skills when I needed them most.

Thanks to Sarah Burton for a fascinating chat over lunch about the nature of imposters which set the cogs whirring.

Thanks to my parents, for taking my sister and I walking up Roughtor when we were children, and for helping me find Lanlary Rock in the fog many years later.

And thanks to Dave for being there through it all, for reading umpteen drafts, and for believing Shilly would come good in the end.